Ryan M Love was born in Kent. Following an education in horticulture, he worked principally as a gardener until a keen interest in modern military history inspired him to begin writing fiction. Having a passion for the outdoor life, he is an avid mountain biker, snowboarder and trail runner. He currently lives in Wales, just outside the Brecon Beacons National Park.

For Mick and Jane

Ryan M Love

THE JACKDAW DETAIL

AUSTIN MACAULEY PUBLISHERS™

LONDON • CAMBRIDGE • NEW YORK • SHARJAH

A CIP catalogue record for this title is available from the British Library.

ISBN 9781398420458 (Paperback)
ISBN 9781398420465 (ePub e-book)

www.austinmacauley.com

First Published 2022
Austin Macauley Publishers Ltd®
1 Canada Square
Canary Wharf
London
E14 5AA

Prologue

13 May 2005
La Convención Province, Peru

Major Hermano Reyes felt the solid crack of wood on leather as if he were holding the bat himself. His chest swelled with pride and a warm glow rushed to his cheeks when his twelve-year-old son struck a good drive for the junior-league cricket team he had just joined that day. It was only a friendly game, but the ball had gone for four and this was sufficient to bring tears to the doting father's eyes. The smell of freshly cut grass, the babbling chatter from the stands: he could recall every sight, sound and emotion of that moment as he thundered above the dense forest canopy in the Sukhoi fighter aircraft.

Twin turbojets vigorously shook the airframe beneath him, the airflow over the cockpit passing with a flat whistle. The gauge showed his indicated airspeed as 290 knots. He navigated between the mountains, flying below the level of the tree line over an endless carpet of lush vegetation. The taller peaks surrounding him remained bare and rocky. He was to the east of Ayacucho, conducting a solo air patrol over the geopolitical region known as the VRAEM – the Valle de los Ríos Apurímac, Ene y Mantaro. These rivers ultimately made their way to the Amazon basin, and the surrounding topography stretched largely unchanged to the borders of Bolivia and Brazil. His eyes scanned for signs of other air traffic without result. He was alone in the sky.

Reyes had piloted the Soviet-built SU-25 for three years in the Fuerza Aérea del Perú – the Peruvian Air Force – and had already seen more combat action than many pilots would ever see. Accordingly, he had developed an exceptional level of flying skill. He was experienced at hunting low-flying aerial targets from a height just above the treetops, an endeavour that required both conviction and finesse. He mused over the relative aeronautical complexity of his role as he made his navigational checks. The American-made F16 Fighting Falcon could cruise to a location ten kilometres above its target, drop its munitions and fly home again. Major Reyes reckoned that an airline pilot could carry out this task. The F15 Strike Eagle could locate an enemy plane with its beyond-visual-range radar, then release a missile to score a kill without even changing course. This was not the case for Reyes. He needed to get in close to engage his targets – he had to chase his prey down.

When Reyes joined the FAP, it had been Shining Path, the communist insurgents, who were the enemy. The guerrilla group still existed but posed a greatly diminished threat since the capture of their leader Abimael Guzmán in 1992. Reyes first piloted the ageing SU-22 fighter-bomber, a relic left over from the Cenapa conflict with Ecuador, but his excellent service was rewarded with transfer to an elite division equipped with superior aircraft. His unit – Escuadrón Aéreo 115 – flew missions to combat the trafficking and production operations of the Peruvian cocaine cartels using the recently purchased SU-25. Designed for close-air-support of ground troops, these had proven highly capable in the role. Reyes was tasked with shooting down cartel transport planes and attacking overtly unlawful ground facilities. These enemies were not the peasant subsistence farmers prevalent throughout Peru's history. They were armed, well-funded and highly organised criminal corporations, with military capabilities that could equal those of a small nation. The cartels were a cancer of his country, greedy and ruthless; they would murder, kidnap or torture in order to protect and nurture their parasitic industry. Their activities must be halted.

He never felt relish for the killing of an unarmed enemy pilot but nor did he feel any remorse. In some cases, where a state-controlled airfield was in range, he would clip the enemy plane with a short burst from the Sukhoi's twin-barrelled 30mm cannon, forcing it to land and be captured. In most cases though, he would shoot the plane out of the sky to ensure the destruction of its illicit cargo. If the cartels were prepared to kill for their sordid purposes, then he was prepared to kill for righteous ones. Reyes' shoulders were broad enough for the job at hand. He had proven this many times.

His eyes flicked momentarily over each of the instruments set into the pale blue coaming. He noted his fuel level and made a quick mental calculation; fifteen minutes of flight time remained before he would wrap up the patrol and head back to base. He would be happy to get out of the cramped cockpit. The pilot's position was encased in a bathtub assembly of welded titanium plate that restricted his space and did nothing for comfort. He initiated a slow, banking-left turn to bring his heading around towards home when he caught a glimpse of movement below at his eleven o'clock, just above the treetops.

He straightened out the aircraft and scanned to reacquire the source. Visibility was limited in the SU-25 due to the low seating position designed for maximum protection, but his sharp eyes found their target quickly. Two kilometres away, flying within the trough of a shallow valley, was a twin-engine light aircraft – a cartel transport. Nobody flew that low without good reason. He adjusted course and depressed the radio talk button to call in the contact, then noticed the second aircraft almost directly below him. Following a few kilometres behind the transport was an armed escort, with camouflage paintwork that made it almost invisible against the jungle backdrop below. Reyes was lucky to have spotted it – it would have been positioned directly behind him if he'd moved in to pursue the leader. This was a cartel tactic. Now he was certain.

Reyes broke right into a wide turn to come around for a better view of his quarry. He couldn't afford to lose his prey during the manoeuvre so he pushed his throttles hard forward to gain airspeed. The vibration within the cockpit intensified and the Sukhoi bumped and juddered as it sliced through the air. The new angle revealed the escort plane more clearly – an Embraer 314 Super-Tucano light attack aircraft, bristling with guns and rockets and painted in military colours. Several of these planes had been bought, stolen or otherwise liberated by organised drug traffickers across South America. Reyes had acquired a target.

He spoke into the mouthpiece contained within his mask: '*Estación Cero-Ocho*, this is *Comadreja Cinco*. I have one light transport, one Super-Tucano escort; approximate grid square: one, eight, lima, x-ray, lima, eight, four; heading east-southeast; both aircraft using cartel procedure. Request identification, priority; over.' Reyes would wait for confirmation before action, as per protocol. The response came immediately.

'*Comadreja Cinco*, this is *Estación Cero-Ocho*. Request acknowledged, priority. Stand by.'

Twenty seconds elapsed before the answer came, during which interval he completed the slow turn and lined up his jet fighter on the heavily armed escort plane.

'*Comadreja Cinco*, identification is negative – they are not ours. You are clear to engage subject to your own judgement; over.' The instruction sounded crackly through the headset but was clear enough in meaning.

'Acknowledged, engaging both aircraft; out.'

The Super-Tucano's pilot had now spotted the jet and broken off in a new direction – the escort's duty would be to waylay Reyes in a game of aerial cat-and-mouse, while the transport aircraft got away with its valuable cargo. The Sukhoi fighter had vastly superior speed, but the little attack plane was more manoeuvrable. If it could evade the jet for long enough, Reyes would run out of airtime and be forced to return to base. The ace pilot had no intention of allowing this to happen; he held the highest kill-count in his squadron for good reason.

He closed on the target, dropping altitude to thirty metres above the canopy and gaining at a rate of 100 knots. Reyes wasn't carrying the Molniya R-60 air-to-air missiles that his airframe supported, but he wouldn't use them even if he was. This newly upgraded version of the Embraer Tucano had a poor thermal signature that the heat-seekers would struggle to follow. Weaving around above the treetops, such missiles could easily miss and be wasted. Instead, he would bring down the enemy plane with his guns and airmanship alone. He would need to be careful though. He carried only 250 rounds of ammunition – enough for just five seconds sustained fire at a cyclic rate of 3000 rounds per minute. Slowing airspeed as he approached from behind, he made a single attempt to hail the other pilot.

'Super-Tucano, identify yourself. I repeat, Super-Tucano, identify. This is your only warning.'

There was no response but the jet gained rapidly and was moments from entering gun range. Reyes steered the Sukhoi to move the green target reticle over his enemy's wing. He clicked off the weapon-safety switch and moved his finger over the stick-mounted trigger. Only moments remained until he squeezed. At the last second, the Super-Tucano pulled up, rolling hard right in a spiral manoeuvre designed to scrub off airspeed quickly. Reyes lost his bead on the target and overshot in an instant. As the Peruvian Air Force jet thundered past, the cartel pilot loosed off a flurry of 12.7 mm rounds from its FN Herstal machine guns. The salvo was far from hitting the fast-moving jet, but the attempt was all the provocation Reyes needed. He pulled up, pushed his throttles forward and entered a steep-banked right turn to come around for another pass.

He took the Russian warplane to its threshold; he would deny the enemy pilot time to plan another move. Maximum wing loading was required. Any more thrust would cause his arc to run wide, any less and he would lose speed during the turn. He gripped the joystick tightly in his right hand as the G-force began to drag his arm down. Blood was forced out of his torso and into his legs, causing a sudden loss of blood pressure in his upper body. His cardiac output dropped and his circulation slowed. Without the tight-fitting trousers of his flight suit, he would soon be unconscious. The periphery of his vision began to fuzz, encroaching further into his eyesight with each passing second. With a hiss, the aircraft's life support switched on, feeding him pressurised oxygen mix through the mask that was attached to his helmet and pulled tight to his face.

He allowed a big gulp into his lungs, then squeezed his diaphragm to exhale against the incoming pressure. The operational G-limit of the jet was given as 6.5 but Reyes knew his aircraft well. As he pulled though the curve, he watched the needle of the G-meter pass 7.5. The metal of the airframe creaked with strain, the wings bending disconcertingly under the extreme load. His left arm was immobilised, pushed down onto the armrest, his vision reduced to a monochrome blur. He worked to control his breathing cycle – an error would force air into his stomach and cause him to vomit. The mental effort to keep concentration was draining, but he refused to succumb to the 'grey'.

This cartel aircraft posed little threat to him, but the extreme physiology of the manoeuvre made him feel fragile, vulnerable, even apprehensive. His mouth had dried up. The G-force diminished as he exited the turn. Blood flooded back into his upper body inducing a near euphoric light-headedness. Stars swam in his eyes as the colour returned to his vision. His focus snapped sharply back to the dogfight.

He scanned around to find that his adversary had changed course again. The escort now flew on a bearing directly opposite that of the transport in an attempt to draw Reyes as far away as possible. The Super-Tucano was turboprop driven – its jet engine powering the propeller rather than providing direct thrust. The craft's airspeed was controlled by changes in the blade angle as the engine always ran at full power. The cartel pilot wanted a faster exit than his propeller would offer and had pitched his nose down in a shallow dive to gain some assistance from gravity.

Reyes felt a flash of anger. He had been shot at; his life endangered. The Sukhoi bore down on the Super-Tucano like a greyhound on a rabbit. He knew that the slippery enemy would attempt to turn off again, just as he entered gun range. He approached from the Super-Tucano's five o'clock, decreasing speed further to allow for the small plane's almost-stationary eighty-knot stall speed. The logical tactic was that the pilot would break left, presenting his aircraft as a smaller target. Instinct and experience told the major otherwise. He acted on impulse. The Super-Tucano twitched left in a feint, then swung hard right and down. But Reyes' jet was already there. *Got you!*

The exposed upper side of the Super-Tucano passed through Reyes' crosshair as he swept down and right in a predictive turn. He squeezed the trigger briefly, firing a one-second burst of armour-piercing shells that slammed into the engine, cockpit and tail section of the enemy aircraft. The heavy depleted uranium rounds first shattered, then ignited with friction, tearing huge burning gashes though the thin-skinned plane. At this low altitude, only four more seconds elapsed before the riddled cartel escort smashed into the colossal treetops of the steep sided valley.

Reyes felt a wave of elation rush over him; the primary threat had been removed. But his pulse kept thumping in his temples. He couldn't afford to relax for a second while the second target remained. He gained altitude and reversed course, following his best guess at the bearing of the transport aircraft. The intensity of the brief dogfight had flooded his system with adrenaline and his senses now ran on overdrive. Absolute concentration was required to regulate his control movements. He glanced at his fuel gauge and saw that he was dangerously low. Determination quickly overwhelmed any concern for safety. He could fly for two more minutes at 400 knots before he was forced to return to base. His eyes strained to acquire the target ahead of him. The Doppler radar was intended for navigation and revealed no sign. He saw nothing but the ubiquitous undulating rainforest. Then a distinctive shape formed at ground level ahead, a stripe cut through the vegetation – an airstrip.

Beeeeeeeeeeeee...

Reyes' elevated heart rate jumped up to a furious hammer as the Sukhoi's active-radar warning sounded with a shrill alarm. He was being targeted. His breath shortened and his mind scrabbled to calculate whether he had strayed into foreign airspace. It wasn't possible – he was three hundred kilometres from the border. He had made no radio contact with Station during the skirmish; the dogfight had escalated too quickly, even for the veteran Reyes. He was about to shout into his mouthpiece when he saw it, coiling upwards out of the jungle canopy like a striking snake.

It was faster than he ever imagined. His heart stopped beating for an instant. A surface-to-air missile streaked towards him at a kilometre per second. Instinctively, he dove his plane down towards it, causing the missile to miscalculate its arc and whip past. His aircraft plunged towards the earth as the projectile performed a neat U-turn back onto his tail. A glance in the rear-facing periscope told him everything: the missile had sufficient energy to catch him no matter how he manoeuvred – he was in the no-escape-zone. Reyes jabbed his gloved fingers at two cockpit buttons, dispensing a random trail of both chaff and flares, but the countermeasures were to no avail. The Soviet Osa missile was controlled by a ground-based launcher unit, which had the Sukhoi illuminated in a beam of active radar like a burglar caught in a flashlight. The missile closed the gap and streaked through the flares in less than two seconds. Reyes grabbed desperately for the ejector-seat handle, but the missile was already on him.

A five-metre proximity fuse detonated the missile's forty-kilogram warhead as it passed under his starboard side, simultaneously rupturing the wing and fuselage fuel tanks. Shrapnel shredded the starboard engine casing. The remaining kerosene fuel instantly erupted, consuming the aircraft in a blazing fireball. The Peruvian Air Force SU-25 struck the ground as a lance of crimson orange fire. Major Hermano Reyes' body was largely incinerated before the 500 kilometre-per-hour impact obliterated his aircraft into a shower of molten debris.

Within one hour, the numerous small fires had burnt out and the smoke had cleared, leaving no obvious indication of the impact site. The immense forest was silent again but for the ceaseless calls of its wildlife. The wreckage was surrounded by a pervasive backdrop of thick undergrowth in a remote, inaccessible location, and the nearest inhabited villages were many miles distant. The evidence of the missile strike would never be found, and the fate of the jet would remain unknown for some time. But this uncertainty would not diminish the significance of these events in the eyes of Reyes' superiors. The loss of his life would not pass without consequence.

Chapter One

Saturday, 21 May
West Sussex, England

Dylan Porter held his right foot flat to the floor in a vain attempt to squeeze some extra power out of the old, battered VW Polo, the engine audibly under duress as he finally crested the top of the hill. The rigid ranks of spruce trees flanking the road gave way to open fields, and finally his destination came into sight. He swung into the dusty, crowded car park of Thresham Down, his suspension chattering as it freely conceded to a series of potholes. It was 9:20 am; the race was due to start in forty minutes.

The registration deadline was nearing and he needed to park quickly. Bumping and weaving the little car through lines of vans, pick-ups and minibuses, he endeavoured to find a last available spot before someone else beat him to it. He jostled impatiently ahead of an immaculate 7-Series BMW and squeezed in to a small space with his left-hand wheels mounting a grass verge. The BMW wouldn't have fitted anyway, or so he told himself. An executive saloon was an unusual sight at this location and he wondered briefly what it was even doing there. Once out of the car, an altogether more familiar scene awaited him, and he took this in for a moment as he stretched the stiffness from his limbs.

The site was frenzied, bustling with activity; it was the busiest Dylan had ever seen it. Almost every bit of spare ground had been taken up as a workspace. The grass surrounding the vehicles was littered with bikes, tools, components and riders making use of the last-minute opportunity for mechanical adjustments. Tyre pressures were checked, bolts meticulously tightened. Shock-absorbers were tested with vigorous bouncing. Those racers not preoccupied with tuning their equipment, instead fiddled with their personal attire. Some wriggled into body armour, others adjusted their full-face helmets or their goggles. Every piece of kit needed to function perfectly during the forthcoming ninety seconds of tribulation. Liveried jerseys displayed every colour of the spectrum, their wearers paying compliment to the hues of their bikes. And these were no ordinary bicycles. These were specialist race machines equipped with front and rear suspension, disc brakes and highly strengthened frame tubing. They were constructed for a single purpose: to travel as fast as physically possible down the roughest imaginable terrain.

An electric ether saturated the atmosphere and high-voltage banter sparked spontaneously around the site. Thrown objects and squirted water accompanied shouts of preliminary heckling between groups of competitors and their attending mates. The younger guy and girl racers were wiry and fit, prerequisites for a demanding physical sport, but present also were the shaved heads and tattoos of tough-looking veterans. This wasn't a points-series race that would attract aspiring professionals, but a one-off, downhill time-trial event with a first prize of five hundred pounds. The promise of a cash prize had attracted a wilder species of animal. From the look of the turnout, Dylan knew that competition would be fierce.

The racers only accounted for half the crowd. A throng of spectators clustered around several merchandise tents that were staffed by marketing representatives promoting the latest overpriced kit. Large-lensed cameras were clutched by professional photographers, and nearby would be their less obvious companions: the magazine journalists. Only a small fraction of those present were locals of Dylan's acquaintance. The majority had travelled from elsewhere specifically to attend the extraordinary event.

Dylan snapped out of his trance; he needed to get a move on. He carefully unhitched his bike from its rack and gave it a final visual check over. Unlike the rusty VW banger, the bike was immaculate and had been polished to a shine. Its hefty aluminium frame was jet-black and set off by matching wheels, silver componentry and a gleaming chain. The chunky-treaded tyres were brand new, fitted that morning for the race. The value of Dylan's push-bike was roughly five times that of his car.

The rest of his kit was less pristine. He wore a faded blue jersey, dusty black trainers and tough but heavily used canvas shorts. His elbow pads, shin guards and spine-protector were all scratched and gouged from their intended use. The black helmet he carried had taken its share of knocks. He gathered up his protective equipment from the rear of the hatchback and was just locking up when the man approached.

'Nice wheels. Looks like you mean business.' The stranger had spoken clearly enough but had caught Dylan off guard.

'Huh?'

'How's it going?' The man was blonde-haired and somewhere in his early thirties, dressed casually in shorts, T-shirt and sandals. Dylan had never seen him before and took him to be one of the many random spectators.

'Oh, right. Pretty good, I guess.' Dylan was shy by nature and didn't exactly relish the attention. Usually, he would avoid such small talk if the opportunity existed to do so, but this stranger was amicable enough and he didn't wish to be rude. The man obviously had something more he wanted to say.

'I was just chatting to the guys at the snack bar. They said you're in with a good shot today.'

'Got the same chance as anyone else, I s'pose. Lot of fast riders here.'

The man gazed over in the direction of the track. 'So what's the tactic? It looks like a pretty tough course.'

'Yeah. Maybe you should go watch about half-way down by the big gnarly stump. That's where it's all gonna happen,' Dylan advised. He was impatient to get under way. He gave the man a curt parting nod as he headed over towards the registration tent.

'Cheers, will do. Good luck,' the man called after him.

* * *

With the registration process complete, Dylan tried to find a bit of free space where he could cable-tie his race number to the front of his bike without being jostled around. A spot near the ten-foot-high wooden start ramp offered a view of the first section of the course. He acknowledged his peers on the way but kept his head down wherever possible. Dylan's reticence belied an intense passion for his sport. He lived and breathed mountain biking, and downhill racing was the main focus of his obsession. He stopped briefly by a marshal to ask which route had been marked out for the race, then moved on silently through the noisy crowd.

For everyday use, Thresham Down had four permanent trails that ran roughly parallel to each other, linked together by a few short connections. Each trail was colour coded for difficulty. The green was for beginners and newcomers to the facility, two red-graded runs were more challenging and the black was a steep, technical route for highly proficient riders. The racecourse had been marked out specially for the day and used elements of both the black and red trails, with a few bespoke modifications thrown in. Dylan – a local and a regular – knew all of these runs intimately and had ridden every possible permutation of route down. There was no practise session for the race but competitors were permitted to walk the track on foot. He didn't bother.

The racers would leave the start ramp one at a time at sixty-second intervals. Dylan would be thirty-ninth to go. He mentally visualised his run as he quietly waited for proceedings to get going. The start ramp led directly into a sizable jump made from shaped-earth, followed immediately by a high-banked corner. These were arranged close together and would force racers to react quickly. From there onwards the course was dug into the chalky subsoil of the open, grassy South Downs hillside, following a series of jumps and switchbacks as it made its way down the increasing incline. The line was narrow and hewn with hand tools, leaving a considerable amount of loose material in the rut. It would be impossible to avoid the rougher sections, and patches of the surface would offer little grip. So far this was part of the red-graded route. At one of the corners, a wooden take-off ramp had been built to transfer the riders onto the tougher black line that cut through the woods.

The forested part of the track was steep, tight and rooty. It weaved between the trunks until it reached the obstacle that Dylan had previously mentioned to the spectator: the 'gnarly' tree stump. The course led riders directly into it before continuing down the slope. The old beech tree had been nearly two metres in diameter with several stems, and the remaining butt was left jagged and uneven. Riders could either bump over it slowly and drop off the back, or ride around it altogether on an indirect route. Dylan's meditation was interrupted by a loud blast from a klaxon horn, followed moments later by the hollow drumming hum of knobbly tyres on wooden planks. The first rider rolled down the ramp. The race had begun.

Dylan inched slowly up the back stairs of the start ramp, pushing his bike before him in the queue of racers. His thoughts were detached from his immediate surroundings. Instead, he scanned the horizon, taking in the crystal-clear blue sky, the city of Brighton and Hove and the calm flat sea beyond. Paragliders lofted from Devil's Dyke and Ditchling Beacon swirled carelessly around in the vacant airspace. He tried to pick out faces that he knew down in the crowd and made an estimate of how many people were present. He recognised the spectator that had spoken to him earlier, now chatting with a fast and consistent rider named Trace. He wondered whether the guy worked for a magazine, thinking that it would be odd that he hadn't mentioned it. His wandering attention found its way back to the race as he reached the top platform. It would soon be his time to go.

He watched the last few riders before him zip down the ramp and his heartrate began to increase. He took a couple of deep breaths, attempting to steel himself for the imminent commitment. Most of the preceding riders took the first jump cautiously, allowing time to regain balance for the following corner. Dylan had other plans. He began to psych himself up and the red mist descended over him – not quite anger, but an aggressive sense of determination. He stepped over his bike and waddled up to the gate, squeezing the handlebars tightly in his gloved hands.

'Thirty seconds,' the start-line marshal called out clearly.

Any sense of fear was now replaced by concentration. He hunched over the front of the machine, left foot on the pedal, counting down the remainder himself. With five seconds to go, he sucked in a deep breath and pulled his right foot up to stand on the bike. He balanced, poised for his sprint down the sheer timber runway.

'3... 2... 1... Go!' the marshal commanded.

Dylan broke off the start line in a snap and pounded furiously down the ramp, hitting the first jump at pace and launching into the air. He sailed gracefully over the dirt mound for a moment, then slammed back down on the other side. The instant his wheels touched the dirt he leaned hard over, sending the bike skittering around the corner like a bobsleigh and firing it along the traverse. His wheels chattered over the broken ground, the bike bouncing over the smaller jumps. Dylan's arms and legs flexed continually to soak up the impacts. There was no need to pedal – he carried plenty of momentum. He charged into the switchbacks with his rear wheel drifting out wide, sending up plumes of dust and gravel as he slewed through. The cheering crowd could already see that he was going to be fast.

A rowdy roar went up as Dylan's bike thumped onto the transfer ramp and sprung into the air, then dropped down into the narrow line beyond. He bumped and wrestled his way through the winding wooded section, wheels pinging off roots, tyres skidding as he dabbed the hydraulic brakes. Breathing hard from the exertion, he knew his goggles would fog up if he didn't maintain enough speed for airflow. Swinging a wide line around a last hairpin bend, he lined up on the big stump. Ten metres to go, he released both brakes and rolled right at it, gaining speed rapidly. At the very last moment, he pulled back on the handlebars and hopped the bike clean over. The line was completely blind but he landed with precision on the steep slope beyond.

His eyes were pinned wide open with endorphin as the bike rattled down the final incline. He gave it everything for the last section, head down over the handlebars, elbows and knees pulled in tight. Forty miles per hour. His eyes watered inside his goggles. The bike bucked violently, shaking him as it skipped over the undulations. His wheels barely kept contact with the earth. Forty-five miles per hour. He topped out, then the gradient relaxed at the base of the hill. Dylan shot over the finish line, scrubbing to a stop in a trailing billow of dust. He grappled urgently with his chinstrap, pulling his helmet from his hot sweaty head before claustrophobia could overwhelm him. He looked over to the finish-line marshal to be informed of his time.

'1:26.05 – that's first place, so far. *Good run!'* The marshal sounded impressed.

Dylan's heart thumped in his chest and a wave of elation washed over him. He had completed a clean run at full pace – that was all he could hope for. Now all he could do was wait and see how fast the others were. He stood on the spot, closed his eyes and exhaled for a moment, then pulled himself together and moved out of the way. In a few seconds, the next rider would arrive at speed and potentially run him over.

Two hours later, back on the top of the hill, a crowd had gathered by the registration gazebo for the prize giving ceremony. The race promoter stood on a table and announced the results through a megaphone while a vendor from one of the merchandise tents handed out the prizes. Trace had performed well and finished in third position. In second place was Amber, a talented girl racer tipped for future success at international level. Dylan had taken the win by a clear second. The locals howled a raucous cheer then accosted their champion with hugs, back slapping, high-fives and handshakes. In an uncharacteristic outburst of exuberance, he let out a long whoop, then took his prize envelope with a beaming smile. He had delivered an impressive performance for an amateur, seeing-off some experienced competition. An array of strangers wished to offer their congratulations. He responded with gratitude but found the process tiring.

After a short while, when the celebration had died down a little, he began his slow and diffident retreat to the car park.

* * *

Dylan squatted by his decrepit VW drying his bike with a cloth. It had attracted only the slightest covering of dry dust but he had washed it again anyhow. Then he had oiled his chain and re-greased his suspension seals. He was more or less finished bar a last bit of polishing. The facility was now two-thirds empty and Dylan could see the spectator heading over in his direction. The man smiled broadly as he approached.

'I spoke to you earlier. Congratulations! That was an incredible run.'

'Umm, cheers. Yeah, it went OK,' Dylan answered modestly, resigning himself to yet another unnecessary conversation.

'Thanks for the tip about the stump. There were a few big crashes and I got some great photos. That move of yours must have taken some balls.'

'I've done it a few times before, but yeah it was scary the first time,' Dylan conceded.

'I'm Tom by the way. Good to meet you. You're Dylan, right?' The man struck out his hand.

Dylan returned the handshake, hurriedly and awkwardly. 'Yeah, that's me.'

'Do you have a sponsor or a team you ride for?'

Dylan wondered why the man was asking. As far as he knew, Tom wasn't anyone of note in the downhill mountain bike scene. He thought about asking who he was outright, but assumed that the information would be divulged soon enough if it was important.

'No, I'm not on a team. I guess I'm kind of self-sponsored, I run a bike shop down in Lewes. It's called Cycl-One; you know it?'

'No, I'm not from around this way. Maybe I'll swing by for a look, sometime.'

'Cool. Drop in if you're passing.' The young racer's reply had only superficial enthusiasm.

'Great. I'll see you around then, Dylan.'

'Yeah. See ya.'

The man waved farewell and headed briskly off, leaving Dylan in peace once again. He returned the bike to its rack on the Polo and secured it with a locking chain, then threw his pads and helmet into the rear of the car through the passenger door. He was famished after the exertions of the race run and the subsequent push back up the hill. He decided to ask around at the canteen and find out if anyone knew who Tom was while getting a half-pound cheeseburger into his belly. The majority of the crowd had faded away leaving predominantly just the local crew. Dylan made his way over to join them and watched with curiosity as the spectator named Tom pulled out of Thresham Down in the staid navy-blue 7-Series BMW.

Chapter Two

Monday, 23 May
VRAEM

Sergeant First Class Raúl Manrique was enveloped by darkness, the void seemingly inescapable if not for the knowledge that his eyes were still shut. His consciousness returned slowly, its listless progression driven by an insistent need: he was in discomfort and he needed to move. The ability to command his limbs remained elusive but he made a half-hearted attempt to open an eye. This wasn't as easy as it might have been on an average morning and it yielded little positive result. Sensation steadily returned to his body, spreading outwards towards his extremities, bringing with it the realisation that he was actually in pain. Anxiety took hold, fuelled by a sickening sensation of being crushed, and panic soon followed. He wanted desperately to move, to escape from the pain and the claustrophobia, but his body was held in a rigid grip. He tried to force his eyes open, but to no avail. Confused and terrified, Manrique floated in a nightmare he was unable to wake from.

Desperation finally overwhelmed his torpor, and his sticky eyelids peeled apart to reveal two fuzzy patches of light in an otherwise shadowy world. With an effort, he found that he could turn his head and by doing so he gained some bearings. He was lying on his front with his face in the dirt. As he looked around, his vision consolidated into a single blurry but coherent image. He recognised nothing that he saw.

Manrique was left-handed and couldn't feel this arm at all, but found that his right arm was functioning normally. He braced it into one half of a press-up position and raised his head fractionally away from the ground. Rotating his head left and right, he found no restriction. *So what the hell is the problem here?* He pushed himself up an increment further, triggering a sharp jolt of pain through his hips and causing him to slump dejectedly back to the floor. His every thought became saturated by feelings of helplessness.

He didn't know where he was but he knew he needed to get free of whatever held him. His movements had triggered an onset of pins-and-needles, now fizzling unbearably through his immobile left arm. He was lying on it, and it occurred to him that the limb had simply gone dead with restricted circulation. He rotated his shoulder joint to encourage the blood flow, then attempted to wriggle the arm from under his torso. The pins-and-needles built to an excruciating climax but he kept going regardless and progressively regained some feeling. With no strength in the muscle, the process was infuriatingly slow and soon the exertion became tiring. He repeatedly blew dirt away from his face to prevent it from entering his mouth as he gasped for breath. Then, in a moment of lucidity, it registered that there was an easier solution. Pushing himself over with his good right arm, he rolled flat onto his back and lay staring upwards and panting. *Where the fuck am I?*

A dark, angular piece of metal rested above him, blocking the light from most directions. He was lying under the wreck of a mangled vehicle. Looking to his left, he could make out dappled daylight, green foliage and the lichen-covered trunks of huge trees. Sounds were coming to him now – birds, animals, the noises of the forest. He deduced that he had been in an accident. *But I'm still alive, so everything will be okay.* He found that he could recall his name but not what he was doing in his present location. Memories appeared in his mind in no logical order, so he tried to concentrate on the basics. He thought about the apartment where he lived some of the time, but then also the barracks. It came to him: he was a soldier. He served in the Ejército del Perú – the Peruvian Army.

There was no gunfire and no shouted commands. He didn't appear to have been shot. By patting his head, he found that he wore a helmet, and a brief check of his face and torso revealed no significant injuries. An attempt to sit up was abruptly abandoned when the vicious pain returned. He was forced to accept that he was injured and he considered ways he could find some help. A mere croak came out when he tried to speak but he thought the better of shouting anyway. First, he would need to ascertain where he actually was. He moved his feet without difficulty, then found he could flex his knees a little, but as soon as his thighs lifted the pain returned. He put his hands either side of his waist and squeezed.

Ooow! He gasped as he found the source. Something was seriously wrong with his hip – possibly a fractured pelvis. *It's not so bad; they can fix it in hospital.* He was already in agony without attempting to move, and it dawned on him that he might not survive the incident without some assistance. It didn't seem possible that he was completely alone.

He lay on his back and tried to piece together his situation from the evidence he could see and from what little he could remember. He knew he was somewhere deep in the forest as there were no discernible human sounds. He could hear no vehicle engines, no aeroplanes, no helicopter. *Of course, the helicopter.* He smiled with relief as a positive recollection emerged in his memory. He had been aboard a helicopter with a team from his unit: the 'Víboras' – the 4th Special Forces.

He visualised the men lining the fuselage, commandos clad in assault gear, fully equipped for a combat mission. He had been sat at the rear of the craft, facing forwards. A piercing electronic tone screamed from the cockpit – a warning. The pilots had shouted, their arms raising up to cover their faces. Then, a jarring impact and the front of the cabin was engulfed in fire. Manrique's memory came to an abrupt stop. His aircraft had been shot down, had broken up, and now he lay in its wreckage somewhere in the wilderness of the VRAEM. The vicinity would not be friendly; he would need to find the rest of his unit for any hope of escape. A voice in his head told him they were all already dead.

He rolled onto his front and dragged himself into the open, over damp, mossy earth and roots. The process was torturous, but his throat was raw and he badly needed water. He wasn't wearing his assault webbing but logic suggested that it would be somewhere close by. He would have removed it in the helicopter to sit in comfort until the three-minutes-to-target warning. A few metres from the crashed craft, he rolled onto his back, propped himself up on his elbows and removed his helmet while he paused for breath.

He had been lying under the rear of the cabin, which had broken off on impact with the canopy. The tail boom stuck out from the wreckage, with its rear rotor stripped off completely. The rest of the helicopter wasn't visible from his position. Epiphytes trailed from the surrounding trees: orchids, bromeliads; some recognisable in bloom. Iridescent hummingbirds darted between them. The chorus of parrots in hundreds. He could tell from the canopy height that he was somewhere below the cloud forest zone. The sun was getting brighter – it was morning. The circumstances of the mission came flooding back to him along with a vivid recollection of his briefing back at base.

A Fuerza Aérea del Perú jet had been shot down in a dogfight with a cartel-operated attack plane – an escort for one of their cocaine transports. The cartel responsible, Del Bosque, conducted aerial operations from a large and notorious production facility that was equipped with an airstrip harboured in a remote highland valley. Del Bosque employees knew this encampment by the name 'La Fábrica', but to the Víboras, it was only referred to by its target designation. They had been en route to seize control of the location and deny use of its runway, just before sunrise to enact a dawn raid. Manrique had been in the first of two helicopters tasked with securing a landing zone for the larger transport following behind. Each would position its door gunner to provide cover while the other disgorged its troops. He hoped that the second aircraft had not shared the same fate.

He could hear a river running close by, no doubt one of the many Apurimac tributaries, and he deliberated whether he should try to reach it for a drink. He decided against, as in his semi-paralysed state he could easily end up in the water and drown. He would need to search the crash site for survival essentials: his webbing, a radio, some ration packs or a first aid kit with some pain relief. Visibility was only a few metres through the brush of ferns and he was forced to drag himself on his belly to move anywhere. Even if he could figure out his bearings, he had no way of knowing where the rest of the craft had come down. Crawling off in the wrong direction could prove fatal. He must be somewhere close to the target facility, probably in the same valley. The severity of his predicament was beginning to get the better of him and he resolved to start moving to distract himself. He had been stationary for just a few minutes and already insects were climbing over him. These were the least of his worries; he'd been through far worse in training. As he wriggled his way back, he noticed his wristwatch for the first time. It was just after 09:00 – he'd been unconscious for over three hours.

It took twenty-five agonising minutes of slowly heaving himself around the wreckage but eventually he found something. Lying motionless on the floor was a fellow soldier, still wearing his webbing. He drew himself up close and located the man's wrist to check for a pulse. He found none. Blood was beginning to pool in the lower parts of the man's arm – hypostasis. The soldier was dead. A lump formed in Manrique's throat. He couldn't see the trooper's face from his position and he didn't want to know who it was. He needed to focus on his own survival.

Unfastening the webbing belt, he pulled it free of his compatriot's corpse and found what he so desperately needed: a water flask. He drunk the entire contents at once, then set about searching the other pouches. He found the troopers first-aid kit and removed a sealed packet containing a spring-loaded autoinjector loaded with 20mg of morphine sulphate. He knew the shot would incapacitate him but he felt utterly exhausted and in so much pain. Without relief he would be able to go no further. He tore open the packet, jammed the tube against his thigh and depressed the button. It took only seconds for the wave of relief to rush over him. He fell back in the dirt and closed his eyes.

* * *

He was alerted by noises close to his position – shouted Spanish voices. His mind had drifted away with the potent effects of the opiate pain killer and he was slow to react. *How long have I been lying here?* Pulling himself up to a sitting position, he found that the pain in his hip had now mostly abated. He checked his watch to discover that two more hours had elapsed. The voices were moving closer and he heard something said about the helicopter. He prayed this was a rescue party but something didn't sound right. There wasn't the usual discipline in the dialogue that was expected from his own unit. He looked for somewhere to hide until he could ascertain who was coming, selecting a spot a few metres away under the overhanging fronds of a tree fern. He rolled onto his stomach and started to crawl, then heard the rustle of a man bursting though the vegetation behind him. *Mierda!*

'Here! There's one alive.'

Manrique was turned roughly onto his back to stare into the face of a weathered looking militia fighter and the barrel of his brandished rifle. Two similarly dressed men appeared at his sides.

'*Get up!* On your feet,' the militia man barked.

'I can't. I'm injured. I can't walk.'

'Then we'll have to make you a stretcher.'

The militia man twisted his shoulder back and swung his rifle butt into the crippled soldier's jaw, the contact producing an audible crack. Once again, Raúl Manrique fell into darkness.

Chapter Three

Tuesday, 31 May
Herefordshire, England

Squadron Sergeant Major Ken McCowan sat silent and motionless in the armchair, positioned centrally in the small room. His hands and feet were not tied but he could not move. He was unarmed, and the three terrorists had him covered from every angle. One stood directly behind him with an AK47 assault rifle levelled on his head. Three metres to his left, a second assailant rested against the wall by a window. Worst of all was the third man, who hid in a corner beside the door wielding a double-barrelled shotgun – a devastating weapon at such close range. His captors were silent and motionless. They would neither negotiate nor sympathise with him. They were steadfast, impassive and completely fearless. This band of terrorists were made from plywood.

McCowan was theoretically in a tricky situation. Before he could go free, his captors would need to be neutralised along with the others spread around the building, and he was unable to assist in the rescue from his position in the chair. The terrorists were nominally wearing body-armour and would not go down quietly. Thankfully, the sheet-metal target had been removed from the room to avoid the risk of ricochet or flying fragments, but an element of danger still existed. This was a live-fire exercise and McCowan's head was positioned directly in front of the wooden target behind the chair. His rescuers did not know his exact whereabouts, or those of the enemy; he could easily be killed by accident if they shot for the figure's centre mass. He could do nothing more than wait and hope for the best, but at least the chair was comfortable. They would not be long now.

As SSM of D Squadron, 22nd Special Air Service Regiment, McCowan was a highly experienced and professional operator. His senior position in one of the world's most elite forces befitted the length of his military career. He did not scare easily. He was able to rationalise his fears to a point where they had little-to-no effect on his performance. But live rounds were live rounds, and their lethality warranted a degree of cautious respect. The SAS practiced relentlessly in their 'Killing House' – a hostage-rescue training facility located at Stirling Lines, their Credenhill barracks. They only ever used live ammunition and often used real people as mock hostages. His breathing deepened. He had no doubts about the abilities of his men, just an impatience to get on with the exercise. The six-man rescue team would be forming-up outside the front, preparing to breach the door with an explosive charge at any moment. McCowan counted the seconds.

* * *

McCowan's upbringing had not been bad in itself, but life was tough in Aberdeen for a poor family. He had shared a cramped household with his parents and four siblings, and his father and older sister had only just managed to cover the bills with their low wages. McCowan forsook school at sixteen years of age with no qualifications, not because he lacked in aptitude, but so he could contribute an income to help raise his younger brother and two younger sisters. To remain in education would have equalled a selfish luxury that his family could ill afford. He found employment labouring but wages were sporadic as appalling weather often put an early end to the day's work. At the age of eighteen, he enlisted in the Army, attracted by the promise of a regular wage that he could send home. He never looked back.

McCowan was a grafter. He carried out everything he did to the best of his abilities and had little tolerance for those around him who didn't pull their weight. He had never spared much time to think about personal ambition, but a baptism of fire in the Falkland Islands awoke the imagination of the young lance corporal. During the assault of Mount Tumbledown, he became personally and closely acquainted with the chaos, confusion and destruction of war. It was here that he first saw members of the United Kingdom's special forces in action – both the SAS and SBS – and discovered the direction his life was destined to take. In 1984, at the age of 23, he completed the six-month selection process for the Special Air Service. A prolific career followed.

Posted in Northern Ireland during the Troubles, McCowan first shot and killed an enemy at the age of twenty-six. An active-service-unit of the

Provisional Irish Republican Army had arrived at a farm in County Tyrone to retrieve a stash of assault rifles and explosives, unaware that the location was under observation by Britain's 14 Intelligence Company – known internally as The Det – and that an SAS quick-reaction-force had been dispatched to prevent their departure.

Eight of the sixteen-man ambush detail took cover beside the farm lane, while cut-off groups were positioned further out to deny any possible escape. The orders given were simple: they were not there to make arrests; none of the PIRA men were to leave. The terrorists' intent was ruthless in nature, as would be the response.

McCowan lay in wait in the rear cut-off position as the two PIRA vehicles rolled past him. Thirty yards…sixty yards…ninety yards…into the kill zone. The main group opened fire, hitting the drivers of both vehicles immediately and preventing any retreat from the ambush. McCowan saw a man roll from a car door to take cover behind its rear wing, directly exposed to his position. He released a volley of 7.62 rounds from the G3 rifle, puncturing the terrorist's body and bringing a swift end to his resistance. Surprised and outnumbered, the rest of the PIRA cell shared a similar fate.

Afterwards, the SAS were criticised for the heavy-handedness of their operation, but it was considered a decisive success within the regiment. An attack on civilians, police or army personnel would have been imminent without the intervention, and therefore McCowan felt little remorse for the terrorists' deaths. The skirmish had only been a brief taste of what was to come.

Desert Storm, the 1991 liberation of Kuwait – Operation Granby, as it was known to the British forces of the 1st Armoured Division. A massive mobilisation of troops and vehicles travelled north into Iraq from Saudi Arabia as part of the coalition offensive. It was the largest amalgamation of military forces since World War II. Challenger tanks and Warrior infantry-fighting-vehicles provided the muscle, with fire support from self-propelled-artillery. Convoys of Trojan armoured-personnel-carriers followed in their wake, accompanied by bridge-builders, bulldozers, tractors, trucks and tankers. Scorpion and Scimitar tracked reconnaissance vehicles went ahead to scout for trouble, with close-air-support provided by Lynx helicopters and fixed-wing jets where required. Meanwhile in the Western Desert, the Land Rover 110 Desert-Patrol-Vehicles of A and D Squadron SAS were already deep behind enemy lines.

McCowan stood on the rear bed of his vehicle, manning the Milan anti-tank missile post as they crept gently forward through the moonless desert night. His patrol had been retasked to scout ahead of the main invasion force. The 3.5 litre V8 engine idled quietly, the driver using first gear to pull them forward in a slow, steady crawl. This close to the enemy even the slightest sound could give their presence away. The front passenger kept the Iraqi position covered with the dashboard-mounted 7.62mm machine gun, but the weapon looked insignificant in comparison to the row of long barrels protruding from the ground ahead of them.

Six T55 tanks of the Iraqi Medina Division sat line abreast in revetments, each within the two-kilometre range of the Milan missile. The relatively small tank had a low profile, and only the flat dishes of their turrets protruded above the thick walls of sandbags. They would make difficult targets. McCowan scrutinised each in turn with the Mira thermal-imaging sight as they approached from the left flank. Detection could easily prove fatal; any one of the barrels might rotate in their direction at any moment. But they were not acting alone.

After a brief radio check to confirm the other Land Rovers were in position, McCowan fired the starting gun. With a screaming hiss, the Milan missile flew from its launcher, the bright flare filling his viewfinder as he attempted to hold the reticle steady on the nearest target. The flash of detonation was followed momentarily later by a similar impact on the second tank. The other Milan team had fired simultaneously, and with better luck. A deafening blast ripped through the air as the second T55 erupted in flame, its unshielded ammunition magazine ignited by the high-explosive warhead of the Milan missile. McCowan's target was still operational, and the four undamaged tanks began to turn their turrets to address the threat. He rushed to reload the launcher but there was no need. The T55 was robust and mobile but it lacked the sophisticated night-fighting suite of the British armour. The Iraqi tank crews were still unaware of the Challengers' presence when the barrage of 120mm rounds found their marks with devastating result. For McCowan, this encounter had provided valuable experience of the chess game of manoeuvre warfare in an open battlefield.

On the 6 April 1992, the Socialist Republic of Bosnia and Herzegovina was granted formal recognition as an independent state by the European Union, following the result of a referendum. The new state received international acceptance but was rejected by the self-proclaimed Bosnian-Serb entity Republika Srpska, led by Radovan Karadžić. In coalition with Serbian president

Slobodan Milošević and the Yugoslav People's Army, Republika Srpska began a campaign to forcibly take control of the state. A major humanitarian crisis then unfolded and the United Nations Protection Force deployed to intervene on behalf of the civilian population.

In 1994, McCowan, by then a sergeant, commanded an eight-man section operating covertly in Bosnia under the instruction of UNPROFOR. Their role was to seek out and remove threats to the UN designated safe zones, which were subject to sporadic attacks by Serbian forces. Sarajevo's Markale market had come under direct and deliberate mortar fire, killing many civilians. Snipers posed a continual threat. McCowan's unit stalked the urban battleground, setting up hides and observation points to identify and destroy the units responsible.

He stared through Steiner 10x50 binoculars as the tell-tale puff of smoke drifted upwards from the distant hillside. Several seconds later he heard the faint echoing thump. It was the second time. They had finally located a persistent and troublesome Serbian mortar team. He gave the order to his radio operator, who then transmitted the request for an immediate airstrike. The reply came swiftly. A pair of F-16s were being deployed from Italy, armed with 1000lb Paveway II laser-guided bombs.

A trooper kept the enemy position centralised in the ten-times-magnification sight of the Pilkington Optronics LF28 target designator, mounted on a tripod for stability, while the remainder of the section guarded the laser crew in counter-sniper formation. The jets were inbound from Aviano Air Base and McCowan fretted that the enemy team would relocate before they arrived, but the mortar team kept up their routine of occasional firing. After what seemed like an age, the radio operator received word from the F16 flight leader: sixty seconds to target. The trooper activated the beam, 'painting' the location of the enemy dugout, then withdrew his hands from the device to prevent any accidental movement. McCowan held his breath for the remaining seconds, then watched the resultant explosion with satisfaction. Finally the double crump reached him, reporting the retirement of the bothersome mortar crew. Members of the SAS remained active in this role until a sustained NATO air campaign – Operation Deliberate Force – helped to bring the conflict to an end in December 1995. McCowan had spent one of the longest periods operating covertly in enemy territory, of anyone active in the British Army.

Sierra Leonne, the year 2000—a combined force of SAS and 1st Company Parachute Regiment pack their bags for home after a successful operation to rescue six Royal Irish Rangers held hostage by the West Side Boys rebel group. McCowan did not leave with them. Remaining behind with three men, he was tasked with tying up a loose end. A key figure in the rebel organisation had escaped the raid and was thought to be regrouping with other survivors. The gang had repeatedly abused their female captives and forced children to fight as soldiers, actions deemed intolerable by the governments of both Britain and Sierra Leone. McCowan was given authority to hunt the man down to prevent such atrocities from happening again in the future.

The target was thought to have gone to ground in one of a series of villages around thirty-five kilometres inside hostile territory. McCowan and his men would be delivered to the vicinity by Land Rover during the night, but the approach to the villages was only possible on foot. To operate comfortably in the sweltering daytime temperatures, the patrol needed to travel as light as possible. Their Bergen backpacks were left behind. Water, ration packs, first-aid and ammunition were stowed in their belt-kits. Just these essentials were heavy enough as each man also wore body armour and carried a M16A2 assault rifle, fitted with the M203 under-barrel grenade launcher.

They covertly observed the villages one by one over a period of twenty-four hours before becoming confident that the WSB stragglers had gravitated to a single location. The primary target was suspected to be ensconced in a small hut at the edge of the rebel settlement. The patrol split into pairs and kept a distant vigil, front and rear, for five further hours until dawn. Finally, the man appeared in the open doorway for a few moments before returning inside. The decision was taken unanimously: they would bring the matter to a rapid close and exit the area as soon as possible.

Two men gave cover while McCowan and the fourth member ran towards the doorway. At fifty yards' range, they dropped to a kneel. McCowan Sighted the M203, fired, reloaded and fired again. The 40mm high-explosive grenades woke the village in an instant, reducing the objective time window to mere minutes. Two bursts of M16 fire crackled behind the assaulters as they stormed forward – the cover team had cut down an armed arrival from a neighbouring abode. Inside the hut, three WSB men had been badly lacerated with shrapnel, including their primary target. Follow up headshots finished the job at point-blank range. The patrol beat a rapid retreat from the village, guarding their rear with salvoes of rifle fire until they were collected by Land Rover and returned to the mission staging area. McCowan had added assassination to his repertoire.

In 2001, McCowan first saw combat in Afghanistan. On his repatriation, he was promoted to squadron sergeant major – the second highest rank he could hold as an enlisted man. Only the unique role of regimental sergeant major remained ahead of him. In over twenty years of military service, he had served on almost every major global battlefield. In 2003, he returned once again to Iraq.

At Stirling Lines, D Squadron now enacted a final simulated mission with 'Special Projects' – the counter-terrorism phase of the SAS duty cycle. The four squadrons were continually rotated between foreign deployments and domestic roles. Their next rostered duty would be 'Team Tasks' and during this period they would be free to engage in special assignments should they become available. This might involve attending international incidents as advisors, or conducting instruction programmes for foreign armies as a contract service. The current training phase had been particularly demanding and McCowan was keen to get this last exercise finished without incident to bring closure to the current domestic posting. He sat quietly waiting in the chair in the first-floor room of the Killing House.

* * *

Bang. The blast of the door-breaching charge shook the very structure of the building. Moments later, it was followed by a series of loud, sharp cracks. Through his earplugs, McCowan recognised the reports of 5.56mm rifle fire, instantly distinguishable from the sub-machine guns they commonly used. The Heckler & Koch MP5SD was fitted with an integral suppressor – a favourite of the SAS for its reliability and quiet operation – but its subsonic 9mm round lacked the punch to penetrate body armour. That meant headshots and follow-ups, more ammo used, more frequent magazine changes: not so practical when speed was critical. Instead, the rescue team were carrying harder-hitting assault rifles – the Colt Canada C8 CQB (close-quarter battle) carbine, known to the British as the L119A1. Fitted with ten-inch barrels, vertical fore-grips and telescoping stocks, these were an ideal tool for room clearance. D Squadron had trained with this weapon on a regular basis during their current rotation. A door was swung open downstairs.

Crack, crack. Crack, crack. McCowan heard the clatter of rounds on sheet metal.

'*Clear!*' a man shouted below, followed by a further fusillade of shots. The team would have split into two groups now to clear the lower building faster, with one man covering the lower hallway and one the staircase.

'*Hurry up!*' McCowan bellowed at the top of his voice. '*I'm being interrogated here.*'

It was only seconds into the exercise but he believed that his team should be training under the maximum amount of pressure, not that they would be able to hear him adorned with their hoods, masks and earplugs.

'*Locked door!*' a different voice shouted.

McCowan counted the seconds: *one…two…three…*

The boom of a 12-gauge rang twice through the house. One of the assaulters carried a pump-action shotgun, loaded with Hatton breaching rounds to rip off hinges and disable stubborn door locks. The three-inch Magnum cartridges were made from a mixture of wax and metal dust, designed to pack a heavy punch but disintegrate on impact, preventing potential injury to hostages. For this exercise, however, McCowan had made an unusual arrangement with the camp's carpenters. Heavy-duty deadbolts were installed top and bottom, and a third hinge was fitted to the middle of the door. The breacher could carry four shells in the magazine plus one in the chamber, and two of this total had been used already. McCowan chuckled to himself while a few seconds passed. '*I'm haemorrhaging information!*' he shouted downstairs.

Another bellow from the 12-gauge sounded. Blasting the lock would achieve nothing further but the breacher wouldn't know that.

'*Don't you waste those fucking Hatton rounds!*'

The big deadbolts were still holding and the door wouldn't open freely. McCowan felt beside himself with his own deviousness. He could almost sense the frustration of the breacher from his position upstairs in the chair. A fourth and final report rang out once the breacher had identified the last hinge.

'Having a spot of trouble lads?' McCowan muttered to himself, hearing the thump of the remaining door being kicked open.

McCowan's mischief was in fact a valuable part of the training process. Hostage-rescue teams needed to be prepared for every eventuality and able to adapt instantly when things went wrong. There was no room for indecision. The SAS practiced every scenario until all their actions were second nature.

There were two more 'Clear' calls before McCowan heard the tread of rubber-soled boots on the staircase. His pulse picked up a notch. The team would already be sweating in their assault gear, and then they would have to wrestle with the folded mattresses jammed in the upper stairwell. There were four upper rooms remaining for the rescuers to clear; McCowan's would be second-to-last. He heard two doors thrown open in quick succession, each with an accompanying volley of semi-automatic rounds. His mouth was dry now. The door in front of him swung open. The salvo of shots was deafening as the terrorist behind him went down, along with the man by the window. Two black-clad, masked men entered the room, weapons up in the shoulder, each peeling left or right.

'*Stoppage!'* McCowan yelled.

The man who had swung to McCowan's right smoothly lowered his assault rifle on its shoulder strap, pulled his pistol from its holster and bought it up to continue his sweep. He fired twice in quick succession, the double-tap taking the shotgun terrorist in the forehead.

'*Clear!'* A man shouted. 'Are you alright, sir?'

McCowan remained seated while the final shots were fired in the room next door, then casually removed his earplugs. 'You took your bloody time,' he eventually replied in his rich Scots accent. 'Who knows what I might have told them.'

'They're all dead, sir,' the masked assaulter replied. 'It doesn't matter what you told them.'

'I don't suppose it does, Jonah. That was some fine pistol work, by the way.'

The rescue team were all carrying the SIG Sauer P226 pistol as a secondary weapon, and Michael 'Jonah' Jones had employed his correctly by switching to it in the case of a stoppage. Jonah nodded briefly in acceptance of the compliment.

'Well I seem to be alive, so let's have a look around.' McCowan rose from his seat and surveyed the room.

The facial area of the wooden target behind him had been obliterated by at least three rounds. The terrorist by the window had fared no better with a cluster of hits to the upper chest – another definite kill. McCowan made his way around the first-floor rooms, the air hanging heavily with cordite smoke in each. He found nothing to kindle any disappointment. All the targets were taken down cleanly and his rescue had only taken a shade over a minute. He made his way downstairs, clambering over the discarded mattresses, and singled out the man carrying the tactical shotgun. The breacher, Trooper Iain Morris, stood with his head hung slightly down and the Remington Model 870 cradled in his arms.

'So, what happened there, Morris?' McCowan barked as Morris' head sunk lower. 'Just messing with you, lad. I meant for that door to be a bastard. You did fine, but let's see how our hostage faired.' A brief inspection behind the breached door revealed a wooden hostage in healthy order. He checked the remaining lower rooms for stray shots or omitted targets while the rescue team stood by for feedback. There was nothing amiss to report.

'Ok lads, I've seen enough. We'll wrap it up here. Get the gear back to the quartermaster and we'll run through the debrief, then you can grab yourselves some scoff.'

McCowan made his way out through the obliterated front door to be met by a small group of onlookers monitoring the exercise. He sought the attention of a man dressed in regular khaki uniform and a sand-coloured beret, Sergeant Calvin Shearman, who had commanded the rescue operation.

'Well, I'm glad we didn't use flashbangs, Cal. My ears are ringing as it is. How did it go down here?'

'By the numbers, Ken, and pretty good on the stopwatch too.' Calvin Shearman stood six foot two with a slim, muscular build and the ebony skin of his West-Indian lineage. He was a natural athlete, destined for a successful career in sport had he not joined the Army with the specific intention of applying for the SAS. Shearman had issued the rescue team their orders for the house clearance and given their final 'go' command.

'And how about the girl?'

'Spot on; she's very capable. Her weapon handling is right up there with the lads.'

They referred to their latest training exchange participant. The SAS regularly sent personnel to train with affiliated foreign forces, and received their members in kind. The Sayeret Matkal are an elite Israeli unit specialising in reconnaissance, counterterrorism and hostage rescue. Controversially, they had sent Elana Govrin as a trainee.

In 2005, the British Army did not use women for frontline combat roles, but that wasn't the case in the Israeli Defence Force. Having national service conscription for both men and women, Israel passed an amendment to their Military Service law in 2000 stating that all positions within the IDF should be open to women. At first, McCowan wasn't sure whether they had sent 'the girl' to be contrary, or to show off that they had women of her ability. On seeing Govrin's performance level, he realised that the latter was the case. She had consistently held her own with his men since her arrival at Credenhill. McCowan called her over.

'Elana, a moment please.'

She stepped up briskly and removed her mask and hood. 'Yes, sir.'

'How did you find our exercise?'

'Your training is very intensive compared to ours, but I think that maybe we do this for real more often.' Govrin was five foot seven and of stocky build, with defined, muscular thighs. Her dark hair was worn in a short, tight ponytail.

'How so?' McCowan interrogated.

'We have a lot of intelligence people and agents operating outside our borders. When they get caught, Sayeret Matkal are deployed to get them back on very short notice. In this kind of operation, it is almost certain that you will need to fire your weapon; you cannot afford to hesitate or miss.'

'Well I'm told that your performance was first class. Good work; carry on.'

'Thank you, sir.'

When she was out of earshot, McCowan quietly addressed Shearman again.

'There's talk of an overseas op in the pipeline, Cal. What are we going to do with her then?'

'Let's cross that bridge when we come to it. Someone here can look after her. We won't let it get in the way of an op, anyway. Why, what have we got on?'

McCowan was thinking about his answer when a member of the administrative staff approached and addressed him.

'Sar' major, the CO has requested a conference call on the secure line with Major Nolan and yourself, at your first convenience.'

'I'm not entirely sure, Cal, but maybe I'm about to find out.'

Chapter Four

Saturday, 4 June
La Fábrica

Coniraya sat alone, bathed in the orange glow of the gas lamps, finishing his last few mouthfuls of supper under the stretched tarpaulin roof of the mess area. It was prior to the start of his late-evening shift and the canteen was quiet. A handful of other men were scattered around the surrounding rows of cut-log benches but there was no conversation to be heard. Each ignored his neighbours and ate in silence, disturbed only by the hiss and trill of jungle insects and the nocturnal serenade of a thousand frogs.

Coniraya was dispirited. The meal had been a small portion of fresh fish – caught from the nearby river – and fried potato spiced with chilli and strong huacatay paste. It was nourishing enough but he wasn't overly impressed with the flavour. He found the camp food repetitive and thought the cooks should make more effort, despite their remote location high on the slopes of the mountain forest.

At one end of the mess, the catering crew used a row of gas burners and an assortment of basic kitchen equipment to provide meals for the whole camp. There were over one hundred mouths to feed in total and so mealtimes were divided into shifts. First to be served were the agricultural workers, who got up before sunrise for breakfast and came in at sunset for their supper sitting. They were followed on the mess rota, both morning and evening, by the production teams. The men on nightshift duty had a different sleep pattern to the majority and were always the last to be fed. Standing, Coniraya weaved his way through the benches to where the chefs kept an open barrel for the dirty dishes and cutlery. He threw his bowl into the tub with a disdainful scowl, then skulked away without offering any thanks or acknowledgement.

The evening air was cool and dry, which was a welcome change from the high humidity felt throughout most of the year. Coniraya stood for a moment and retrieved a pouch of coarse tobacco from his shirt pocket, then took a pinch and rolled it into a dirty-brown paper. He lit up with a match and took a long hard pull of the harsh unfiltered smoke. It scorched his throat but he felt a flush of pleasure regardless as he exhaled through yellowed, chipped and missing teeth.

Adjacent to the mess was the accommodation tent – an envelope of timber, rope and taut canvas erected to sleep everyone in the camp bar the officers. Inside, each employee was allowed a small space to sleep and store their possessions, identified by their personal blanket laid out on the heavy ground sheet. The conditions were bearable but far from comfortable. Outside of the rainy season, some of the men preferred the open air to the confines of the crowded marquee, and thus a number of hammocks were stretched between nearby trees. Coniraya scanned his eyes around these as he smoked, to see which were occupied for the night ahead.

The point where he stood was near the centre of the cavernous clearing. He gazed upwards towards its barely visible ceiling. In the poor light, it was impossible to appreciate the scale of engineering that had gone into its construction. The manmade glade was arranged to disguise the enclosed structures from overflying aircraft. A set-up of its size could never be invisible, but it was obscured sufficiently to make aerial targeting difficult.

Massive trees had been felled or reduced to standing structural poles; a pair of these served as masts for the accommodation tent. The overhanging canopy from the surrounding trees covered the area, forming a thick leafy ceiling twenty metres from the ground and upwards. Multiple layers of camouflage netting were stretched below this, woven with cut brush to cover gaps and conceal the activity below. At last light, the expanse felt like the interior of a massive cathedral, not that Coniraya believed in any gods. He was just there for the money.

Coniraya was of indigenous Quechua ethnicity, as were the majority in the Apurimac region. Born near the city of Andahuaylas into a poor community of subsistence farmers, his family grew their own crops and raised chickens to provide a small monetary income. Cockfighting was a popular pastime in rural Peru, and there was always demand for strong two-year old roosters. Coniraya, however, gained no satisfaction from this life of basic agriculture. As a young man, he left the family home to follow a different career path entirely.

He sucked on the last of his cigarette until it burnt his lips and fingers, then flicked the stub at a compatriot resting in a nearby hammock. *'Allin tuta,'* he disingenuously wished the man goodnight.

Strutting into the accommodation tent, he made no attempt to be careful or quiet. Stealing was a punishable offence in the camp and it was one of his duties to deal with offenders. Hence, he strode through the marquee like an overlord, shoving into anyone he considered to be in his way. From his bed, he picked up the Zastava Arms M21 assault rifle, issued to him as a patrol weapon, then held it in the air and cocked it melodramatically. In reality, he was unlikely to fire it for any other reason than machoistic self-expression.

Heading out from the marquee, he made his way over to a cluster of smaller tents, most of which provided accommodation for the camp's officers. The one he sought stood apart from the others and was adjoined by a satellite dish and a tall radio antenna. A dim but steady light emitted from its doorway. Nearby, the thrum of the devoted diesel generator could be heard. He entered the command post and reported to the duty-officer using Spanish, the language of the camp, rather than his native Quechuan tongue. His pronunciation was poor and laboured, mainly due to a lack of effort. Nicolao barely looked up but addressed him curtly.

'Ah Concha, all-positions check for you. Take a radio. Get going now and come back here when you're done.'

Coniraya had earned himself the nickname 'Concha' amongst the Spanish-speaking Peruvians. He realised there were derogatory connotations but didn't take the slight to heart. It wasn't his language and he was too thick-skinned to care, anyway. Not that he could do much about it – all of the officers used the name. He nodded acquiescence, took a radio and stepped out of the command tent. It was a similar routine most nights. Coniraya was a guard at La Fábrica – the largest cocaine production facility of the Del Bosque cartel.

The Del Bosque organisation was a cartel in the true sense of the word – a syndicate of competing businesses, uniting strategically to pool their resources. Wealthy plantation owners and exporters had joined forces with criminal elements, and the alliance offered many advantages: it streamlined transport, gave bulk-buying power for chemicals and equipment, facilitated bribery of officials, and allowed the sharing of expensive assets such as aircraft. As a result, the syndicate's cocaine growers had reduced their costs and increased production massively, while Del Bosque itself had become a politically formidable entity.

Coniraya did not consider himself to be a member of a drug gang. He saw himself as a soldier in an army, defending the region's farmers and businessmen. In his eyes the government was a corrupt and unjust oppressor, only attacking the cartels in order to encourage the payment of bribes. In any case, during Coniraya's youth Del Bosque had been the only viable employer. He stood outside the command tent and performed a brief radio check, wishing that he was holding a bottle of cold beer instead of the handset. He always had a thirst for alcohol, but it was strictly forbidden on duty and harsh retribution awaited rule breakers at La Fábrica.

His patrol route would take him on a circuitous tour of the facility via each of the stationary lookout positions. If he found anyone to be absent, drunk or otherwise slacking he would relish and maximise the opportunity to administer some discipline, with the full backing of the duty-officer behind him. He walked back past the marquee to the western end of the clearing where the production utilities and storage huts were located. The lamps weren't lit at this hour and Coniraya's eyes were slow to adjust to the darkness, but the solid, dark outline of the agricultural workshop stood out from the gloomy backdrop. He made his way northwards towards the coca fields via the western road – a narrow vehicle track that was cut like a tunnel through the brush at low level. Coniraya squinted to focus on the faint light emitting from the fields beyond to maintain his direction in the darkness.

In contrast to the arrangement within the clearing, the activity in the plantation was brazen. The cultivated area was extensive, spreading across and up the more open hillside where less felling had been required. The crop was Huánuco coca, which grew strongest in humid forest clearings but produced better quality product from drier, cooler, higher slopes. La Fábrica utilised both environments with its sprawling plantation. Cuttings were propagated in the forest, then planted out in blocks on the hillside above. Coniraya saw no reason to hide the crop anyway – the plant wasn't even illegal. Coca had been grown in Peru for centuries as a medicinal herb, chewed with lime to alleviate pain, fatigue and altitude sickness. Now the fresh leaves were approaching readiness for the second of three harvests. The first and biggest was always after the rainy season in March, the last usually carried out in late October.

Coniraya's first port of call was in the southwest corner of the plantation. The mortar pit was dug into the hillside with high mud walls on three sides, remaining open at the rear to allow rainwater to drain downhill into the forest.

Housed in the pit was an American-made M30 mortar, ready to fire with only the removal of its rain cover. The weapon was originally purchased by the Bolivian Army, subsequently stolen, and then smuggled across the border on a mule train along with several cases of 107mm ammunition.

La Fábrica's militia used a simple but effective method to aim the potent device. Schematic diagrams of the coca plantation and the surrounding hillsides were mounted inside the pit on laminated cards. These cards were annotated with the required elevation and azimuth settings to hit each area. Operators would receive instruction by radio on the location of hostile forces, then set the relevant trajectory on the mortar's base plate. The initial calibration had been carried out by test-firing rounds and charting their impact points. If faced with an enemy assault, men from the clearing could run up the western road to man the position in a matter of minutes. Government forces, either advancing on the ground or attempting to land helicopters, would be met with a rainstorm of high-explosive shells and burning white phosphorous. Coniraya's only responsibility was to check that the position was in ready firing order.

He made out the silhouette of the guard as he approached – one of four men positioned around the headland to provide warning of any incursion. Other roaming sentries continually patrolled between them using various circuits and an irregular pattern of rotation. Omar stood dutifully on station with a radio handset clipped to his belt. The VHF transceivers were notoriously unreliable and rarely used to check-in. Instead, at the first sign of trouble, Omar would discharge a burst of gunfire into the air and wake up the camp like a hive of bees. He carried an ageing Belgian-made FNC assault rifle slung across his back, ready for the job.

As Coniraya approached, he swung his own rifle off its strap and cradled it to his chest as if he expected to use it. His M21 was one of the latest batch to reach the camp; thirty had been delivered to Del Bosque in a single consignment, then distributed around their various operations. The cartel possessed the necessary money, influence and smuggling contacts to acquire almost any export firearms package, but in this case a simple bribe had diverted a few crates of infantry weapons headed for the Ejército del Perú. Ironically, this meant that the rifles' end users were ultimately destined to fire them at the very forces that had purchased them in the first place.

Coniraya had only fired the Zastava a few times for practice, finding it roughly similar to the old Kalashnikovs but with an improved, more modern mechanism. Nonetheless, he still saw it as a status symbol that affirmed his superiority over the other men. Only those at the top of the food chain were rewarded with the newest kit. The only firearm in the camp that held more prestige was the futuristic-looking assault rifle brought back from the downed helicopter by the search patrol, and this had been confiscated by the officers and hung as a trophy in their mess tent. Omar was doing nothing that Coniraya thought worthy of comment, so he strode past with his head down, without so much as a greeting.

He continued the long trudge up the western headland to the next lookout's position, passing line after line of two-metre-high coca plants. The crop was oldest at this end of the plantation – around eight to ten years in Coniraya's estimation. Long straight branches profuse with tapered oval leaves obscured the sight lines eastwards between the rows; the dark blanket of foliage could easily conceal an army without him being any the wiser. The gentle breeze encouraged a light but constant rustle.

He finally reached the northwest corner of the plantation, its highest point, where the watchman reclined in a plastic chair. Coniraya paused for breath, taking in the night sky to the south while he rolled a cigarette. The dark outline of the next ridge of towering mountains, many kilometres distant, cut into the backdrop of pinprick stars. Beneath these, the lush sea of coca plants ran gently down to the edge of the forest from where his patrol had begun. In his own time, he continued around the headland, checking the remaining positions without incident. When his duties in the plantation were completed, he made his way back to the camp via the eastern road.

* * *

He crossed the clearing from north to south, passing the entrance to the cavernous bunker. The dugout was supported with sawn timber and had a ramp of earth leading inside, giving the appearance of an old-fashioned mine entrance. The ceiling of the interior was reinforced by the remaining root networks of the felled trees above, creating an underground garage for safe storage of the camp's military vehicles. A glimpse of the silhouettes secreted within spurred Coniraya with heady hubris. Housed inside was the armoured pick-up truck – an improvised fighting vehicle with a pair of pintle-mounted machine guns on its roof bars. Two men could mount its rear bed and hose down attackers with showers of hot lead, while a slotted steel sheet over the windscreen protected the driver. But the menacing little truck shared its sleeping quarters with an even more malevolent bedfellow: the monstrous, six-wheeled, mobile missile launcher. It sat safe from sight and harm in its underground lair but could be driven in a moment to a number of firing locations. Twice it had fired a rocket and twice it had obliterated the target. He knew that the Russian beast made them invincible.

Adjoining the eastern end of the clearing, at the furthest extent from the tents and structures, was a swathe of hillside where only the taller trees had been felled. Smaller shrubs had been left standing to provide the cover of foliage at ground level. From inside the area, the absence of canopy opened up a huge window to the star-spattered sky above. The launcher was brought here to perform radar sweeps of the airspace to the south, and the cartel had many sources that would provide forewarning of military aircraft operating in their neighbourhood.

Coniraya continued down the incline via the snaking hairpins of the southern road, a route that eventually joined the airstrip at its northwest corner in a cleared apron under the forest's edge. The apron was used to store the plant equipment used in the construction of the facility: an excavator, a bulldozer, a big four-wheel-drive tractor that was now used for manoeuvring planes and towing supplies up to the camp in its trailer. Coniraya always looked forward to this part of the patrol. A small band of men were permanently garrisoned here, and far from the vigilant eyes of the officers there was a good chance of some alcohol going around. They stood by a small fire, prohibited in other parts of the encampment.

Coniraya joined them to roll a cigarette, chatting idly for a few minutes and making a rare attempt to be amiable. Present were the crew of the second pick-up truck and the operator of the Cascavel armoured car. The truck was mounted with a .50 calibre Browning machine gun on its rear flatbed, but was mostly used for light logistics and ferrying personnel to and from the main camp. The armoured car was immobile due to a seized transmission. It sat buried up to its turret in the corner of the airstrip, ready and waiting to swat any unwelcome visitors to the runway with its fully functional 90mm cannon.

'Oye, Concha!' The voice came from Coniraya's left. He looked up from rolling his second smoke to be handed a small bottle of locally brewed rum. This was exactly what he'd been waiting for. He took a long swig of the potent hooch

until he nearly gagged, then handed the bottle back while wiping his mouth with his sleeve. Satisfied that the temporary halt had achieved its purpose, he made an unnecessary comment about the importance of his patrol then set off across the airstrip itself.

The airstrip was another noteworthy piece of construction engineering and was no less obvious than the coca fields. At a kilometre in length, the runway was designed for heavy transport planes to land, turn around, then take off again when empty – no mean feat for the pilot considering the reduction in lift that occurred at this altitude. Its surface was graded, levelled, grassed and periodically mown to provide smooth passage for the rugged tactical aircraft it accommodated.

Processed cocaine was flown out of La Fábrica on light aircraft, but larger transports had been required to bring in the plant equipment and military vehicles. During the camp's establishment, the first workers had brought chainsaws, augers and explosives via mule train. Initially they had cleared an area where helicopters could drop supplies and machines. Then came the first small runway, which had expanded incrementally in line with the increasing needs of the cartel operation.

Coniraya felt pleasantly light-headed as he made his way down the track to the river, albeit with a touch of nausea. He needed to check in with the river guard, the man who reportedly suffered the worst duty in the entire camp. Time served and obedience translated directly into seniority with Del Bosque. Coniraya had been at La Fábrica for three years and had earned himself a preferable regular assignment, but he could vividly recall the monotony of the river guard position. The area was completely inaccessible. From the west, there were too many rapids for a boat to navigate upstream; from the east, the river came gushing down through the rocks of the mountains which in themselves were difficult to traverse. The inescapable security of the location meant that the river guard had nothing to watch out for, and thus was guaranteed to be catatonically bored for the whole of his shift. The camp joke was that anyone brawny enough to reach La Fábrica via the river would easily overpower the lone guard anyway.

After a brief but sympathetic chat with the sentry, Coniraya made his way along the narrow strip of gravel beach, rounding a bend in the river to where the canoes sat on the shore. These could only be used to travel downstream but were employed to run errands, or by men taking leave at times when aircraft weren't available or economically justified. After enduring a few hours of bumpy ride, the canoeists would eventually join the main Apurimac River, where they could switch to road vehicles at one of the many small settlements. Returning canoes were dropped back at the camp by the scheduled supply aircraft, then dragged down the track to their embarkation point near a calmer section of water. Coniraya now had only one remaining lookout position to check on. He headed away from the beach and made his way upwards along the cliff path.

The cliff had been created by a large slice of land falling away from the hillside, the resultant landslide flattening the brush below and forming a scree slope running down to the beach. Hundreds of years of subsequent erosion had covered the slope in fine gravel from the shattered rock face, leaving only the occasional larger rock exposed and preventing the re-establishment of the forest flora. The face of the cliff was just a few metres high to begin with, increasing as the path ran up its edge. The path itself was just over a metre wide and snaked along the broken edge of the rock. Regular machete work was required to keep back the encroaching brush.

The final guard position was considered to be most critical for the defence of La Fábrica. It was referred to as 'El Sillón' – The Chair. The Chair sat on the highest part of the cliff edge and benefitted from both the vantage point and the lack of trees growing below, giving an unrestricted vista looking westwards down the river valley. This had proven invaluable when the army troop helicopters had attempted to approach the camp from this direction, flying low up the course of the river. The lookout stationed in El Sillón spotted the incursion at several kilometres distance, giving adequate warning for the missile crew to move their machine to a firing position. A swift end was brought to that raid.

Coniraya passed the entrance to the back path – a shortcut to the clearing avoiding the hairpins of the south road, used from the main camp to access the river on foot. He was sweating heavily from the exertion of trudging up the steep slope, his breathing laboured and his head feeling the rum. He turned a corner, his view opening along the path before him, and he froze in his tracks. He almost stopped breathing while he tried to get a grasp of what he saw. A man was sat in the wooden framed chair, hands in his lap, with his head lolled forward. Coniraya crept slowly closer for a better view, considering if the guard could be rolling a cigarette. He didn't think so. The lookout hadn't moved in a while and the long rifle rested on the stony ground beside him. Coniraya felt a tingle of excitement and a flicker of an involuntary grin.

As he stalked closer, he became confident that the man was asleep. *Who is it?* To Coniraya's straining eyes it looked like Temetzin. He struggled to breathe quietly to avoid waking the man prematurely, creeping to within a few metres where he saw for certain that it was Temetzin. *Oh brilliant!* Coniraya sniggered to himself. *That smug bastard thinks he owns this place.* Temetzin was a supposed big shot sent over from another camp. Coniraya hated him.

He crept behind the chair with his heart pounding so loud in his chest that he thought it would wake the sleeping sentry. But no, it was too late now. He took one last careful step, planted both hands on the back of the chair and violently heaved the man forward. Temetzin's sleeping legs buckled under him, his arms flailing desperately as he tipped off the cliff face. The half-conscious sentry let out a brief shriek, before a low thump silenced him and signalled the end of his fall.

'Ha haar!' Coniraya burst into laughter and clapped his hands repeatedly. Camp rules were arbitrary: any man caught sleeping in El Sillón could be pushed over the edge without recrimination for the patrol guard. Coniraya couldn't believe his luck.

Still grinning, he peered over the edge and scanned for a body; the vertical drop was over ten metres before the upper scree slope. He picked up the long rifle – a Galatz 7.62 – always held by the lookout in case any worthwhile game strayed onto the gravel beach below. Fixing the lifeless form in the scope, he saw that Temetzin had gone down head first. The impact had snapped his neck back like a twig. Even if he had survived the fall and dragged himself back to the clearing, he would most likely have been executed as an example anyway. Coniraya pulled the radio off his belt clip.

'Command, come in. This is outer patrol.'

'Si Concha, que tal?' Came the crackly reply.

'We need a new man in The Chair. Temetzin fell asleep.'

'Do we need a new chair as well?'

'No, I held onto it,' Coniraya said with considerable pride.

'Okay, Concha, wait there. I'll send someone down the back path.'

Twenty minutes later, the new guard arrived to be politely handed the long rifle and ushered into the wooden chair.

'Don't fall asleep,' were Coniraya's departing words as he headed off on his return to the clearing.

He swore and stumbled as he picked his way up the steep, rocky path in near total darkness, but nothing could spoil his mood. He clambered up and across the short wooden ladders and bridges, installed to get over the many obstacles. He nearly fell twice but didn't lose the spring in his step. In all Coniraya's three years at La Fábrica, this had been his best shift.

Chapter Five
Monday, 6 June
London

Didier Morin stood by the dark-wood service counter of his small but highly acclaimed restaurant, polishing wine glasses from the rack beside him and watching the handful of customers. He was immaculate in appearance, dressed in a crisp white shirt, black waistcoat, black trousers and gleaming black-leather shoes. His dark hair was slicked back, his face clean shaven except for a fine, carefully shaped moustache. The image blended perfectly with the décor – polished wood, etched glass and artwork that was quirky but still classically French. He glanced nonchalantly down at the open reservation book that sat beside him, mostly for effect as he could easily recall all of the day's bookings. It was half past midday, still quite early for lunch sittings, and only two tables had ordered food so far. The young Hungarian waitress had served these along with the odd coffee. Didier awaited the day's first noteworthy customers, whom he expected to arrive shortly.

Chez Morin was situated just off Eccleston Street, Belgravia – one of the more upmarket areas of West London. Its location, high pricing and relative privacy made it popular with clientele averse to the scrutiny of the public eye. Today, this included the table for three booked by the personal assistant of Simon Tidewell – the Minister of State for the Armed Forces. It wasn't uncommon for Didier to receive officials from the Ministry of Defence, or from the security services. Such people frequented Chez Morin for their less-formal engagements as there was a relatively low likelihood of being eavesdropped by unwelcome parties. Didier envisaged that this air of intimacy had attracted Tidewell's party, and that they might be sufficiently relaxed in the setting to discuss matters of a sensitive nature. His interest was aroused accordingly.

A black Jaguar pulled up outside and a tall, balding man got out, attaché case in his free hand and The Times newspaper under his arm. He was well dressed in a navy blue, pinstriped three-piece, finely tailored in Savile Row or thereabouts. Didier moved swiftly to the front door, opened it and ushered the minister inside as they exchanged the usual cordial greetings. Tidewell was a regular at lunchtimes and the two men knew each other on first-name terms. Didier showed his customer to a vacant corner and proffered a chair, his movements smooth and precise, almost theatrical. He would serve this table himself and leave the others to the waitress.

Tidewell was broad shouldered and formerly athletic, but a lifetime of office work and restaurant lunches had rewarded him with a heavy waistline. He needed to shuffle around to get into his seat. He ordered coffee, put on his glasses and read quickly to fill the minutes until his two summoned companions arrived. Didier knew the man to be both sharp minded and well educated, having attended Radley College and Oxford University, details the restauranteur had ascertained during a previous visit.

It was only a short while before the second man arrived on foot. Didier recognised him immediately through the glass frontage. The man's name was Daniels, one of the spooky types that came over from the Vauxhall Cross headquarters of the Secret Intelligence Service – commonly known as MI6. He was unusual in that he appeared to report directly to Tidewell, leading Didier to the impression that he was a liaison officer of some kind, serving as an intermediary between SIS and MoD. Daniels was average in height and of slim build. His blond hair was neatly styled and he wore pale khaki cotton – lightweight, single-breasted and almost certainly off the shelf. Didier had a quick eye for such details. Daniels had a direct and confident manner and took himself quickly to Tidewell's table. Didier left the two men to exchange pleasantries while he fetched the coffee. They were unlikely to get down to business before the third man arrived.

Didier did not recognise the third man but the upright posture and brisk manner suggested a military background. He was short, weathered and fit looking, and wore a herringbone tweed jacket with sharply creased grey trousers. Didier took a guess that the man was Army, an officer, and fairly senior as the grey-tinged hair suggested an age in the forties. He held the door, then politely ushered the man when predictably asked for the minister's table. Daniels and Tidewell stood for the new arrival while introductions were made.

'Colonel, good to see you. This is Tom Daniels. I take it you may have met before.'

'Yes, I believe so. In passing at Sandhurst and briefly in Westphalia,' the older man replied.

'That's correct, sir. How have you been?' Didier took note that Daniels had a military background and most likely held a commission.

'Just fine, but please, it's Alan.'

Tidewell then introduced Lieutenant-Colonel Pearson-Roberts to Didier, announcing the later as the proprietor of one of the finest brasseries in West London and prompting the restauranteur to give an elaborate appraisal of what his chef had to offer. Didier accepted any compliments with good grace and an appropriate affectation of bored professionalism. He didn't wish to appear too keen to loiter by the table. At the first break in the conversation, he slipped away to make tea for the lieutenant-colonel.

By the time Tidewell's party had ordered their first two courses, Didier had learnt that Pearson-Roberts was the current CO (commanding officer) of 22 SAS, a fact that seemed likely to be pertinent to the agenda. He also gathered from their food orders that they planned to be sitting for a while. Didier checked with the waitress that she could manage serving on her own, told the chef not to rush his table's entrées, and retreated to his office via its key-coded door.

At his desk, Didier activated the control console of the Racal Wordnet multi-channel voice logger and pulled a pair of Sennheiser headphones over his ears. He selected the input from Tidewell's table, checked momentarily for volume and clarity, then activated recording. The men were still discussing relative formalities. Didier switched his headset to receive the audio feed from each of the other tables for a few seconds each, quickly dismissing their chatter as inconsequential, then returned his attention to Tidewell's table. Pearson-Roberts was asking Daniels what he'd been doing since being seconded away from the Army. This conversation would be of interest to Didier.

* * *

After a childhood in Sainte-Foy, Quebec, aspiration and adventure lured Didier to Paris as a teenager. There, he undertook classical chef's training, followed by two years of arduous work at the bottom of the '*brigade de cuisine*' ladder. His passion and commitment earned him the respect of his mentors and a fledgling career took flight. In his mid-twenties, opportunity attracted Didier to London, where his culinary skill further improved his prospects, but only so far. He was sufficiently capable, either in the kitchen or working front-of-house, but the level of competition prevented him from acquiring a position of any significant prestige. He switched employers regularly in the hope of finding an entry point to one of the more renowned establishments. Didier had recently taken a job as maître d' for a newly opened and fashionable central London restaurant when his big break occurred.

The process had begun when a man and woman, evidently not a couple, sat for dinner. Before leaving, she had asked Didier if he would join her for a late-night drink after his shift. The young and red-blooded Didier accepted with enthusiasm, but just five minutes into the rendezvous the woman's male companion reappeared. The pair announced that they were officers of Britain's domestic security service: MI5.

They were polite, business-like and reasonable in their requests. A wealthy and frequent customer at Didier's new workplace was suspected to have sympathies towards a certain less-than-moderate political group. Didier was asked to surreptitiously place a listening device at the person's table when they sat for dinner, which would then relay the conversation to a vehicle stationed outside. Of all the opportunities available to Didier at that point in his life, this one had seemed by far the most enticing.

He exceeded all expectations and completed the task with ease. Fitting the device to a champagne cooler, he had wheeled it to the customer's table and captured a perfect recording. His performance was so polished and natural that the MI5 officers recruited him to their ranks shortly afterwards. After a transitional period and some essential training, Didier was awarded an almost unique position within MI5; one that also allowed him to fulfil his more everyday ambitions.

Chez Morin was housed in a state-owned building that was administered by the home office. The business was set up in an experimental scheme as an intelligence gathering asset, situated conveniently within walking distance of several foreign embassies. With no capital of any note, Didier couldn't hope to own his own premises, and especially not in such an expensive area. But as MI5's agent-restauranteur he could have his cake and eat it. He had run the brasserie for six years, diligently eavesdropping on conversations with microphones hardwired into the seating areas. He had become adept at identifying which parties might be worth attention and served those tables himself, slipping out back to initiate the recording process. Didier carried out this espionage while always maintaining his charade of being the consummate professional. MI5 had gleaned many morsels of useful information from the enterprise, and the establishment even made a modest profit.

* * *

Didier's headphones were turned up to considerable volume, ensuring that he didn't miss a single word or inflection. Notes were scribbled in rapid shorthand. His ears were sensitive to minor differences in accent and could easily distinguish the three men's voices. Tidewell's was both deepest and loudest, and had the drawl of public-school education. Pearson-Roberts had a rasp to his voice and generally spoke quickly, sounding almost impatient at points. Daniels was relatively youthful in comparison to the other two men, conspicuous in his upbeat and inquisitive tones. It transpired that Daniels had been cherrypicked by the MoD as a young lieutenant, early in his career as an officer. Presumably he had displayed unusual prowess of some kind, perhaps a trait that was revealed by his essays or exam results. Now he headed a pointedly ambiguous department within the Defence Intelligence Staff named Limitation and Remuneration – or L&R – the purpose of which he attempted to elaborate to Pearson-Roberts.

'I work with 'Six' on a day-to-day basis – they gather the intel on the defence market – but I'm answerable to the MoD.' Daniels used the abbreviation for MI6. 'Our aim is to ration the egress of British technology to our foreign competitors, or at least maximise the revenue gained from it. So, that could involve making sure defence contractors meet licence criteria during export sales, for example, or negotiating contract specifics with oversees customers. It sounds a bit mercenary, but it's quite important for national security.'

'Yes, I can see how it might be.' The lieutenant-colonel sounded indignant. 'It still baffles me that we gave away our Chobham armour. But is there really that much work in it?'

'You'd be surprised how much we get involved in. Export equipment quite often needs a few software modifications before it gets shipped, generally to reduce any potential future threat to our own forces, but also to maintain our industrial advantage. Someone has to make sure the manufacturers toe the line.'

'Sure, but don't you miss some action? It just sounds a little administrative for a man of your background.'

'Far from it, sir. There's often some conflict of interest with the buyers, some of whom do business through intermediaries. In significant cases, direct measures can be required to prevent undesirables from gaining access to our technology. I coordinate with Six when I'm overseas, and occasionally we have to call in some help and get our hands dirty. I've been the bearer of bad news in some less-than-friendly locations and had some pretty tense moments.'

Didier listened intently as the conversation progressed. It was a long while since he last obtained product of this value, and that made him even more eager to learn the specific purpose of the meeting. He knew that DIS requested information from MI5 on occasion, but the current didn't necessarily flow both ways. And besides that, inter-service rivalry wasn't completely dead. He checked his watch to see how much longer he could remain at his headphones before returning to serve in the restaurant.

'Right, let's get down to business: Peru,' Tidewell let the word hang for a moment. 'Alejandro Mendez' government is currently engaged in process of reformation aimed at tackling corruption, organised crime and drug trafficking. They've been enjoying some measure of success against the cocaine cartels – burning coca fields, shooting down planes, seizing assets, et cetera. But their enemy are resourceful and well-funded and as always, they find ways to fight back for their survival. So we, Her Majesty's Government, intend to support Mendez' endeavour by offering a suitable package of training and equipment to the Peruvian Army – the Ejército del Perú.'

'Sounds fairly regular. What are we giving them?' Daniels asked.

'Colonel,' Tidewell prompted.

'We're sending a troop from D Squadron to work with their 5th Mountain Brigade and 4th Special Forces. They'll cover weapons drills, movements, tactics, as well as assessing their current training practices for weaknesses. It's the usual routine, really. The EP will then integrate those abilities into their regular training as they see fit.'

'Why do they need that from us?' Daniels queried. 'I mean, their own SF are already highly capable and they know their home turf far better than we do.'

'They'll still take an opportunity to train with another elite unit, especially our SAS,' Pearson-Roberts countered. 'No general turns down resources for his command, whether that be men, equipment, intelligence or expertise. What's less common is the political will to spend one's budget on foreign services – these packages are expensive. But we have a foot in the door on this job. We made a good impression with the Japanese Embassy crisis.'

Didier thought back to when the matter had been in the newspapers. A large number of high-level diplomats, officials and businessmen had been taken hostage by the radical MRTA group at the residence of the Japanese ambassador in Lima, some of which were held for months. The SAS sent advisors to help bring the situation to a close, and with their assistance a largely successful rescue was conducted.

'They've had a recent setback,' Tidwell took over. 'An army helicopter was taken down by a surface-to-air missile during a raid on a cocaine production facility operated by the Del Bosque cartel, killing twenty troops and the flight crew. It's the biggest single loss of life they've had for a while. Now both Mendez and the military leadership are facing serious criticism for their approach to the conflict. The press has torn him off a strip and the public are angry.'

'What kind of missile are we talking about?' Daniels asked.

'Alan can explain the detail better than I.'

Pearson-Roberts spoke tersely. 'Two Mi-17 'Hip' transport helicopters were carrying the advance element of an assault force through a region of cartel control. They were flying low up a river gorge to avoid detection. As they approached the target, the first of the pair was struck with little-to-no warning by a command-guided SAM. The missile hit head on and the helicopter crashed into the ravine, leaving no possibility of survivors. The second of the pair picked up the active radar burst used to target the first aircraft, saw it go down, and was able to reverse course and abort the mission. The data suggests that the missile system used was the Russian SA8 'Gecko'.'

'The SA8: that's a worrying piece of kit. Can't they hit the site from a fast jet?' Daniels suggested.

'It's not an option they're considering,' Tidewell answered. 'They'd need to drop a lot of ordnance to have any hope of hitting the launcher – there'd be a lot of dead farmers. Del Bosque would then publicise these civilian deaths. The public would conclude that the crooks had outsmarted the authorities by forcing them to resort to indiscriminate bombing. Let's remember that coca farming is historic in Peru; it's neither illegal nor entirely unpopular.'

'It now appears that this wasn't the first such incident. The Fuerza Aérea del Perú lost a Su-25 'Frogfoot' in the same region prior to the failed raid,' Pearson-Roberts resumed, sticking to his use of NATO reporting names.

'The *'Grach'*, or so the Russians call it,' Daniels added.

'Quite. At the time, the jet was believed to have either crashed or been shot down during a dogfight with a cartel plane. That's why the assault force was going in: to deny Del Bosque the use of the airfield.'

'Turns out that the enemy were a lot better prepared than expected,' Tidewell surmised.

'Assumption is the mother of all cock-ups!' Pearson-Roberts's voice had an angry growl.

'I take it a land assault is also out of the question?'

'The terrain is difficult. Infiltration would be a slow process and government forces could expect to come under fire from ground-attack aircraft once their intentions were identified. This particular cartel has access to some worrying hardware.'

'Mendez' administration won't survive the political backlash if they continue losing the lives of their soldiers.' Tidewell again. 'The matter has gone too far. He has requested our help. The ideal solution is for the Ejército del Perú to overrun the Del Bosque operation using standard military procedures. Mercenaries killed, cartel members arrested, drugs impounded, and colour pictures for the press; all carried out with the bare minimum of further casualties.'

'And of course, our lads will be doing a bit more than just training.' Daniels's voice had a cocky edge to Didier's ear, even a bit arrogant; but he sounded likeable anyhow.

'Unofficially, yes,' Pearson-Roberts answered. 'A second detachment from D Squadron will be tasked with disabling the missile launcher, along with some other defences, to allow a successful repeat raid by the EP's special forces. We'll be using the designation Operation CATHODE for this covert action.'

'I take it the DSF is in the loop on this,' Daniels asked.

Didier's mind raced for a moment to identify the acronym, then found it quickly. *Of course, Director Special Forces.*

'Regrettably, the Brigadier wasn't available to join us,' Pearson-Roberts answered. 'But yes, our orders will be coming via the normal chain of command.'

Didier heard the faint sound of pages being flipped through the sensitive microphones. Tidewell had apparently taken some paperwork out of his attaché case. 'Moving on, I've been talking to Alan about this new equipment, and we both feel that CATHODE may be an ideal opportunity to put it into action.'

'You've been liaising with the manufacturer on this; is that correct?' Pearson-Roberts asked.

'The Jackdaw, yes,' Daniels answered. 'We think that integration with some of our regular army units could lead to international sales in the future.'

'Other militaries are experimenting with this approach, the Americans fairly extensively. We'd like to demonstrate that our forces not only have the capability but are leading the field.' Pearson-Roberts stated this with an undertone of unnecessary melodrama.

'What sort of timeframe are we looking at?' A hint of scepticism was clear in Daniels' voice.

'We would intend to carry out the raid during August, their driest period. The Peruvian Army training programme has been scheduled to coincide with this window. That gives us two months to get up to speed on the Jackdaw. How soon can it be made available?'

'We'll have prototypes available within three weeks,' Daniels answered, now adopting a more positive note.

'And will the manufacturer provide the necessary instruction?'

'No, I'll bring in an outside contractor – a specialist that can also assist with the design refinements,' Daniels paused. 'And the associated equipment listed here is mostly self-explanatory but will come with the relevant handbooks.'

'Don't we already have someone qualified for this within the Army?' Pearson-Roberts queried.

'Yes, possibly, but we couldn't control the talk. We'll keep things quieter with a contractor.'

'I concur – we'll stick with the contractor,' Tidewell confirmed. 'Summing up then, I'm keen for the Peruvians to take the complete package: the training, the covert action and the equipment. It's of considerable value to the Treasury and there's potential for further business in the long-term. D Squadron will provide both the instruction and assault teams, deployed under Alan's command. Tom, you'll accompany the two units to Peru, manage the financials, and negotiate from the MoD's position. Your contact on the ground will be General Juan Carlos Torres, commander of their 3rd Division. In the meantime, report to

Hereford with the equipment and get the necessary instruction under way as soon as possible. Are we all agreed?'

'Agreed,' both men affirmed.

'I don't need to remind you that this whole operation needs to be conducted in complete secrecy, with plausible deniability for the covert action if necessary. We need zero press exposure on any part of this. Don't assume that anyone is aware of CATHODE, either here or in Peru – that's apart from our two teams and General Torres himself. Right, let's go over some specifics.'

Above Didier's head a red LED bulb lit up, snapping him out of his trance. The light signified a call from the chef to announce that the entrées were ready. Didier had been so absorbed in his table's discourse that he'd forgotten all about the time. He snatched off his headphones then stepped out from the small office into the kitchen. He would listen to the whole recording again later, before typing a concise abstract on his heavily encrypted computer and sending it to Thames House. He needed to ensure that he hadn't missed the tiniest relevant detail when reporting a matter of this significance; it would be a late-night finish. A courier would be sent to collect the hard copy – it was someone else's responsibility to catalogue and store the intel. MI5 didn't employ Didier to snoop on their fellow services specifically – it was simply his job to spy on anyone he deemed to be of interest. And the day's events had been particularly intriguing, so far. He strode purposefully back into the restaurant, courteously serving his table's starters: pan-seared foie gras for both the lieutenant-colonel and the minister, cured trout in watercress velouté for the intelligence officer.

Chapter Six
Tuesday, 7 June
Lima

Luis Oneto was dropped directly outside the front of the small restaurant, located a short distance from the coast on a quiet side street in Barranco – the affluent but bohemian district renowned for attracting tourists with its colonial buildings, street art and floral displays. The rain had held off for a few days and he suspected that the numerous night spots would be well populated without being overcrowded. As usual, the venue had been chosen for anonymity and not convenience; a repeated occurrence that Oneto found increasingly annoying with each new episode. He paid the driver and headed for the entrance – late, surly and frustrated to be summoned. He needed to bring an end to these ongoing arrangements. The situation was becoming untenable.

He stepped inside to be met with terracotta floor tiles, dark-wood furniture and colourful hanging tapestries of alpaca wool. Folk music blared from small speakers, combining a mix of Spanish and indigenous influences. The premises was narrow, with just twelve tables in two rows, only four of which were taken. Oneto glanced briefly at each of the faces of those seated, a procedure necessary to quell his easily triggered neuroses. By the entrance, an elderly, bald-headed man sat alone and overdressed, slowly spooning soup to his lips. A couple sat adjacent, heads leaned toward each other, engrossed in amorous communion. In the far corner, four young backpacker types – plainly American – were chatting loudly in English. Oneto reassured himself that no one present would recognise him, apart from the man sat at the remaining occupied table. After an enthusiastic welcome, the establishment's hostess took him by the arm and led him through the restaurant, but her greeting was restrained in comparison to La Rosa's. He stood up, arms outstretched wide, a beaming smile across his face.

'My old friend, so wonderful to see you. It's been three months, has it not?'

Alfredo La Rosa had the carefree air of a successful man. His expensively tailored and slightly outlandish jacket was draped over the back his chair. He wore no tie and his shirt was partially unbuttoned. A chunky gold watch protruded from beneath his sleeve. He was tanned, muscular and energetic; only his silver-grey hair betrayed his true age. Oneto briefly and reluctantly returned the shorter man's embrace before sitting down impatiently. La Rosa knew full well it was three months. It was always three months.

'I believe congratulations are in order, Luis. You've come a long way since our school days.'

'Gracias,' Oneto uttered gruffly. They had never really been friends but he did remember the bullying. As a youth, La Rosa had been quick tempered and eager to put his physical strength to use. Consequently, he was never far from trouble. Oneto had not been surprised by La Rosa's chosen career path; it was just a logical progression.

'The new job comes with more responsibility and a shift in priorities. Some changes need to be made, especially regarding our arrangements.'

'Relax, Luis, we've the whole evening to talk business.' La Rosa had maintained his wide smile. 'Let's order some food and catch up a little. I've chosen the wine already.'

The bottle of Argentinian red was of good label and stood opened alongside two glasses, one of which was tinted with faint burgundy traces where La Rosa had tasted the wine for quality. Adjacent on the table rested an ornate, heart-shaped chocolate box of a handmade variety. The hostess filled the men's glasses as they sat, then returned a short while later to take the food order. Oneto suspected that her husband would be out back in the kitchen, as was typical for a small family business.

'So, tell me, how are you enjoying the benefits of your new position? It's undeniably an impressive sounding title. Have they finally put you in charge of something?' La Rosa chuckled amiably as he teased his mirthless companion.

'I've worked in government for twelve years. It's a promotion, yes, but not undeserved.'

'I see that your modesty hasn't grown with your salary.' La Rosa let out a short roar of laughter, his cheeks reddening with genuine amusement. 'But what exactly does it mean, in plain language?'

'I prepare documents outlining the government's instructions for the military, and I process applications to and from congress.'

'You must feel out of your depth – a civilian surrounded by so many uniforms.'

'You can forget that. I answer to the defence minister; their medals don't impress me.'

'*Ha ha!* Too much of a big shot now, eh? Then I assume you must have the confidence of Admiral Ballesta?'

'Of course. He's the Head of the Joint Command. His office is on my floor. We work together on a daily basis.' Oneto's self-satisfied manner affirmed that the posting appealed to his ego.

'And therefore you have access to his strategic planning. This will prove very useful, going forward.' The humour had disappeared from La Rosa's voice. He knew exactly what Oneto's role entailed.

'You are, of course, referring to classified information that I would be prosecuted for disclosing, even if I wished to do so.' Oneto's tone was firm and emotionless.

'You've never been a man to worry about rules, Luis, and besides, our continuing cooperation is in the nation's best interests. A balance is required, between governance and commerce, to maintain the status quo. This new agenda of so-called reforms will do nothing but hinder the economy and undermine our successes. A wealthy man like yourself would be unwise to rock the boat.'

Oneto felt tense, agitated, his discomfort increasing exponentially as La Rosa applied the inevitable pressure. He ran a manicured hand through his carefully styled hair. 'Since when did you become the conscientious public servant, Alfredo?'

'Politicians come and go very quickly,' La Rosa continued, ignoring the slight. 'They only think of themselves and the immediate future. They have no concern for the long-term implications of their actions. We must think about the bigger picture, as patriots and as influentials.'

'What's your point?'

'These recent changes in policy have been costly – harmful to my organisation. We employ thousands of hard-working citizens, mostly from poor communities. Do your colleagues ever consider what happens to them? Then there's the considerable revenue generated by our exports – money that neither your masters nor the wider population would wish to give away. So now our syndicate is forced to act for the good of the country, and that means steering the path of this fickle government. It's fortunate that you and I are such good friends, to facilitate this process.'

La Rosa was a solicitor by trade but rarely practiced any actual law. He had found his true vocation acting as negotiator and trouble-shooter for the Del Bosque cartel. He paused to drink his wine, then pushed the ornate box gently across the table.

'Please, give these chocolates to your lovely mother with my kind regards. It's been too many years since I've visited.'

Oneto ignored the box. He knew it contained no chocolates, but ten thousand in US dollars.

'This has to stop,' Oneto said flatly.

'I'm sorry?'

'This has to stop – all of it. The chocolates, these meetings; it's ridiculous to think we can go on like this forever. A man in my position cannot…'

'A man in your position?' Alfredo snapped aggressively in a hoarse whisper; his smile replaced with an angry scowl. *'How dare you!* You think you can take my generous gifts for all these years and then just tell me to *fuck off? Hypocrite!* You'd have achieved nothing without my help; you would never have even escaped your debts. *The ingratitude…'* La Rosa seethed as he barked across the table in hushed tones. 'Do you think I'll let your family live like royalty in that big house while you destroy everything that I've worked for? Maybe I should be sending your mother a box of tiny fingers, instead of chocolates. Is that what you want?'

Oneto's face turned pale, his anger and confidence deserting him. 'No, of course not, but it's just not possible to keep on like this. You have to be realistic.'

'You'll give up everything you have for that prick Mendez and his pathetic conquest? I'll leave you with nothing, and I mean *nothing.*'

'Please, look, it doesn't have to…' Oneto's head sunk and his words trailed off.

La Rosa glared into his adversary's eyes for a moment longer then sat back and appeared to relax, his anger abating. 'I'd much rather we settle this as friends, Luis, but I'll need to explain exactly what it is that I want from you. There can be no misunderstanding.'

Oneto trembled slightly. He wanted so badly to resist but couldn't find the strength of heart. He had never been able to fight La Rosa face-to-face. He nodded weakly in acquiescence.

'*Bueno!* Obviously, you are aware of the recent attempt by the Ejército del Perú to attack one of our agricultural enterprises. This misguided endeavour bore no result but the deaths of good soldiers, men who should be tasked with defending our country. One would expect that the imbecile president would learn from this public failure, but it appears to have only encouraged him. He thinks he can make amends for his mistakes with the ruining of our operation. So, now I expect to be made aware of any planned action against our infrastructure or real estate, either by the Army or Air Force. If they wish to go around burning peasant farmer's crops, so be it, just so long as those crops don't belong to us. I don't give a fuck about the National Police or the borders – we can handle them anyway – but these attacks on our aircraft and property will stop. You'll do everything within your considerable new influence to prevent this aggression or our friendship will cease with all that entails. Is that clear enough for you?'

Oneto held his head in one hand, propped up by an elbow on the table, his mind assaulted by terrifying glimpses of the possible ramifications for disobedience. Consequences that would be suffered by his family. It was a simple choice: *plata o plomo* – silver or lead. He perked himself up in an attempt to cover his distress from the returning proprietress.

'I understand. Let's change the subject.'

'That's better.'

La Rosa smiled warmly at the hostess as she served the men's food.

* * *

Oneto left the restaurant and walked the short distance down to the cliffs above the sea front. He had the physique and gait of a fashion model, but now his stylish suit draped limply off his body like rags on a scarecrow. His expensive leather shoes barely cleared the ground as he trod. La Rosa had settled the bill and offered the services of his driver but Oneto had protested that he needed some fresh air. The chocolate box, which he'd been expressly ordered not to forget, nestled under his left arm. He sat down on the rocky edge and looked out over Playa Barranco and the dark, choppy Pacific Ocean. He began to cry.

Chapter Seven

Friday, 10 June
Lewes, England

Dylan Porter stood sullenly behind the counter of Cycl-One, the euphoria of his race win having long since passed in the three weeks following the event. It was 4:32pm and he counted the minutes until he could shut up shop, retreat to his flat and switch on his video game console for the evening. He'd spent the whole afternoon dwelling on his numerous problems, most of which were financial, and now he needed an escape from the mental turmoil. It had been yet another bad day for sales, and to make matters worse he'd received a letter from the bank warning him that his overdraft limit had been exceeded. This wasn't the first occasion. Dylan would have been doing well to be running his own bike shop at twenty-four years of age, had it actually been a profitable business.

Dylan's parents had separated when he was just nine-months old, and he hadn't seen or heard word of his father since. His mother had been relatively young at the time, and had subsequently struggled to raise him alone in a series of properties funded by the welfare state. He loved her dearly but their relationship had always been a volatile one. By the age of nineteen, incessant arguing forced him to move in with his elderly grandmother in a small flat at the rear of a bric-a-brac shop in Lewes.

His grandmother owned and ran the shop for most of her senior life, staffing the premises just by sitting in her front room. It had only ever attracted a trickle of trade. There was not much space in the flat and the arrangement was limiting for Dylan's social life, but it did provide a roof over his head and a necessary respite from the quarrelling with his mother.

During this period, Dylan had worked daily in a large, well-established bike shop in nearby Brighton, serving customers alongside the owner. The two were polar opposites and had quietly disliked each other. Dylan had an appreciation for a well-engineered product and was fascinated by the science that led to upgrades in performance; his boss was a career businessman who didn't care what he sold as long as the margin was right. The owner neither had interest in Dylan's personal development, nor his opinion – the young lad was simply used as cheap labour. Dylan had a good memory for technical detail and possessed an almost encyclopaedic knowledge of mountain bikes and their componentry. While this proved advantageous for sales, his heart was never in the job. Ultimately, he aspired to run his own outlet.

After three years spent living with his grandmother, she passed away quietly in the night. When her last will and testament was executed, it decreed that the small shop and its contents were left to Dylan. With no intention of personally selling the miscellany of ornaments and trinkets, he offloaded them in one job lot via an auction house. Then, with an empty property, he had set about turning his ambition into reality.

Dylan's venture had been hampered from the outset by a lack of capital. Only limited credit was available to him. A bank loan against the property had covered the cost of the security shutters and basic shopfitting modifications, and he needed a regular turnover just to afford the repayments. Without any trade connections, he had no way of acquiring a sufficient range of stock to generate the necessary income. Cycl-One became popular with local riders but lacked the top-end merchandise that would attract bigger spenders. Unwisely, he had entered into a deal with his previous employer. The businessman provided some items for Dylan to sell but the rate of commission was tiny. As soon as Dylan began to accumulate any revenue, a new bill would arrive and absorb his profit. The venture only just managed to cover its overheads and Dylan himself lived on a shoestring.

He was snapped out of his melancholic trance by a person entering through the front door. Usually, the only customers at this late hour would be locals dropping in for puncture-repair kits, brake pads or replacement tyres; so he was especially surprised to see it was Tom – the curious spectator from the Thresham Down race. Dylan's enthusiasm was at low ebb but his mood lifted significantly at the prospect of a sale, especially as Tom was smartly dressed and looked like someone with a reasonable budget. He would stay open as long as was necessary.

'Afternoon, Dylan.'

'Hey, Tom. Wasn't expecting to see you today. You need a bike?'

'Just thought I'd stop by for a look.' Tom approached the counter to shake hands, then took a slow stroll around the small shop. 'How's business?'

'Yeah, great.'

'Not quite what I was expecting in here,' Tom said, referring to some uninspiring stands of clothing and helmets. 'I thought you'd have a load of those flashy racing machines for sale.'

'I'd love to, but that kind of stock is too expensive to have sitting around. I can order something in for you, though. The stuff on those racks isn't actually mine – I have an arrangement with a business partner.' Dylan made the term sound derogatory, shrugging his shoulders to absolve himself of any responsibility for the choice of wares on display.

'I see. Great performance the other Saturday,' Tom acknowledged, changing the subject. What are you spending the prize money on?'

'Just bills, unfortunately, and it's already spent.' It was hard not to notice that Dylan looked utterly depressed.

'These things look more your style,' Tom commented, gesturing to some new suspension forks hanging on the wall.

'Are you a rider then, or do you work for a magazine or something?' The man's presence was becoming irritating and Dylan decided to opt for a more direct approach.

'I used to race cross-country when I was younger, but back then it was more about physical fitness than technical ability. What you guys do nowadays takes a whole different level of commitment.'

'But that's not why you're here now, right?'

Tom stepped back up to the counter. 'No, not exactly. I came to make you a proposition – some work that I think may interest you. I was hoping you could spare me an hour to elaborate. You must be closing up soon. How about I buy you a pint and something to eat in that pub over the road?'

'Actually, I don't drink alcohol,' Dylan replied quickly, then the implications of the offer sunk in. 'But to be honest, I could really do with some food. Can I lock up here and see you over there in ten?'

'Great. Take your time. I'll find us a table.'

Dylan nodded approval and the spectator named Tom left the shop without further comment.

* * *

The Hooden Horse had a limited menu of the usual pub grub. Tom ordered steak and ale pie and a pint of Guinness; Dylan chose scampi and chips with a pint of orange juice and soda. While they waited for the food, Tom enquired about the business arrangements at Cycl-One. Dylan wasn't normally forthcoming with his personal affairs, but he felt frustrated at the shop's lack of progress and needed to get matters off of his chest. For some reason this stranger appeared to be interested, and Tom's occasional reassuring comments were welcome enough. Making the most of the sympathetic audience, Dylan then explained his general financial predicament and his lack of current options.

'Sounds to me like you're being taken for a ride,' Tom quipped, light-heartedly. 'But I think I can help you out.'

'So what's this about then? I mean, you can't be here to offer me a sponsorship deal – I'm not even a professional racer.' Dylan's history of business failure had left him sceptical; the concept that Tom would make him any kind of worthwhile offer seemed too hard to swallow. 'You don't seem like part of the bike scene, anyway. You still haven't told me what you want.'

'Okay, I'll get to the point.' Tom handed Dylan a business card with the lettering:

Tom Daniels

Limitation and Remuneration

The HM Government logo was positioned in the top left-hand corner of the card, and two phone numbers and an email address were printed below the wording. Dylan sat speechless and was manifestly none the wiser for having read it.

'I arrange training schemes for people working in the public sector, amongst other things.' Daniels' business card gave no indication of his military credentials, and he deliberately neglected to mention them. 'Currently, I have a small group that need to learn the kind of riding techniques that you displayed at the race. If you're interested, I can offer you a short-term commission as a paid instructor.'

'You want me to teach people how to ride?' Dylan felt both relieved and incredulous in equal measure. The reason for Tom's visit now seemed surprisingly uncomplicated.

'That's what I'm saying, yes.'

'Doing what exactly?' Dylan pressed, rapidly gaining confidence in the proposition.

'My aim is to set up a programme to train fit but relatively unskilled amateurs to ride quickly and safely in mountainous terrain. The course needs to be as short as realistically possible, and that will make it very intensive for both the trainees and the instructor. Once the first group are up to scratch and we're in a position to repeat the process ourselves, then your work would be complete. Sound okay so far?'

'But I have to run my shop,' Dylan objected with a hint of dismay.

Daniels removed an envelope from his jacket pocket, extracted the letter it contained and handed it over. Dylan took the single sheet, unfolded it hastily and read, discovering that the commission offered a sum of £4,000 for the estimated four-week period.

Dylan sat upright on seeing the bottom-line figure. 'I don't make that much in three months.'

Daniels continued: 'You'll need to live on site for the duration and be readily available when summoned. Assume you'll be working long days, seven days a week, with no free time as such. Everything will be provided and you won't need any money of your own. We want to get started soon, so you'd better arrange for someone to staff your shop while you're away. In the meantime, put together a list of everything you think we'll need to get the first group of riders up to speed. It doesn't matter how you write it, just make sure you don't miss anything out. You can e-mail it over to me; the address is on my card. When it's time to get started, we'll send someone to collect you and your luggage, and when it's all over we'll bring you back home.'

Dylan stared at his plate and toyed with his few remaining chips, bewildered and uncertain. He calculated roughly what the figure equalled per day, reasoning that he could close the shop for the entire period and still come out better off. He struggled to think of some other questions he should probably ask, but his mind was blank. Daniels spoke again, freeing him from the moment of perplexity.

'There's one more thing. This programme is not to become public knowledge at any point. The offer is dependent on your agreement not to disclose any details to anyone – not its whereabouts, who you are working for, what training has been carried out, nothing. Your payment may be withheld if you breech these terms; so if you want the job, you need to take this commitment seriously. I have a document here for you to sign, which acknowledges that you understand these conditions.'

'Got it. Don't tell anyone. That part, I *can* manage.' Dylan stated positively.

Chapter Eight
Wednesday, 15 June
Herefordshire

'You've got to be kidding me,' McCowan said to the other two men. They had spent the last thirty minutes in a briefing room at Stirling Lines, now reserved for the CATHODE operation.

'What do you think?' Pearson-Roberts asked the squadron sergeant major.

'I'd love to pull it off but I need to know more. Let's go through it again, from the beginning.'

Pearson-Roberts stood at the back of the room, scrutinising some of the material that had been prepared in readiness for the planning session. Spread across the tables and mounted on the cork boards was a compilation of data that was relevant to the mission. There were large-scale maps, aerial photographs and infrared satellite images, many of which were enhanced with coloured pins or marker pen annotation. Printed sheets detailed the expected enemy strength, their known equipment and their tactical capabilities. On a table, in the centre of the room, stood a large plaster model of the target facility, showing its location within the surrounding mountains. McCowan and Daniels stood side by side in front of it, contemplating the topography. McCowan was the shorter man by a small margin but was much heavier set. He continued.

'We can't get a helicopter within miles of this place because of the surface-to-air missile system – that's a fact.' McCowan spoke clearly and with authority, even in the presence of his superior. 'Parachute insertion is also unrealistic, as the only safe landing areas are the plantation and runway, both of which are permanently guarded. Our men would be spotted and engaged the moment they hit the ground, and if they got blown off-course that would probably be worse.'

The other two men nodded agreement.

'The river below the camp is unnavigable, and the surrounding jungle would take several days to penetrate. Therefore, the only viable infiltration method is to be dropped by helicopter at a safe distance, over the crest of this mountain range, then approach the target on foot from the north.'

'That's correct,' Pearson-Roberts confirmed.

'How far exactly are we talking?' McCowan asked.

'There's a known route over, formerly used by indigenous tribes for llama trains. It should vaguely resemble a footpath. You'll need to meet up with that. It's not that far as-the-crow-flies but the path traverses about a bit, as you'd imagine given the terrain. So on foot, you'd be looking at a hike of about twenty kilometres.'

'How long would that take you, Ken?' Daniels queried, staring at the model mountains.

'Tabbing over uneven ground in the dark, at altitude, with frequent stops to scan ahead – at least five hours. We'd have to slow right down for the last kilometre before the plantation, then conduct close target reconnaissance to locate these sentries in the coca fields.' McCowan pointed to a thermal image of the plantation with marker-penned rings around the tiny red dots that indicated a human presence.

Daniels looked at him. 'You'll need to remove those guards, I'm assuming?'

'Yes, Tom. The marksmen can take care of them, but they'll be using subsonic ammunition to keep the noise down, and that reduces the effective range. They'll have to sneak up nice and close to guarantee clean shots.'

Daniels thought on this point. Most of the 'crack' from a rifle is generated by the round breaking the sound barrier as it leaves the barrel. Fitting a suppressor, or so-called 'silencer', will muffle the sound generated by the explosive propellant in the cartridge, but does not reduce the noise of the bullet itself. A subsonic round is therefore inherently quieter, but the slower-moving projectile will travel a shorter distance before its accuracy degrades.

'How close?' Pearson-Roberts asked.

'Within a hundred metres – closer the better. Then, after clearing the plantation, there'll still be some distance to cover before our team reaches the camp itself. That's a bare minimum of seven hours' darkness used up before we even get started. No go.' McCowan shook his head. 'They would have to lie up outside the plantation for the whole day and move again the next night.'

'And that brings its own set of risks and complications,' Pearson-Roberts added.

'So, the concept you are trying to sell me, is that we can complete the approach phase faster using this new piece of equipment, which is more or less purpose built for the role, if I understand it correctly.'

'They've been designed from the ground up for fast, quiet, tactical insertion,' Daniels confirmed. 'The Jackdaw looks similar to a motocross bike – knobbly tyres, large mudguards, a narrow bench seat – except without the engine and built much lighter. Then there are some military-specific features.'

'Such as?' McCowan leaned forward, listening intently and clearly curious.

'There's a rubber-lined holder between the frame tubes, in the space between the seat and the handlebars. A short weapon will sit there securely until you need to use it. You just grab the grip and pull it out when you need to fire. The tyres are filled with a semi-setting foam to resist punctures; they won't go flat even if they are shot. There are handlebar mounts for infrared illuminators, to facilitate riding with night-vision goggles. It's been well thought out and solidly built for tough mission conditions.'

'Will they be usable on the terrain, though?' McCowan pressed.

'Obviously we're going to need to test them out for ourselves, but I've seen what recreational riders can do in the name of sport and I'm very confident. They hold races down slopes that you couldn't even walk down. It's not a matter of whether the Jackdaw can handle the kind of ground that you'd negotiate on foot: if the terrain is too rough for them, you'll be using climbing gear anyway.' Daniels' optimistic appraisal was met with silence by the two army men, but no conspicuous scepticism.

'Can we peddle these things like a normal bicycle if we need to?' McCowan would want to know every detail.

'Yes, you can pedal them, but they only have two speeds – just a high and low gear. A normal bicycle chain and derailleur mechanism is too fragile and noisy. Instead, they have a belt drive, attached to something called a planetary gear held within a casing up front. The system is silent, robust and can switch gear while stationary.'

McCowan seemed satisfied with the answer and appeared to relax for the moment.

'Okay, that might be feasible. We're saying that our men can sit on these things with all their heavy kit, and roll themselves down to the plantation in a fraction of the time it would take on foot.'

'And they'll still be fresh as a daisy when they get there,' Pearson-Roberts put in.

McCowan looked at him disbelievingly.

'Then what?'

'Even if they discard the machines at that point, it would have been worthwhile. We can recover them later,' Daniels proposed, his tone enthusiastic. 'But it might prove advantageous for the team to stay on them. There's a long distance to cover, to get right through the camp. The quicker they can move the better, right?'

'The enemy move around the site using vehicle tracks cleared through the brush. We've approximated their locations.' Pearson-Roberts indicated a satellite photograph marked with coloured lines. 'There'll be little chance of navigating through the undergrowth anywhere other than these routes. If the team are compromised, they'll have to fight their way out with the enemy closing in around them.'

'Whereas, you are suggesting that we can ride right into the camp unnoticed, plant our explosives, and be gone before the balloon goes up.' McCowan continued. 'After all, we'll be using night-vision; the militia presumably will not. And if someone does get a glimpse of our boys on these Jackdaws, they're not going to have a fucking clue what they've just seen.'

All three men laughed loudly for a moment.

'But this approach could also allow us to use shorter fuses, if we get the timings right,' Pearson-Roberts speculated. 'It won't matter if they shoot a few guards on the way through the camp. By the time the militia realise something's happening, they'll look in the wrong place and find a nasty explosion instead. In fact, we could deliberately lead them from one spot to the next, following a trail of destruction.'

McCowan stared pensively into empty space for a long moment, then nodded decisively.

'Sounds risky but I like it. It's right up our street. Let's proceed for the moment on the basis that it's a viable method, at least until we find otherwise. We'll make up a team from our Mountain and Mobility guys; both their skillsets would seem relevant. With your permission sir, I'd like to get the troop captains in here along with Sergeants Shearman and O'Neil, then we can knock out some details. I'll order us up some tea while I'm at it.'

Each of the four operational SAS squadrons were further subdivided into four troops. Each troop, consisting of roughly sixteen men, specialised in a particular method of insertion and was commanded by a captain who would normally remain at headquarters to arrange support and logistics. The troop captains' direct superior was Major Nolan – the current Officer Commanding of D Squadron – but he was absent, having travelled to North Africa to resolve a diplomatic complication. It would be Sergeants Shearman and O'Neil, the ranking NCOs on the ground, who would plan, direct and carry out the operation.

'Carry on,' Pearson-Roberts replied in his normal brisk manner.

After a short recess, the architects of Operation CATHODE were ready to resume the session. The four new arrivals milled around the briefing room, running their eyes over the images until McCowan got the ball rolling.

'Let's begin with a brief summary of our current intel, then we'll have a look at the target facility's defences. We can move on to tactical planning a bit later. We have all the usual maps, photos, facts and figures; kindly put together for us by the Slime,' McCowan referred to the 'Green Slime' – the Army's nickname for the Intelligence Corps. 'Plus, these wonderful satellite images supplied by Mr Daniels.'

'Where did you get these, Tom, if you don't mind my asking?' Pearson-Roberts queried.

'I have a desk in the MI6 building,' Daniels answered matter-of-factly. 'Six borrows scraps like these from the Americans from time to time. We couldn't ask for anything too specific in case we aroused their interest. After all, they'd love to be doing this raid themselves – if they knew it was on.'

'Wouldn't they just,' agreed McCowan.

'They'd want to blow up the whole ruddy mountain,' Pearson-Roberts added dismissively.

'And who could blame them,' quipped a captain.

'The lieutenant-colonel also has something for us. If you wouldn't mind, sir,' McCowan prompted.

'Yes, quite informative this,' Pearson-Roberts held up a folder. 'We have a first-hand report from a captured cartel member who's been to the target facility, which he refers to as 'La Fábrica'. The transcripts of his questioning are here. He describes an extensive arrangement of tents and structures hidden beneath the canopy. The cocaine processing utility is at the camp's western extent, the mess area and sleeping quarters are adjacent, and a tent with a large metal aerial is located in the centre. His sketch of the layout is included. He hasn't seen any missile launcher but believes there may be a vehicle garage at the eastern end of the camp, although he's not been inside it himself. He confirms our impression from the thermal imagery, that there are three main vehicle tracks to move about the site, and he also mentions one narrower footpath that leads to the river.'

'Do the cartel know we have their man?' McCowan asked, stroking his thick, dark moustache with his thumb.

'No. He was shot by General Torres' men on a raid elsewhere and left for dead by his compatriots. He hasn't seen daylight since and won't do until this is all over. Downing that chopper made Del Bosque very unpopular with the 4SF. The informant is now being shown their best hospitality.' Pearson-Roberts glanced around the room at the facial expressions of the other men, confirming that each seemed satisfied with the credibility of the source.

'There's one other thing. He claims there's some kind of gun position in the corner of the airfield but his description is very vague. We'd better look into that.'

'And that brings us neatly on to the defences,' McCowan announced.

'Several of the thermals show activity in the northwest corner of the airfield, just under the forest canopy,' Sergeant Shearman gestured to an infrared image. 'If there's a fixed gun, that's where it will be.'

'Have a look at this horseshoe shaped structure at the edge of the plantation – just here.' Sergeant O'Neil tapped his finger on a high-resolution photograph pinned to one of the corkboards. 'I think it's a mortar pit, set up to cover the approach from the north.' The others stepped over to join him.

'Looks that way,' Shearman agreed.

'If there's a mortar it will have to go, along with the guard presence in the plantation,' McCowan stated.

'They'll be able to move fighters around quickly using the vehicles, and there's at least one technical.' Shearman referred to a modified pick-up truck, parked alongside a light aircraft in one of the aerial photographs.

'We'll want to find a way of blocking those routes, seeing as we can't avoid them altogether. And also disable their communications set-up – otherwise there'll be reinforcements turning up halfway through the raid.' McCowan was going over old ground to a certain extent, having already scrutinised all of the intelligence.

'If the SAM is in a sealed garage structure, then we'll need some method of entry – materials for explosive breeching,' O'Neil recommended.

'Agreed.'

'The airstrip will almost certainly be guarded,' someone mentioned.

'We can assume they maintain an armed presence there around the clock. Anything else?' McCowan seemed eager to move on.

There was little more that could be discerned from the evidence without digressing into unnecessary speculation. One by one the men nodded to McCowan to indicate they were happy to proceed.

'Then let's put it together.'

Ninety minutes later, a preliminary plan of action had been drawn up with input from all parties present. The group sat while McCowan orated the end result for their confirmation, his usual bellowing voice easily filling the briefing room.

'Right then, I'll recap what we've suggested so far. We will deploy a troop-strength unit to approach the target from the mountains to the north, potentially using Tom's new bit of equipment – the Jackdaw – if it shapes up as promised. On reaching the plantation area, they'll then split into four patrols each with their own objectives, which are as follows:

'Delta One will consist of two marksmen and two spotters. They will clear the plantation covertly and secure a helicopter landing site for the general's forces – designated LS-1.

'Delta Two will plant a delayed diversionary charge on the mortar assembly, then proceed to the main camp via the western track – call sign RED. There, they will plant a second timed charge in the cocaine processing area, then exit the main camp via the footpath designated YELLOW. This will lead them to the cliff face above the river, where they will neutralise any sentries, descend to the riverbank, and take position to approach the airstrip from the south. The mortar and production area targets will be identified as RED-1 and RED-2, respectively.

'Delta Three and Delta Four will access the camp via the eastern track – call sign GREEN – and immediately locate the missile launcher. Delta Three will then plant delayed charges to disable the radio equipment and any vehicles in the expected garage structure. We will label these targets GREEN-1 and GREEN-2. Delta Four will move ahead down the road to the airstrip – designated BLUE.

Here, they will set up an ambush with vehicle mines and wait to be joined by Delta Three.

'The missile system will be referred to as WHITE, regardless of location, as it's our primary objective and must be removed before we can be reinforced. At least one patrol must be in position to destroy the launcher the moment the diversionary charges are blown.

'At a given fixed point, the RED-1 charge will wake up the camp. We can expect the militia to advance through the production area en route to the now-defunct mortar, at the same time making attempts to use the radio and man the vehicles. Bad luck on all counts. The RED-2 and GREEN charges will be timed to detonate shortly after, maximising enemy casualties and confusion. At this point, we anticipate the militia garrisoned at the airstrip will mount up in vehicles and head for the main camp via BLUE, where they'll trigger our mines and be ambushed at BLUE-1.

'Finally, Deltas Two, Three and Four will converge on the airstrip from both directions to secure the second landing zone – LS-2. The fixed gun emplacement will be destroyed and reported as BLUE-2. Then we hold positions and wait for the Peruvian special forces, who will ferry in by helicopter as soon as they receive signal that WHITE has been disabled. Job done.'

Pearson-Roberts stood and took the front of the room.

'Thanks for that, Ken. I think that's as far as we can go at this point in time. Does anyone have anything further to add?'

The two sergeants and two troop captains shook their heads.

'Then that gives us just six weeks to get trained up and thoroughly prepped for this. Plan every detail, with actions-on for every possible contingency. We only have vague intelligence on what to expect in there, so leave nothing to chance.'

'We never do, sir,' McCowan acknowledged.

'Then you have your orders. Make it happen.'

Chapter Nine

Tuesday, 28 June
Cusco, Peru

Derrick Carver oversaw as the engineer prepared the helicopter for the impending flight. Just a few more minutes were needed before the fuelling process was complete. The black and turquoise body of the Eurocopter EC135 had been hosed down and now gleamed in the late morning sun, and the interior had been thoroughly vacuumed in readiness for the charter. A quick check of his Gallet wristwatch told Carver that take-off was scheduled in fifteen minutes; his flight bag was already stowed aboard. He expected that his passenger, Alfredo La Rosa, would arrive at the small aerodrome just moments beforehand.

Carver was born in the United States to an American father and Peruvian mother, but had spent most of his working life in Peru since qualifying as a pilot. His business catered mostly for oil and mining companies, who paid well to access remote locations. And they needed to pay well, because flying in mountainous terrain with rapidly changeable weather was a skilled and dangerous job. These customers tended to be security conscious as kidnappings had not been infrequent in the past; hence they tended to stick with contractors that they trusted, even if the cost was high. In this respect, Carver's American upbringing often gave him a competitive edge with prospectors from the States.

The Del Bosque syndicate was another customer happy to pay his high fees, but for entirely different reasons. For them, it was discretion that was paramount, rather than personal security. They had their own aircraft, but the syndicate's members occasionally needed use of these assets at conflicting times. When this occurred, Carver would get the call, usually with the bare minimum of forewarning.

But despite the prevalence of paying clientele, Carver still had financial challenges to overcome. The Eurocopter in reality belonged to the bank. To fully repay the loan would take a lifetime's worth of flying, and then there was the depreciation to consider. The value of such a machine fluctuated according to rental demand and the availability of similar aircraft. Carver was therefore engaged in a constant battle to ensure that the net worth of his asset stayed higher than the remaining debt owing. The quicker he made repayments the less interest he paid, and the better his prospects of selling up one day to an adequate retirement package. Therefore, he was happy to take anyone's money, and the Central Intelligence Agency had plenty of dollars to spend.

He gave regular reports to his handler, Johnson, on anything the CIA might care about. Movements of cartel members, locations of facilities, details of equipment he'd seen; they even took an interest in the oil people's whereabouts. They were more than happy to pay, and this side-line provided a small but welcome boost to Carver's income. If it ever became known that he informed on the cartel then his life would come to a swift end, but he knew that Johnson was a professional who would ensure protection of his source. The CIA never acted on the information anyway, as far as he could tell. It was seemingly just collated to augment their vast database of foreign intelligence. Carver didn't worry about the potential consequences. He'd lived his whole life taking risks for money.

He climbed aboard as soon as the helicopter was fully fuelled, beginning the sequence of pre-flight checks, flicking switches to activate the electrical and hydraulic systems. He wondered where the destination would be this time; as per usual, he hadn't been told in advance. He didn't wait much longer before a black, executive-model SUV with heavily tinted windows pulled onto the apron. His client got out of the rear with only a leather shoulder bag for luggage, allowing the SUV to speed away again the instant the door was shut. As La Rosa strode purposefully across the concrete to the aircraft, his stocky frame reminded Carver of a bull terrier. He swung open the door and clambered up into the empty front seat.

'Good morning, Mr Carver. It's a fine day, yes? Thank you for accommodating me on such short notice.'

'De nada, Señor La Rosa.'

Carver waited patiently while La Rosa manoeuvred himself into the four-point seat belt.

'Where are we headed today?'

'Northwest – you haven't flown to this destination before. Get us out of the city and I'll give you coordinates once we're airborne.'

It was quite common for survey teams, naturalists and occasionally even the wealthier tourists to head out into the mountains without a specific destination. Carver didn't need to register a flight plan – he would simply contact air traffic control at Alejandro Velasco Astete Airport to request a flight path out of the city. He fired the ignition of the twin turboshaft engines individually, their whine reverberating inside the cabin then escalating as the four-bladed rotor began to revolve. The noise was bearable though; the EC135 was in fact a relatively quiet helicopter.

Fifteen minutes later they were clear of the city's outskirts and soaring northwest over agricultural plains and the lagoons of Huaypo and Piuray. Carver was always appreciative of the Eurocopter's high service ceiling, which was in excess of 6000m, but he would keep his altitude as low as safely possible to avoid the need for supplemental oxygen. The city of Cusco sat at an elevation of 3400m, and to reach the coordinates that La Rosa had supplied they would need to pass between the towering snowclad peaks of the Vilcabamba mountain range. He would keep to the easterly side of the colossal monolith Salkantay, which dominated the view through the cockpit glass, then pass to the north of the smaller peaks Pumasillu and Choquetacarpo. Then he would bear westwards for the remaining leg of the journey, over the steep and craggy forested valleys of the Apurimac tributaries.

'I believe you have a good future in this country, Mr Carver. A man with clear motives can be relied upon.' La Rosa's voice broke into Carver's thoughts, the patronising tone immediately annoying the pilot. 'But those who confuse themselves with ideology become unpredictable, untrustworthy, so much more difficult to work with.'

'Reliability is essential in my business; my customers don't like to miss their engagements.' Carver reeled off the answer like a line from a cheap television commercial, but he knew exactly what the cartel man was really saying. La Rosa liked people whose integrity was for sale. His respect wouldn't be so forthcoming if he knew that the arrangement worked both ways.

'Not like that fool Mendez, huh? What are his motives? What's *he* trying to do to this country?'

'I don't pay much attention to politics,' Carver lied.

'You should, Mr Carver, you should. Our prosperity as businessmen depends on the stability of our economy. You have many foreign customers, yes?'

Carver simply nodded. The east face of Salkantay loomed like a massive white pyramid in his left-hand cockpit window. The skies were crystal clear – no sign of bad weather ahead.

'My organisation also relies on foreign customers to buy our products, and they don't like to be let down either. Failures in supply would soon invite competitors into our market. Reliability is an essential quality for all our businesses, therefore we *must* have the cooperation of the government. There will come a time that we need to address this Mendez problem, for the sake of maintaining our substance, if nothing else.'

Carver stayed silent but paid careful attention to La Rosa's words. He would be making a call to Johnson later that evening. Of that much, he was sure.

* * *

The ground elevation was above the tree line at the given coordinates. A few small lakes, shining iridescent blue, were held captive by huge crests of bare, weathered rock. Taller peaks, a few kilometres away, wore a light dusting of snow. Carver was mindful of katabatic airflow pushing his aircraft downwards, but with the sun so high in the sky he knew there wouldn't be a problem. Flying here at night would be a different matter altogether. He didn't have to look too hard to see that the desolate area was completely uninhabited.

'I need to announce our arrival before we cross that next ridge ahead. Please slow down while I make a call. Circle around if you have to.' La Rosa's voice was clear and loud in the headset.

Carver didn't deliberate. He tipped the aircraft into a wide turn that would steer them away from the outcrop. La Rosa pulled a chunky, modern-looking sat-phone from his leather bag and attempted to achieve a connection. It took a minute before the response came.

'La Fábrica, go ahead.'

'It's La Rosa, I'm at the eastern ridge. I'm about to enter our airspace.'

'Acknowledged, Mr La Rosa. You are safe to proceed.'

Since Carver could hear the exchange, La Rosa simply pointed a thick finger to indicate commencement of their journey. The pilot brought them around sharply, simultaneously using the left-hand rudder pedal with a firm tweak of the cyclic stick. He then pushed forward on the stick and raised the collective lever to increase lift and accelerate, tipping the cabin downwards at a disconcerting angle. For a brief moment, the two men stared at fissured rock rushing past, just twenty metres beneath the aircraft's nose, then they passed over the crest and the ground dropped away beneath them. The effect was dizzying, almost vertigo inducing, for pilot and passenger alike. The Eurocopter levelled out, revealing a sea of lush green vegetation stretching for many kilometres into a gigantic, wide valley. The cobweb-thin glint of a river was barely visible writhing through the gully below. To their front, an expansive cultivated area dominated the hillside. Carver knew that this would be a coca crop, and their destination.

'Let me give you one piece of advice, Mr Carver, that I strongly suggest you take heed of.'

Carver looked expectantly into the stony face of La Rosa, feigning a level of interest that wasn't present in reality.

'Never fly into this valley without myself or one of my colleagues aboard.'

'Okay, got it.' Carver nodded acquiescence.

'Down there, if you please. You will see the airfield.'

* * *

Carver spent the better part of two hours on the ground in close proximity to the Eurocopter. Three guards kept a watchful eye on him throughout. Dressed in faded, soiled denims and cotton shirts, each man had an automatic rifle slung over his shoulder. Their swarthy faces displayed a lack of merriment that effectively repressed any desire he had to wander around. A quick visit to the brush to urinate was as far as he dared stray.

He gazed around in all directions as subtly as he could manage in the circumstances, hoping to identify something that would interest Johnson. There was nothing to see but the narrow, rectangular, grass runway and the road leading from it in the distant northwest corner. Had he been instructed to land at the other end of the airstrip, he undoubtedly would have noticed the 90mm gun turret concealed at the edge of the forest, but from where he stood it was as good as invisible.

Each of his watchmen had gratefully accepted an American cigarette, offered when he needed a light, but otherwise there had been no interaction with them. This lack of hospitality wasn't a problem for Carver. He always carried a packed lunch and a flask of coffee during charter flights and was perfectly content to spend the extended break reading his newspaper.

La Rosa had been driven off the airfield in a pick-up truck and had given the pilot no indication of when he might return. Carver could do little more than wait, and suspected that he wouldn't be free to leave even if he wished to. At one point, the monotony of the interval was interrupted by the ominous sound of a single gunshot echoing down the hillside. He glanced over at the nearest militiaman, whose face was framed by long, dark hair and a felt cowboy hat. It registered no alarm or concern. Carver hoped that the sound was an everyday occurrence and not the sound of someone's violent dismissal. He couldn't help wondering what else La Rosa carried in his leather shoulder bag, other than a sat-phone.

* * *

The return journey went smoothly and with the absence of any conversation. La Rosa seemed content to sit and brood, staring out of the door window. The sun at their rear threw long shadows. The mountain slopes to their front shone brightly. Carver didn't disturb La Rosa. He preferred to concentrate on his dials and the feedback from the aircraft. As they rounded Salcantay, he radioed in to air traffic control and was pleased to make it back to the aerodrome comfortably before dusk. He was perfectly capable of flying at night but it never made things any easier, especially after a long day in the cockpit.

On landing, La Rosa thanked him politely and instructed him to send the bill as usual. He wouldn't care how much it was for. Carver would charge the waiting time at full rate. La Rosa's SUV arrived almost as soon as the skids touched the ground. Moments later the cartel man was gone. The journey had been trouble-free, *easy money,* but Carver was still relieved it was over.

He handed the aircraft back into the care of his engineer and headed for the building. His personal assistant and mistress Catalena was waiting for him by the door with a message, seemingly glamorous and beautiful as always. She kissed him on the cheek as he entered.

'You had a call from Mr Thomas Daniels, a British gentleman, enquiring about a charter. Could you call him back in London this evening? He will take a late call.'

It was an everyday request. There were always prospectors, eager to exploit the resources of a nation less proficient at exploiting them for itself. He yawned and vaguely nodded assent.

'He said you were recommended by a Mr Johnson.'

Carver stopped in midstride, his mind snapping into focus. Johnson wasn't in the habit of endorsing his business; at least, he had never done so in the past. They avoided all contact unless Carver wished to make a report. He cursed as his mind hunted for a plausible explanation. *Is there someone else called Johnson?* He felt the first inklings of panic creeping into his chest. This Daniels might be a genuine customer but he had no way of knowing. *Surely, Johnson wouldn't expose me.* He winced at the thought of the possible connotations. He took the number from Catalena and went briskly into his office, unintentionally slamming the door behind him as he entered. He checked the time in London: six hours ahead – approaching 11pm. It was getting late but he placed the call anyway. He wanted to get this matter dealt with before his nerves could get the better of him.

'Daniels.'

'Good evening, Mr Daniels – Derrick Carver Charter. I understand you need a helicopter.'

'Hello. Thanks for returning my call. Yes, that's correct. I'd like to make a series of journeys departing from and returning to Cusco. I have a list of dates here to check with your availability.'

'Of course; that won't be a problem. But first could I ask how you came across my company? My assistant mentioned a recommendation.'

'Mr Johnson gave me your details. He tells me that you have a working relationship.'

Carvers heart sank. This was it – he was going to be blackmailed. The beginning of a slow death sentence. He would never have believed that the CIA would betray him. *They can't be doing this to me.*

'Don't worry, Mr Carver, Johnson and I have a common interest in the region. My business in Peru is also of a private nature. You can rest assured that both you and I face unwelcome consequences for a lack of discretion in this respect.'

In an instant, Carver understood. This wasn't blackmail – this Brit was a fellow spook, probably coming to spy on the cartels. If the man's purposes were discovered, he would not be seen again. Daniels simply wished to ensure Carver's silence. He breathed a sigh of relief and his shoulders relaxed. This was a situation he could manage.

'I understand completely, Mr Daniels. Anonymity is a requirement for many of my clients. It comes guaranteed with the service. Go ahead. Give me the dates, times and destinations.'

Chapter Ten

Tuesday, 5 July
Stirling Lines

Lance Corporal Christian Bryce stood atop the scaffold platform with his legs astride the Jackdaw, its handlebars gripped tightly in his gloved hands. The wooden deck was one-metre wide, around twelve metres long and elevated two metres from the ground. Waiting in line behind him were Jason 'Match' Marchant, Iain Morris and Gavin Riley. Each man stood over an identical machine and wore one of the lightweight ballistic helmets that had been issued for the exercise. To their front stretched six metres of runway followed by an abrupt drop. Two metres from the end of the scaffold, a pile of earth was shaped and compacted into a landing ramp. This was the initial obstacle of the morning's training session and Bryce was first in line to try it out.

The drop was considerably larger than the ones they had practiced the day before, and Bryce felt a flutter of trepidation; but he had no intention of letting the other men see that. He had watched Dylan demonstrate the feature three times, once on his personal mountain bike and twice on the Jackdaw, each time landing without difficulty. All Bryce had to do was leave the ramp's edge at the correct speed. He felt sure it would be easy enough. The fear factor even added a bit of excitement to the morning's lesson. Mostly though, he was just keen to be getting on with the programme after the problems of the previous day, and relieved to finally be making some progress with the new equipment.

'Watch how it's done, Match.' Bryce was Australian born and his accent had retained a thick twang throughout his nine years of residency in the UK.

'Get on with it,' came the reply.

He took a deep breath, stood up on the bike and began to pedal forward. Four hard strokes and he was up to speed. The drop appeared to grow before him as he coasted towards the end of the gangway, the gap widening as he neared the edge. He sucked air into his chest and braced for the landing, his arms and legs bent to take the brunt. His wheels left the scaffold, for an instant he was airborne, then his tyres touched down on the dirt. The Jackdaw's plush suspension soaked up the impact comfortably, requiring surprisingly little physical effort from Bryce. He exhaled hard with relief as he rolled away from the landing ramp.

'Yeah, spot on, Bryce,' Dylan called over from his position next to the obstacle. 'Match, you're up.'

Bryce was one of sixteen men chosen to carry out Operation CATHODE, eight of whom were selected from Mountain Troop and eight from Mobility. This combined unit were now detailed to the Jackdaw training programme – a course of instruction in advanced cycling skills for the navigation of mountainous terrain, utilising the new equipment. This was welcome news for the Mobility Troop members, who were the squadron's off-road vehicle experts, and this included Bryce and his three training companions. Mobility Troop were already proficient in the use and maintenance of Land Rovers, ATVs, Unimog trucks and off-road motorcycles; each man was capable of manoeuvring quickly over rough terrain, in the dark when necessary. This new vehicle would add another string to their bow. But the appeal of the module also went further: the Jackdaw programme provided an opportunity for some good old-fashioned competition.

The man following Bryce was a tall and sinewy trooper whose dark hair and beard were trimmed to a uniform length, inspiring the nickname for his resemblance to a matchstick. He was lauded as the most talented motorcyclist within the service, having spent much of his childhood perfecting his trials riding – the art of maintaining balance on a bike while scaling rocky slopes and collections of improbable obstacles. Match was expected by everyone to perform well on the Jackdaw, but the other men would be equally keen and would fully commit to the course. Bryce was stronger, more athletic and quite determined: he wasn't going to let Match steal the show without a fight.

Match pedalled slowly along the runway, looking more relaxed than Bryce had been. As he reached the lip, he compressed the machine's suspension and bounced smoothly from the ramp and down onto the dirt mound. A perfect landing. *Damn,* Bryce thought, *he's not even trying! Gunna have to step yer game up, Brycey.* Morris and Riley also took their turns without incident, and when each member of the group had repeated the drop two more times, they moved on to the next in a series of increasingly daunting obstacles.

After arriving at the former RAF base early on Saturday morning, Dylan had spent the whole weekend working tirelessly to create a training circuit for the Jackdaw riders. Equipping himself with a sketch pad, a pencil and a can of engineer's marker paint, he then requisitioned the help of a digger driver to pile and shape the required mounds of earth. Large rocks and logs were manoeuvred into position, then the camp's carpenters completed the arrangement with ramps and platforms built of scaffold and planking. Dylan claimed that each feature was designed to practice a particular riding skill.

However, these considerable efforts were initially to no avail as the planned consignment of Jackdaws failed to arrive on time. Just five out of twenty units were delivered on the Monday morning in their hard travel cases, and these first went to the squadron's mechanics to be assembled and checked over. Lacking the equipment to train with, Dylan was instead asked to hold a briefing session outlining the objectives of the course. After starting with enthusiasm, he soon ran into difficulties and the first of two heated arguments with McCowan.

Bryce could clearly recall the uncomfortable atmosphere in the briefing room as the presentation steadily fell apart. Dylan began the lesson with an explanation of the mechanical features of his own personal mountain bike, which rested polished and gleaming at the front of the room. The oversized frame tubing provided the strength to take impacts; the big disc brakes dissipated heat, allowing continued braking on long descents; the long-travel suspension made it possible to ride quickly over rough ground without being shaken to pieces. The Mobility Troop men listened intently, despite being familiar with the subject matter, but not everyone present could see the benefit of the lecture.

Elana Govrin had been included in the module, reputedly just as a convenient way to keep her occupied. She was uninterested by the prospect and visibly bored to tears. Sergeant O'Neil was vocally sceptical about the practicality of using bikes in the mountains. But most significantly, McCowan himself was unconvinced. Twice he interrupted Dylan, telling him to move on to a new topic. When Dylan then played a video, highlighting the skills the trainees would need to master, McCowan irritably switched off the television set after just a few minutes. As the session progressed, Dylan became increasingly flustered. He attempted to continue with a series of whiteboard drawings showing positions of the bike and rider, annotated with names for the manoeuvres and arrows to indicate movement. Once again, it wasn't long before McCowan intervened.

'Dylan, I don't see the relevance of these 'tricks' for getting us down a mountain in the dark. We need to learn how to ride safely and quietly, not how to show off.'

'They're not tricks!' Dylan's face glowed red with exasperation. 'They're skills you use all the time.'

Despite Dylan's protests, McCowan brought the briefing to a premature close. Before anyone was out of earshot, he began to openly question Daniels about the suitability of the training. Bryce filed out of the room with the others, feeling disappointed with the breakdown of the lesson and sympathetic for Dylan.

The second argument occurred outside in the training area, where the mood had otherwise been improving. Dylan gave a demonstration of the practice circuit using his own mountain bike, negotiating the obstacles with such speed and precision that he received an enthusiastic applause from the Mobility Troop men. Even McCowan seemed to appreciate the level of talent on display.

'I still fail to see that these abilities are necessary for my men, Dylan. We'll never encounter obstacles like these in the field.'

'But you'll use the same techniques. You don't get much time to think when you're riding fast. If you practice here, over and over, it will happen automatically when you need it.'

'I can certainly understand that maxim, Dylan. Continue then, please.'

McCowan remained placated until the five Jackdaws were made ready and handed over to Dylan to commence the tuition. Bryce was in the first group of four to test the device, while the others were rotated onto other training until their turn came. The Australian was impressed as soon as he saw the bombproof build of the machine, the detailed engineering and the disruptive-pattern camouflage in matte black and grey. Dylan's flashy downhill racing bike seemed like a toy in comparison to the burly, militarised Jackdaw. However, it was Dylan's turn to be critical. He lifted one up.

'They're way too heavy,' he declared flatly.

'I'm sorry?' McCowan's temper began to fray.

'It's like…more than double the weight of my bike.'

'They weigh whatever they weigh, lad. We've spent a lot of money on this. You're supposed to be a professional who can work with such things.'

'It doesn't matter what they cost. I'm telling you they're too heavy. Some of these obstacles I've built just won't be possible.'

'Well they are what we have – we can't make them any lighter, for heaven's sake. Just bloody get on with it and stop throwing your toys out the pram.'

'Okay fine, but nobody is going to be quick on one of these.'

'As I *keep* telling you, Dylan, we don't care about being quick.'

Once again, Bryce was dismayed by the faltering proceedings.

In practice, Dylan had shown no real problems in sending the heavy Jackdaw over the smaller obstacles, and before long the first group of trainees were completing laps of an easy circuit. Bryce and Match successfully negotiated the course after just a few attempts, only attracting minor tips from Dylan. Bryce found it took a little forethought to adapt his riding style to a pedal powered bike, more so as he became exhausted from sprinting the bike between the obstacles.

'It's harder to keep your balance when you're out of breath,' Dylan had advised. 'Carry more speed through the corners and you won't need to pedal so much.'

Dylan made them work for a solid hour. Bryce was soaked in sweat by the time he handed over the Jackdaw and rotated onto other training. The intense session was repeated with each group until the entire detail had mastered the basic circuit. Despite the problematic start, the first day had ultimately ended on a positive note.

* * *

Bryce and the others had woken Dylan at 5:50am to accompany them on their daily four-mile fast run around the base perimeter. Dylan protested profusely but they wouldn't take no for an answer, insisting that he needed to appreciate their routine to target his training effectively. In reality, they just wanted to pay him back for making them sweat. He vomited after the first mile and was unable to continue, giving the D Squadron men a good laugh.

Again, Bryce's group were given the first session, and Dylan took them straight to the larger obstacles. Bryce now felt positive with the first task completed, but the difficulty and risk were increasing with each feature. The next challenge was a test of nerve and balance. A narrow wooden ramp ran up to a height that Bryce could just touch with his fingertips, then levelled out and sloped sharply back down again. The width of the entire platform was less than thirty centimetres. They had successfully wobbled the bikes across narrower beams the previous day, although much lower down and without the same consequence for error. Bryce didn't think the ramp looked safe but he wouldn't dare admit it out loud. *That's a fair way to fall, mate.* Reassuringly though, he was last in line and that boosted his confidence, as did yet another series of effortless demonstrations by Dylan.

Match went first, and true to form he tackled the challenge with conviction. He powered up the ramp with just the right speed to coast slowly across the top, then held his balance until the bike tipped onto the downslope. Bryce felt nervous. Morris and Riley took their turns, both looking less stable but getting over safely with some laughs on the other side. Now Bryce was under pressure. *Everyone else has completed the thing; I can't let the side down.*

He pedalled away for a run-up and his pulse began to hammer in his chest. *Shit! Why am I so damn scared? The others made it look easy.* He resolved himself to stop thinking about it and get moving. Hesitation just made things worse. *Come on Brycey, let's get this fucker done.*

He rode at the ramp as hard as he could, hitting the upslope fast but tensed. The Jackdaw crested the ramp quickly, but Bryce was off-balance. He twitched his handlebars left then overcompensated hard right, skewing the front wheel over the edge of the platform. The tyre's knobbly treads hung up for a brief moment as Bryce tried to steer back, then the rubber lost its grip with a snap. The front of the bike plunged, pitching him forwards, and man and machine fell. Bryce's hands slipped from the grips as the front wheel struck the ground, but they were unable to protect his head from the subsequent impact. There was a sickening crunch for all to hear as the ballistic helmet met the hard, compacted earth. Bryce lay still, in agony throughout his upper body. He heard McCowan's voice bellow from somewhere above him.

'Get a stretcher here, *quickly!* He's in a bad way.'

* * *

It was late in the afternoon before Bryce returned to the barracks – sore, downbeat and groggy from pain relief medication. He was annoyed with himself; he should have been able to control his nerves. Now he wouldn't be able to complete the training. He went to look for the rest of the team but found Dylan's mountain bike first. The formerly elegant machine sat mangled and discarded on the concrete pathway outside the lecture room. It took only a brief inspection to see that the aluminium frame had been torn open by nine-millimetre rounds, along with the wheels and tyres. *What the hell has happened here?* Bryce asked himself. He stepped into the building and soon found out.

The rest of the detail were sat around inside, looking glum and presumably waiting for something. McCowan, Dylan and Daniels were all absent. Normally Bryce would have expected a thorough ribbing after a training injury, but apparently no one was in the mood at that moment. Morris jumped up to usher him into the room and check him over.

'Alright bud. We were wondering when you'd be back. They fix you up, okay?'

'I'm not doing great. They had to relocate my right shoulder. Hurt like hell, but the doc said I could use it again in a month with some good physio. But this one,' Bryce raised his left arm fractionally, which was wrapped in a cast and supported by a sling. 'I've fractured the ulna at the elbow. I've got the cast for six weeks minimum, then I'll have to build up exercise gently. Doc said that if I'm operational in three months I should be happy about it.'

'That's crap; sorry mate. Looks like you'll be getting some R&R.'

There were sympathetic noises from around the room.

'But what the hell's been going on here? Why are you all sat inside and why is Dylan's bike full of holes?'

'The shit hit the fan after your crash,' Morris answered. 'McCowan blew a fuse. Him and Dylan had a stand-up row and you can guess who came off best. McCowan accused him of conducting a needlessly dangerous exercise, and Dylan said he warned him the Jackdaws were too heavy. So then McCowan drags Dylan's bike over to the firing range and puts a whole clip in it with an MP5. He said it was to demonstrate why the Jackdaw needed to be built so much stronger. Things went downhill from there onwards. The CO is with them now, getting it straightened out. We've been told to wait in here for further instruction, but if I was you I'd go grab a beer while you've got an excuse.'

Bryce sunk down in a plastic chair instead. He was part of the unit and wanted to know the outcome as much as anyone else did. He resigned himself to the wait, even though he was unlikely to have any further participation. His thoughts drifted to that cold beer and he began to wonder what he could do with his time off.

Chapter Eleven

Wednesday, 20 July
Cusco

Tom Daniels had endured sixteen hours and two fuel stops aboard the Lockheed Tristar before it eventually began its descent into Cusco's AVA Airport. The sprawling mosaic of orange-clay tiled roofs that spread through the shallow valley below were a welcome sight. The mild but inescapable scent of recycled air and upholstery cleaner had left him feeling faintly nauseous. Finally the hiss of the engines and the hum of electrical motors was broken by the vibrato whine of the landing gear lowering.

Accompanying him on the long flight from RAF Brize Norton were the twenty-one soldiers and supporting staff that comprised the tactical development unit now referred to as the TDU. The assault team remained behind at Stirling Lines and would follow at a later point. He had filled the time chatting with the troops until the first refuelling stop in the Azores – mostly with Staff Sergeant Yates, who held authority over the training procedure – but then successfully got his head down until they reached the South American land mass. He felt jaded, but was wide awake again as they made their final approach to the runway. The pilot had already informed him of a radio communication: General Torres would be ready to receive them and their equipment as soon as they touched down.

Daniels spotted the line of olive-green canvas-backed trucks rushing out to meet them before the Tristar even stopped rolling, their presence mitigating one of his principal concerns. There were numerous crates of valuable kit in the hold and nothing could be allowed to go astray. Stowed amongst the regular equipment was the materiel required for the covert phase of the operation, some of which would be very difficult to justify for a unit that was supposedly engaged in training.

Most of the raiders would carry the C8 CQB assault rifle, as its short barrel and telescoping stock made it an ideal fit for the Jackdaw's weapon holder. Sixteen of these were packed, along with magazines and a few thousand 5.56mm rounds. Other crates held the SIG Sauer 9mm pistols that would be carried as secondary weapons. Also included were two newly-purchased Heckler & Koch HK417 rifles, along with suppressors and several boxes of match-grade 7.62mm subsonic ammunition – the chosen tool of the designated marksmen to engage their targets silently. The assault team would carry explosive charges made up on site from the General's resources, but timers, detonators and appropriate satchels had been brought along to ensure familiarity and reliability. Daniels was glad there would be no customs check.

Making his way down the metal steps, he could see Torres standing in front of the row of trucks, now arranged with their open backs facing the aircraft. The general was tall, heavily built and imposing, appearing neither lean nor toned. A rigid, stern expression gave the impression he wasn't a man to be trifled with. He wore camouflage overalls and a matching cap; only the rank insignia on his sleeves gave indication of his authority. He stood hands behind his back, feet shoulder width apart as he stared at Daniels over his dark, bushy moustache. He remained motionless until they stood face to face, then thrust out a large hand.

'Señor Daniels, I am General Juan Carlos Torres – commander of the Región Militar del Sur and Third Division. Welcome to Peru. These men will now assist in loading your equipment to my helicopter. It will then take us to the training facility where you will carry out your work.' Torres spoke good English, but with a deep gruff voice and a heavy Hispanic accent.

'Good to meet you, General. We have...'

Torres did not wait for the reply; he turned away once the introduction was complete and began directing his men, rapidly barking orders in Spanish. Daniels couldn't avoid the impression that the British team were not entirely welcome, but this kind of judgement could be saved for later. Tidewell and Pearson-Roberts had invested time and effort in putting this deal together, and he had been assured that Torres was fully committed to their plan of action.

The RAF loadmaster supervised the transfer of the crates while Torres' men assisted with the manhandling on the ground. Daniels had little to do but observe, and felt like a spare part. He stood stationary in the crisp winter air growing increasingly cold from the inactivity. In barely fifteen minutes, the gear was loaded onto the trucks, with a few accompanying troopers in each. Daniels hopped on board the last in line and the procession began rolling slowly around the airfield perimeter. He was slightly curious that Torres had mentioned his helicopter in the singular; at least, he was until he saw it.

As the truck swung around to face its rear to the lowered tail-ramp, Daniels took in the enormity of the Russian MI-26 'Halo' helicopter. He had heard about these things, read about them, but the vast bulk of the machine was still surprising in the flesh. The aircraft stood eight metres high and forty metres long, its eight-bladed rotor measuring more than thirty metres across. The truck that Daniels sat in could be parked inside its cavernous load space twice, without any struggle. He whistled softly to himself in appreciation.

The soldiers dismounted hurriedly to transfer the equipment to the helicopter's empty fuselage, now sharing the task between the two units. Torres led Daniels to the front of the aircraft. The general paused briefly by the cabin door and signalled to the pilot, then ushered Daniels up the passenger steps to take a seat behind the cockpit. The twin 11000hp turbines throttled up to an incredible roar and the blades began to rotate. When the last crate was loaded and the last man aboard, the flight technician raised the loading ramp and closed the twin rear doors. Torres took the seat beside Daniels as the gigantic machine gently lifted from the ground. The general passed over a headset and indicated a socket for the intercom. When Daniels could finally hear over the roar of the engines, the big man spoke.

'Mr Daniels, allow me to greet you properly.' Torres took his hand and shook it again, more vigorously than the previous time. 'There would be people watching at the airport; maybe even listening. The scale of corruption here is reaching unprecedented levels as the cartels squirm to avoid their destruction. It's preferable that I don't appear overly enthusiastic to receive you.'

'I understand completely, General. We'd like to keep a low profile ourselves.'

'So, how do you like my helicopter? It can lift twenty tonnes.'

Daniels looked around the interior. The craft looked half empty with nearly forty passengers and all their equipment inside.

'It's a beast of a machine. Would you mind if we borrow it?'

'*Haha!*' Torres laughed heartily at Daniels' half-joke. 'You would be most welcome, but I think we should be more discreet or people will suspect your purpose here. Don't worry, I shall lend you a less conspicuous aircraft.'

'What do you have in mind? Our men will be carrying a lot of gear.'

'This is not a matter of concern; I have several ideal machines at my disposal. Until recently I had one more, but Del Bosque took it from me along with the crew and twenty of my best men.' Torres face set in a hard scowl that revealed the extent of his disdain for the cartel. 'And since this event, many members of our government have lost the political will to take decisive action against Del Bosque, and therefore would not approve the operation we have planned for your second team. In fact, there have been many objections to your presence here in a training capacity alone.'

'We'll be bringing the assault team over on civilian flights,' Daniels clarified. 'And I've arranged for a private charter helicopter to take us to our forward operating base. I'll use the name 'Outpost' to refer to this location.'

'Understood. The presence and location of your assault team must become known to no one except ourselves. Not even our congress is aware of the plans for the raid. They are angry enough that they were not consulted about the purchase of your training services, especially as their permission is required to allow foreign troops on our soil. Fortunately, the budget for this project is available from unspent funds previously allocated to the EP for expanding our special forces.'

'How far up does the corruption go? Do the cartels have influence within government?'

'We don't wish to accuse our politicians directly, but there are many secretaries, assistants, support staff; any one of which can be a security risk. Our congress has one hundred and thirty democratically elected members, each with their own office. If they vote on a law or policy to combat organised crime, the cartels will be aware of the results the moment they are counted. For this reason, President Mendez has used his authority as Commander-in-Chief of our armed forces, and given orders for this operation directly to my superior. We are the only people that understand the full extent of the assistance you will provide. Both the Defence Ministry and Joint Command have suggested that the Ejército del Perú has nothing to gain from your instruction. Neither would sanction foreign military assistance here. That's why we're having this conversation in my helicopter.'

'The men of the TDU know enough to prepare the munitions for the assault team, but they won't speak a word of it to anyone. Secrecy is like a religion for these guys. The other team will be bringing some specialised kit with them, but all our weapons are in these crates. We'll need to get them moved over to Outpost before the operation commences.'

'I have already made arrangements for this, Mr Daniels.'

'Please, call me Tom.'

'Very well, Tom. Elements of my Mountain Brigade will be garrisoned with you for the duration of the training assignment, but 4SF – the Víboras – will travel from their own barracks to attend. The eyes of both the cartel and my political adversaries will be on your team here, allowing me to stage the covert element of the raid from elsewhere unobserved. We'll prepare the explosive charges as if it were a routine exercise, then a helicopter will drop them to your second team along with the weapons. The Víboras will travel frequently between the two bases, and this will disguise the movement of the equipment. For the assault itself, I'll send a transport helicopter to ferry your men to their insertion point. When I receive the signal that the missile system is no longer operational, I'll dispatch two more with enough troops to clear and hold the enemy camp. There will no longer be any need for subterfuge at this point: I will announce the launch of an official operation.'

'I'd like to finalise our plan of attack with you. We'll be able to talk privately at our destination?'

'Yes, there's an office we can make use of. But perhaps you would tell me something now about the specialist equipment that your other team will be bringing.'

'We intend to use this raid to demonstrate some new technology of British manufacture and our ability to use it in action. If you like the results, we can add further modules to the training programme, to give your forces this capability in future.'

'Ahh ha!' Torres's face broke into a broad smile. 'So you intend to sell me this curious 'technology'. We shall have to see if it works first. I admit, I am intrigued.'

* * *

The ponderous aircraft set down lightly on an area of levelled gravel adjacent to the nucleus of the training camp. A series of wooden huts and containers were arranged on the shore of a crystal-clear lake, perched in an area of desolate highland at the northernmost extent of the Altiplano – the Andean high plateau that stretched through Bolivia to Chile and Argentina beyond. Spread around the site were the usual canvas-backed trucks, a few 4x4's, an American Humvee and an amphibious armoured personnel carrier. An unmade track could be seen running down the hill in the direction from where they had just come. The encompassing landscape was dotted with tufted grass punctuated by towering structures of craggy rock. The snow-clad peaks of massive mountains rose above them kilometres distant.

Daniels was shepherded on a brief tour of the site and given a breakdown of the available facilities by a Mountain Brigade master sergeant. The Peruvian troops were free to train in this bleak wilderness – a giant's playground – and could use live ammunition without any concern for civilian presence. The vehicles could be used to access terrain ranging from dense rainforest to sheer faces of ice. The sergeant pointed out a ragged column of rock close to the camp, forty metres in height, on which a platoon-strength party were performing climbing-rescue exercises with simulated casualties. The official title of the training area was condensed to an acronym, but it didn't take long for the British troops to brand the site with their own more-fitting nickname: 'War Mountain'.

The men of the TDU were shown to the quarters they would inhabit for the next few weeks. To comply with the unavoidable regulations, Torres insisted that their equipment crates were registered and stored with the camp quartermaster – weapons and ammunition could not be unaccounted for or carried freely. He gave his solemn promise that they would not be interfered with in any way, and that they would be kept in the most secure possible containment.

After familiarising themselves with their surroundings, the SAS men made their way to the canteen. They had time to kill before the training procedure started and they intended to use it getting to know the soldiers they would be working with. The first few days would be spent accompanying the Peruvian forces on a series of typical exercises, to watch how they worked and identify areas of potential improvement. Foreign military training needed to be of flexible format and tailored to the requirements of the individual units attending.

Daniels joined them for just long enough to gulp down a cup of coffee, then sought the general's ear to gain approval for the existing plan of action. He had other business to attend to and didn't wish to linger at the camp any longer than was necessary. Torres guided him into a small office at the rear of one of the huts, stationing a guard outside to guarantee their privacy. Once the door was closed, Daniels produced a sleeve containing aerial photographs of the target, and a folded, A2 sized diagram.

'What I have here is an outline version of a much more detailed plan that's been put together at headquarters over the past few weeks. We've identified the critical objectives, prioritised them and allocated them between four teams. Team one will secure and maintain a landing zone for your men, to the north of the target in the plantation. Team two will enter the production area at the western end of the facility and create a diversionary explosion, in order to reduce the effectiveness of the militia response. Team three will disable enemy communications, neutralise any mobile defences, then locate the SAM launcher and destroy it. Team four will block the road from the airstrip to protect the other operations from counter-attack.' Daniels drew his finger around the diagram to indicate the movements. 'These three teams will then clear and hold the airstrip as a second landing zone.'

'Thorough and ruthless, as I would expect. Your SAS has much experience in this kind of work. However, there is something that you've missed, another objective I must insist you carry out.'

Daniels was surprised at this revelation. The Intelligence Corps had been through the intel with a fine-tooth comb back at Stirling Lines. Every element had been scrutinised, every eventuality planned for.

'We'll do whatever's required to get the job done. What are we missing here?'

'You must destroy one hundred percent of the cocaine stored at La Fábrica, either by fire or using an appropriate explosive charge. Whichever way, this must happen before my teams arrive.'

Daniels looked uncomprehendingly at Torres.

'You don't trust your men with the cocaine?'

'I trust my men absolutely, but I do not trust the process that will follow when we take control of something worth many millions of dollars. There will be procedures dictated to me over which I have no control. People will wish to test it, weigh it, transport it for controlled disposal. As you can imagine, there are many opportunities for this process to run astray. Some of it will make its way back into the hands of criminal gangs, and I cannot begin to describe to you the damage that this substance has done to my country. Of course, I could have my men burn it themselves on arrival, but it would be a violation of protocol on my part. It would make things easier for me, politically, if the product was entirely destroyed by the time my men arrive.'

'Where will the cocaine be stored?' Daniels asked, turning back to the diagram.

'There will be a structure adjoining the production huts.'

'Okay, that could work to our advantage. I'll need to run it by the team, but maybe they can put a charge in there big enough to blow the stuff all over the site. At that concentration, I imagine it would be debilitating for anyone caught nearby. Our team will just need to make sure they're not too close downwind when it goes.'

'Can I count on you that this will be done, Tom?'

'We can't allocate the cocaine storage the same priority as the defensive targets or the launcher, for obvious reasons. Nor can I guarantee how the mission will pan out on the day – these operations are always subject to an element of chance – but I can promise you that we'll make this the primary objective when positioning the diversionary charges. We don't take our responsibilities lightly.'

'Then my mind is at rest; thank you.' The general turned away from the diagrams and began to gather his personal items from the top of the desk, as if to indicate that the meeting was over. As he held the door open for Daniels' departure, he made a parting remark. 'I sincerely hope that the element of chance favours your men better than it favoured mine.'

* * *

The next morning, Daniels set out for Cusco in a borrowed Toyota Land Cruiser. He had an appointment with Derrick Carver and it seemed neither appropriate nor discreet to ask Torres for a helicopter to be laid on. The journey wasn't so far in a direct line, but with the meanderings of the road the drive was double the distance. Narrow, winding and poorly delineated, the route required focussed attention and constant gear changing. While the going was slow and treacherous, the views were breath-taking.

Daniels relished the opportunity to take in the landscape. A vast, turbulent ocean of tormented rock stretched out to the horizons, its extent revealed only in glimpses when the height of the carriageway allowed. Just a sparse dusting of vegetation softened the scarred and fissured terrain. A large bird soared overhead. *Was it a condor?* It was too difficult to tell while driving the vehicle.

The sun shone brilliantly from a pale blue backdrop, adding to his enjoyment, and the temperature was mild at seven degrees centigrade. The minor road joined a highway, passing settlements and banks of agricultural terraces on the shallower slopes. It was a full three hours before he pulled onto the concrete apron of the small airfield.

Derrick Carver's office building was nothing more than a single-storey extension adjoined to the side of a small hanger. The black and turquoise Eurocopter sat outside. Behind it, through the open roller-shutter doorway, Daniels saw a man in overalls rummaging in the drawers of a tool chest. He made his way inside through glass double doors. The receptionist smiled warmly in welcome, inviting him to take a seat while she notified Mr Carver of his arrival. The pilot emerged promptly wearing a thick, wool-lined flight jacket and hiker style boots, suitable clothing should he need to exit the aircraft in the mountains. Daniels had chosen similar attire, and hoped he would pass for an oil industry type to any attentive eyes. They shook hands, exchanged pleasantries and briefly went through some paperwork relating to payment and insurance. It wasn't until they were seated inside the helicopter with the doors shut and the engine winding up that there was any kind of recognition that they shared each other's secrets.

'So, Tom, I'm curious why you mentioned your association to Mr Johnson over the telephone. If you'd just booked the charter, I'd have no idea who you are or what your business concerns.'

'No, but someone may have asked you to find out. It wouldn't be long before you deduced enough to jeopardise my security. I wanted you to appreciate the consequences from the outset – a problem for me is a problem for you. The location we're heading to can't be revealed to anyone. Lives depend on it.'

'Yeah, yours and mine, apparently,' Carver quipped with a sardonic smile.

Once again, Carver steered the Eurocopter to the east of Salcantay before heading northwest into the steep, wide valleys of La Convención Province. Daniels intended to use the Eurocopter to ferry the assault team and their Jackdaws from Cusco airport to Outpost unnoticed, while the TDU remained under the spotlight at the training camp. A Víboras patrol had chosen the location for its physical attributes and its remoteness. The assault team would be able to rehearse weapons drills, practice bike handling and prepare for the operation in complete isolation. When the time came to launch the assault, Outpost was only eighty kilometres east of their drop-off point.

The helicopter dropped altitude, scattering a herd of vicuña grazing on the grassy alpine tundra, and soon they were below the tree line. Carver notified Daniels that they were approaching the given destination. It took a moment before either man spotted the objective but it was easily recognisable when they did, and right on their current bearing. The natural clearing was spacious enough to accommodate a helicopter and level enough for a landing.

'That's where we're going. Put her down there,' Daniels instructed.

The pilot simply nodded and wheeled the craft around to approach from the angle he favoured. Carver was experienced at flying in these mountains; he could slot her into a gap much smaller than this and often had. It was only a few more minutes before they were on the ground with the rotors slowing. Daniels jumped out onto the stony surface, leaving Carver to power down the helicopter's engines.

Torres' men had chosen well. The vegetation wasn't so dense at this altitude but still gave enough cover to conceal the assault team's tents and equipment. The ridge above Outpost was mostly dominated by flaky-barked polylepis trees, while further down the incline the forest thickened with Andean alder and coniferous podocarps. Wild papaya bushes were dotted around, reaching a few metres in height. Patches of bare rock were left exposed in many places. Daniels spent nearly an hour inspecting the location on foot before he had seen enough. He noticed the extra exertion required to move around the steep hillside in the thin air and wondered how it would impact the twenty-kilometre descent from the drop-off point to the target. The men would need to acclimatise, here as well as at the training camp. With no further business at Outpost, Daniels re-boarded the helicopter and asked Carver to lift-off and commence their return flight to Cusco.

* * *

Most of the day had passed by the time Daniels returned to the training camp. He brought the borrowed 4x4 to a halt by the guard post for a brief security check, then was granted access through the barriers. He had spent much of the return journey mulling over the ancillary responsibilities of his assignment. In order to identify potential for further equipment sales, he would compile an inventory of all the kit that the Mountain Brigade soldiers were currently using, also making note of its condition and suitability for purpose. Collating and recording this information would eat up a fair slice of his time, so the sooner he got started the better. He only had one leg out of the vehicle when the SAS corporal ran over.

'There's some Rupert turned up – top brass; been giving the general grief about us lot. You'd betta get in there.' The soldier referred to the arrival of a high-ranking officer, no doubt intending to make his presence felt. Daniels had expected this. His work often attracted bureaucratic difficulties.

He was shown to Torres' office, where Admiral Ballesta – Head of the Joint Command – was waiting to see him personally. The Joint Command is the executive arm of the Peruvian military leadership and the interface between government and the armed forces. It is responsible for carrying out the instructions of the Defence Ministry. Each of the three services has its own chief, who in turn is answerable to the Head of the Joint Command. Ballesta had previously commanded the Peruvian Navy, but now also presided over the Fuerza Aérea del Perú and the Ejército del Perú.

He stood in Torres' office in black dress uniform, its cuffs adorned with gold bands denoting his rank. He wore a white cap with a shiny black peak, and displayed a ribbon bar pinned to his chest. He looked out of place to Daniels, given the surroundings – everyone else at the camp wore camouflage fatigues. However, his position required a certain gravitas of appearance and his Marina de Guerra del Perú uniform fulfilled the role aptly. Ballesta was a lean man with a hawkish nose and tanned, weathered skin. He was not happy.

After a cursory introduction and handshake, he confronted Daniels accusingly.

'I'll get straight to the point, Mr Daniels. I've spent my entire life in military service and I'm neither naive nor foolish enough to believe that your men will restrict their activities here to purely tutelage.' While Torres' English was good, Ballesta's was immaculate. Daniels suspected a British university education. The admiral continued.

'Your SAS are renowned for the assistance they have provided to other nations in dealing with subversives. No doubt your men will be on exercise with General Torres' forces when you 'unintentionally' run into a cartel operation and are forced to defend yourselves, destroying it in the process. Let me make it completely clear to you now, that this type of activity will not be tolerated on Peruvian soil. We do not need your assistance to destroy the cartels; our difficulty is in navigating the political channels that will allow us to do so. Your presence here only causes further complications. Then there is the matter of national sovereignty. No Peruvian citizen, criminal or otherwise, will be executed without trial at the hands of a foreign soldier. I won't allow it.'

Daniels remained quiet as it seemed unlikely that Ballesta had finished.

'I have a directive from the Minister for Defence requiring that I prevent your soldiers from engaging in any operational action during your stay. It's within General Torres' remit to waste his budget on your instructional services if he so wishes, but I'll be implementing measures to limit your movements to areas where they can be monitored.' Ballesta maintained the indignant tone throughout his monologue. 'Within this facility, your men are free to do as they please, but exercises elsewhere must be scheduled and approved by my department in advance. If your men are found to be armed, outside of this base in an unexpected location, you will be treated as a hostile force. Are my rules clear enough for you?'

Daniels was unabashed. He had negotiated in countries where a man could go missing for failing to reach a satisfactory agreement. Neither the Admiral's rank nor his hostile disposition were of any great consequence. The British involvement was requested by President Mendez. They had nothing to fear from Ballesta.

'Admiral, I appreciate your concern, especially given the reputation of our elite forces, but you misunderstand our intentions. The instructional services that we offer are second to none and will increase your capacity to fight these cartels. If you didn't need our help, we would not have been asked to come. I can give you my word that our training unit will not take part in any offensive operations. In any case, I have no authority to order these men into a firefight.'

'The matter of your authority I also find quite fascinating. You appear to be in charge of this rabble holding the mere rank of lieutenant, whilst a captain who outranks you has been on the telephone to my office arranging nothing more than your landing permission. Who is actually in command of these men?'

'My military background has no relevance here; I'm a representative of the Ministry of Defence. It's my job to communicate General Torres' needs to my superiors, so they can provide the relevant services. Staff Sergeant Yates holds rank.'

'A non-commissioned officer…'

'All our counterterrorist and counter-insurgency work is carried out by troopers and NCO's – it's the expertise of these men that you're purchasing.

Commissioned officers in the SAS only bear arms when deployed at war. Their attendance isn't necessary.'

'I'll take you at your word for now, Mr Daniels, but I'll be watching closely.'

Ballesta strode from the room with the bare minimum of further formalities. When he was out of earshot, Torres broke his prolonged silence.

'Now you see one of the many problems I have to deal with.'

After leaving Torres' office, Daniels found Yates and asked him to round up the troops for an emergency briefing. When everyone was together in a reasonably secluded location, he explained the developments in reduced tones.

'Here's the score: You guys are forbidden from taking part in any active ops – no surprises there – and you'll have to toe the line because there'll be eyes-on at all times. Those of you working with 5MB, carry on with your planned exercises, but if you're outside the camp make sure you're not carrying or you'll be getting deported. Those working with 4SF, cancel whatever's scheduled first and move weapons and demo drills forward. Make sure they're all held right here on base in plain sight. We need to get the raid gear prepped up and sent over to the Víboras barracks before it can get locked down. You've met some of the 4SF guys, yes?'

'Yeah, we were out running with them this morning,' a trooper answered. 'They're a sound bunch. We'll get on fine.'

'Good, because we're going to switch the assault kit into their crates at the end of each session. Our boxes will be staying here under the supervision of the quartermaster. We'll fill them up with whatever bits of kit 4SF doesn't need themselves. Let me know as soon as you've worked out the course revisions. I'll need to get them authorised by the general before we get started.'

Over the next three days, twelve men of the TDU accompanied a company of Mountain Brigade soldiers on combat exercises in a valley several kilometres from the training area base camp. This served Daniels purposes perfectly, offering a convenient focal point for the admiral's scrutiny. The remaining instructors worked tirelessly with the 4SF commandos, first on weapon handling then demolitions. At the close of this phase, the assault equipment was prepared. Every weapon had been individually stripped, cleaned, reassembled and checked. The communications gear had been tested for clarity, battery life and range. Charge packs were assembled from American M112 C4 plastic explosive blocks from the Mountain Brigade stores, each labelled for its nominated target. Then this equipment was crated up with the Víboras gear and sent on a helicopter ride. Daniels could only hope that the crates would arrive at Outpost, and not end up an expensive gift to the Ejército del Perú.

Chapter Twelve

Friday, 22 July
Brecon Beacons, Wales

The fading light stripped the hues from the grasses that covered the upper slopes, and obscured the pinkish tinge of the earth into shadow. The pale-grey sandstone, fractured by tectonic movement into flat sheets and oblong chunks, darkened steadily to an ever more imposing disposition. The grazing sheep, ubiquitous throughout these hills, became indistinguishable from the sea of tufts and hillocks, and only the glistening streams still announced their presence through the encroaching gloom. The helicopter thundered over the mountain at dusk.

Elana Govrin stood by the closed door of the swaying Puma HC1, her strong legs braced wide apart to maintain balance as the pilot simulated a high-speed combat deployment. She kept a firm hold of the handrail. With a final swinging turn, the aircraft settled into a hover over the drop zone – the peak of Pen y Fan. At the loadmaster's nod, she grabbed the Jackdaw's handlebars and lifted it onto its rear wheel, so that the front wheel was braced against the inside of the door. The rear brake was held on for stability. A man to her right adopted the same position, as did two more behind her at the opposite door. She wore camouflage fatigues, body armour, webbing and the new proprietary ballistic helmet. Kevlar pads protected her elbows, knees and shins; each held in place by thick Velcro straps. She felt utterly claustrophobic.

'Get ready!' McCowan's booming voice struggled over the roar of the turbines. *'Night-vision!'*

Govrin snapped down her NVGs, turning her world into a hazy green void. The unit tugged at her head continually with the bobbing of the aircraft.

'Wheels!'

The four soldiers rocked their machines back, lifting their front tyres clear just as the doors were slid open. Govrin felt the blast of cool air surging into the cabin. She clenched her teeth, squeezed her eyes shut and tried to remain steady.

'Go! Go! Go!'

* * *

After a relentless week of training at Stirling Lines, the detail had relocated to the steep, grassy hillsides of the Brecon Beacons to test the equipment in open ground. This had been an eye-opening experience for the trainees, who were led by Dylan down increasingly rugged terrain at breakneck speeds. The benefit of the practice sessions became pointedly clear when the riders were made to negotiate a variety of rock features with little or no preparation. They rattled over the uneven ground for another full week, tripping and tumbling until they wore collections of painful cuts and bruises. Then they progressed to night training. Just as the unit felt they were becoming somewhat proficient, the bar was raised by an unforgiving increment.

The monochrome display of the night-vision viewer caused a loss of perspective that made reading the ground frustratingly difficult; even Dylan was reduced to a crawl while he grew accustomed to the synthetic image. But these were the newest batch of NVGs to be acquired by the MoD, manufactured lighter and with a faster refresh rate than the previous version. The usual format of two large light-amplification-tubes had been replaced by four smaller ones, giving a much wider field of vision and better spatial awareness.

The Mobility Troop men all agreed that the unit performed significantly better than the older type, which they had used extensively for riding off-road motorcycles in the dark. The Jackdaws were also fitted with twin infrared illuminators on the handlebars, each unit about the size of a soft drink can. They emitted a wide-angle beam that was invisible to the naked eye but shone like headlights when viewed through the night-vision goggles.

The trainees had come a long way in terms of their ability, and throughout the process McCowan had steadily gained confidence in the vehicle as an insertion method. This was now the final exercise – a series of high-speed manoeuvres down the pitch-dark hillside, devised to test the system in simulated mission conditions. Split into rotating teams, each participant had a turn in one of four roles: Escape, Chase, Follow-up and Objective; while McCowan spectated from his ringside seat, airborne in the helicopter.

Escape Team were led by Dylan, who would flee the summit at a given signal and head for the objective via any route he chose, his riders simply trying to follow his line. They wore Cyalume chemical light sticks on their backs, allowing the other teams to home in on their position. Chase Team then deployed from the hovering aircraft to give pursuit, and would attempt to catch up before Dylan could reach the bottom. Follow-up Team kept track of the hunt at their own pace, navigating the mountain with greater care and forethought, splitting up if necessary. Their task was to respond promptly to any accidents, locating casualties from either team and reaching them wherever they fell. They could not afford to sustain any injuries themselves.

Objective Team waited to receive the others, spread out far below in the bottom of the valley. They would regard Escape Team as friendlies and Chase Team as hostile, fulfilling no active role but assessing how easy the three groups of riders were to detect, aim at and provide covering fire for. The concluding fourth round was now about to start, with Shearman, Jonah and Carr joining Govrin on Chase-Team. Highly competitive by nature, she was absolutely determined not to finish last.

* * *

Govrin could see nothing. With her left foot on the Jackdaw's pedal, she shoved the handlebars forward and pushed out of the aircraft. The bike dropped and the ground rose up, then the thump of the landing winded her, jarring her whole body as her arms and legs buckled. She was stunned but unhurt. *Okay, I'm down. Get moving!* The image in her viewer formed into focus as she scanned around the stony mountain top. *Damn!* The other three were already under way and Dylan's lights had dropped out of sight.

She pedalled frantically to pick up speed until gravity began to take hold, pulling her downward into line behind the others. Her Jackdaw bucked down a series of ragged steps used by farmers and hikers alike. The suspension adequately absorbed the impacts for the moment, but the pace would soon become more frenetic. Dylan had turned off the path and into a steep chute, heading almost directly down the escarpment.

Shearman was fast – he was breaking away. Carr was behind him but losing ground. Jonah was within reach, but was more composed than Govrin in his bike handling. She followed at the rear. The chute was steep enough for a man to fall down, and to slow their descent the four riders swung their bikes from left to right like off-piste skiers. Desperate and frustrated, Govrin rode badly and seemed to hit every bump. She tried a reckless move to overtake Jonah, but the rough ground shook her badly off balance and nearly sent her tumbling. A better line of sight was needed if she was going to get ahead. *Keep it steady! Hang back for the moment.* She wrestled the Jackdaw back under control, applying the big disc brakes to lessen her speed, settling into a more sustainable rhythm. Despite the cool air she was sweating profusely and already breathing heavily from the exertion.

The camouflage clad riders and their dark steeds weaved through the rocks like wraiths in the night. Carr charged up on Shearman but wasn't close enough to follow the same line. The craggy surface shook him like a ragdoll, then, *pop!* Carr's front wheel stopped dead, flipping him clean over the handlebars to bounce down the grassy slope below. Whatever he had hit, he was out of the running for the moment. He would need to scramble back up the hill to his Jackdaw to continue. Govrin wasn't sorry. *One man down.*

Carr waved to indicate that he was okay as Jonah whipped past – they had orders not to stop anyway. The three chase riders were now separated by sixty metres. The gradient was easing. Shearman rode like a man possessed, gunning for Escape Team. He zeroed-in on a vague foot-worn track and exploited its relative smoothness to accumulate speed. Govrin followed Jonah with the bit between her teeth. She saw Shearman make a tight left turn ahead as the track switched direction onto the opposite traverse. She saw her moment.

Jonah was headed fast in the direction of the hairpin. Shearman was coming the other way, almost directly below her. She took a chance. She steered from the path and down a sickeningly steep fall-line that cut off the corner. For a moment, she panicked, unable to control her acceleration as her rear wheel locked up and skidded. She wobbled frantically to keep balance, sliding her inside foot on the ground as she neared the point she must turn. The bike slewed haphazardly onto the lower track. The manoeuvre wasn't graceful, but it had worked. She cranked her pedals a few times to regain momentum and fell into line behind Shearman. Now she was ahead of Jonah.

Govrin tailed Shearman as closely as she could, hoping to conserve the last of her energy. His bike hurtled along the path just ahead of her. The air rushed through her helmet with a roar, depriving her senses. Her lungs screamed for oxygen and her thighs burned. She was losing her grip on the handlebars, her hands and forearms now completely numb. The constant shaking of the NVG unit was straining the muscles of her neck. She would not be able to hold on much longer.

Shearman's furious pace had brought them close behind their quarry, and there was still enough distance before the objective. They were going to catch them. Nobody had caught Dylan yet. Shearman could taste the kill and re-committed himself, abandoning his brakes and carrying more and more speed into every corner. Govrin *had* to keep up. They were too close to fail.

She watched Dylan take a glance backwards over his shoulder, his team in a tight line on his tail, then he effortlessly increased speed and began to pull away. She sensed Shearman's desperation as he could find nothing more to give. He ran wide on a turn, careering into the rougher ground and almost hitting a hefty rock. Immediately behind him, she followed the same line. Dylan cut off the footpath toward the objective, with only a few hundred metres remaining. Within seconds, Shearman and Govrin were lost amongst scattered boulders and were forced to slow down. She looked back to see a single set of headlamps; Jonah was still a fair way behind. Her body cried with pain and she could no longer feel her brake levers. She was completely spent. After a few more moments of agony they reached the destination. The exercise had lasted just nine minutes.

'Bad luck – you were close.' Corporal Haynes was first of the Objective Team to console them, speaking in his usual flat monotone. 'Bet you thought you had them.'

'Sorry, Chase Team. Nice try,' Dylan shouted over.

Govrin sighed to herself. *You never had a chance. What were you thinking?* She patted Shearman on the back sympathetically. He looked devastated.

The Puma lowered in briefly to drop off McCowan before scooting back up the hill in the direction they had come. He waited for the noise of the helicopter to subside a bit before he shouted to the group.

'Listen in, please. That is *End Ex*. Great job everyone; that was fucking superb. We'll pack it up here and get everything onto the trucks. I want all this kit checked off and accounted for before we leave. You can get your heads down when we get back and we'll do the full debrief tomorrow. Again, well done, that was a solid performance throughout.'

'Where's Carr?' Jonah called out. 'He came off. We left him behind.'

'The Puma's gone back up to get him. Bent his thumb back in the fall. Might have pulled a ligament but he's fine. O'Neil's with him; everyone else is here.'

Shearman turned and spoke quietly to Govrin.

'Looks like you've changed your tune about this assignment as much as Ken has.'

'Sorry, please explain.'

'You've had a big old smile right across your face ever since we got down.'

* * *

After the morning run, they congregated in the briefing room along with Pearson-Roberts, Major Nolan and the troop captains. Short but optimistic speeches were made by the commissioned officers. Purportedly, from a mechanical perspective, the Jackdaws had stood up well to the night of solid abuse and had therefore proven themselves as a concept. Some video footage was played without a great deal being clear. Then McCowan gave the final analysis, evaluating the execution of the given tasks.

The pursuit had only been a small part of the overall exercise – in their operational use, the Jackdaws were intended to be ridden safely and stealthily. The main objective was to demonstrate the effective navigation of the terrain, especially for the Follow-up Team who didn't need to rush. The expected standards had been met and surpassed. McCowan was particularly impressed with the helicopter disembarkations, which were all carried out swiftly and without mishap. After summing up, he handed over to Dylan for his comments on the teams' performance.

'Okay, well you all did alright but you've still got a long way to go, I'm afraid.'

There were a couple of groans and McCowan looked disappointed, but for once didn't vent his feelings verbally.

'Sorry,' Dylan continued. 'But I wasn't actually going *that* fast. I had to make sure my own team kept up without crashing. I just took it steady on all four runs. You all do okay when you're following someone, but then mess up when you try to find your own route. It's no good riding along staring at your front wheel; you need to look further ahead and chose the right line in advance. None of you are doing that – that's why I never get caught.'

The room was silent, the team now focussed on Dylan's words without exception.

'I'm told that next week you're taking these things out to South America or somewhere – the terrain over there will be something else altogether. I've been to the Alps and they make the hills we've been using look like molehills. We haven't trained on snow, we've barely ridden in the wet, and we've only spent a few days in the woods. You need to learn to read the ground better or you'll be in a world of trouble. I won't be around to help you anymore.'

A few heads hung down as McCowan took back over.

'You all heard Dylan. You've made a good start but now you need to redouble your efforts. Put in the necessary practice and get yourselves up to speed. We've done everything we can here, so now it's up to you. Dismiss.'

As the detail got up to make their way out of the room, McCowan pulled Dylan aside to speak to him privately.

'Dylan, I'm correct in saying that your contract was for four weeks, right?'

'Er, yeah,' answered Dylan nervously.

'And you've been here for three weeks?'

'Uh huh.' He winced, anticipating that McCowan would inform him of a reduction in pay.

'Good. Then you can go with them and set up a local practice routine.'

Dylan stammered, his mind unable to process the unexpected suggestion.

'But...you'd have to pay for my flight.'

'Well of course we will, lad. We'll pay for everything.'

McCowan shouted to regain the ears of the room.

'Could I have everyone's attention again for a moment, please? Dylan has just volunteered to accompany the team to continue the training on location. He'll be joining you on the trip.'

A loud cheer voiced their approval.

Once the proceedings were done, Govrin sought a private audience with McCowan. She wanted to know what was in store for her next. In all likelihood, she had been put on the Jackdaw programme as a way to keep her occupied, but she had been excluded from all planning relating to the forthcoming operation. Bryce's injury had left the team short by one rider, giving her a place in the final exercise. Now, the rest of the unit were headed overseas for further training. She wanted to go with them, but it would take a small miracle to square the possibility with McCowan.

'Sir, I just wanted you to know that my superiors at Sayeret Matkal have no objection to my travelling internationally in the continuation of this training, if that's an option at all.'

McCowan looked solemn.

'It would be great to have you along, Elana – we're a man down and you've completed the course admirably – but it's not the training over there that I'm worried about, if you catch my drift.'

'In that case, may I quote my commanding officer with this statement: "Sayeret Matkal is wholly committed to the prevention of terrorism and organised crime, both domestic and foreign in nature. It is our permanent and unwritten objective to bring the perpetrators of such acts to justice, wherever the opportunity may present itself. In keeping with this objective, while our operator is in your care you may employ her as your own," sir.'

McCowan narrowed his eyes in contemplation. Her pitch was unexpected, and undoubtedly had been planned and rehearsed. He pondered over the motivation behind it, less on the part of Govrin herself than of her superiors.

'Then it sounds like I need to give your boss a call.'

Chapter Thirteen

Monday, 25 July
Lima

It could have been a tense situation. Sergeant Calvin Shearman led the first patrol to make landfall in Peru, having touched down at Jorge Chávez International Airport prior to their connection to Cusco AVA. It was critical that their arrival went unnoticed for Operation CATHODE to proceed. Each of the four soldiers pushed a heavy, wheeled flight case containing a dismantled Jackdaw towards the customs control point. They had no authorisation for military activity in Peru and they were posing as civilians. If their real intentions were discovered they would certainly be detained and possibly arrested. However, Shearman remained unfazed, focussed, level-headed; he wasn't prone to bouts of nervousness. His senses were heightened by the adrenaline of the moment but his face showed no outward sign of concern. He unhurriedly approached the uniformed officers.

The ruse to smuggle in the raid gear was a simple one. The Jackdaws had been covered in brightly coloured decals of the type used for signwriting vehicles. The matt black and grey disruptive-pattern frames were now obscured by lurid stripes and logos that would be peeled off later at their destination. A peek in the top of the cases would reveal what looked like typical extreme-sports equipment. If asked, Shearman's unit would claim to be recreational mountain bikers travelling for an adventure holiday. They could even provide the name and phone number of a bogus travel agent, with a receptionist on hand to take the call. Their cover story would be authenticated by the expected luggage for such sporting enthusiasts.

As British subjects they required no visas for tourism in Peru. They had already cleared passport control, collected their luggage and filled in the obligatory forms. Now they just had to wheel their flight cases through the checkpoint and into arrivals. The problem was that not all of their materiel could be so easily disguised. Each man held items that had potential to become troublesome if discovered.

The ballistic helmets and body armour were packed in around the Jackdaws. They were also adorned with deceptive vinyl transfers, but anyone familiar with police or military equipment would recognise them easily enough if they were removed from the flight cases. Camouflage overalls were rolled up with other clothes and secreted deeply into the civilian hiking rucksacks they carried. The infrared illuminators were indistinguishable at a glance from normal bicycle lights, except they would not appear to function if a curious customs official attempted to switch one on. The risk that these items would be discovered was considered to be acceptably low.

The night-vision goggles, however, had proven impossible to conceal sufficiently. The newly acquired devices were necessary for the training and had been retained by the assault team up to this point. Stowed in binocular cases and buried in the rucksacks, they would be immediately identifiable if the cases were opened. Security at London Heathrow had consented in advance to let the team through unhindered, provided they carried nothing that went 'bang', which at least removed the risk of the electronic gear being detected on departure. Once through customs, Shearman's party would need to repeat the baggage check-in process for their connecting flight. There would be no grounds for suspicion, but the briefest of inspections would soon arouse some.

'*Buenos días.*' Shearman's Spanish was clumsy and the sober-faced customs officer stared at him briefly.

'*Vacaciones*?'

'*Si, Si,*' Shearman responded with a smile and an enthusiastic nod. The officer quickly waved him onwards.

On the other side, Shearman held his breath while the others followed. He didn't look around. One by one, Match, Morris and finally Riley appeared casually beside him – his patrol was through without a hitch. Each group of four had flown via a separate route, and Shearman hoped that the other men would have a similarly stress-free experience. He checked the overhead signs for domestic departures and pushed his flight case onwards.

* * *

116

At Cusco AVA, Shearman's instructions were to proceed to the standing area for light aircraft and helicopters that adjoined the small terminal building and its taxiway. They would encounter more police on the way but having passed all security controls they were unlikely to be approached. The air was thin, and the extra effort required to haul their luggage soon became apparent. At the eastern end of the concourse, they shunted their cases through a set of double doors leading back out onto the concrete apron. They didn't need to look far to find their transport; the black and turquoise Eurocopter awaited nearby. Its pilot, Derrick Carver, identified them promptly by their distinctive luggage and waved them over.

Even dismantled, the Jackdaw was large for a bicycle. The four rectangular cases would be a difficult fit. As Carver flew solo, one man could sit to his right in the adjacent seat. Behind them, facing backwards, was a row of three seats for the other men. Two of the cases were slid in upright, in front of the rear passenger's knees. The other two were put in through the rear clamshell doors and stacked flat. The other baggage was squeezed around the passengers wherever it could fit. There wasn't much room left in the cabin but it would suffice for the journey. Shearman took the front seat as the Eurocopter began to spin up its twin turboshaft engines. Carver would need maximum power to get the heavy payload airborne at this altitude.

* * *

Their deliverance at Outpost was initially a disappointing event. They were dropped on the side of a remote mountain with no survival equipment, limited water, and a collection of cumbersome luggage. The vegetation was sparse enough to move around the landing site, but the hillside below them stretched down into a vast and seemingly impenetrable forest. They were 3000m above sea level, and although the temperature was mild it would drop sharply below freezing overnight. They had been assured that events would run to a precise timetable and that a supply drop would soon follow, but this was of little comfort as they watched the EC135 depart to the southeast. Shearman could only hope that Daniels was in control of things at his end. For the moment, they were stranded and helpless.

He was faced with a simple decision: they could either stay in the open and leave the vivid decals on the bikes, maintaining the impression of being sportsmen; or they could hide up, at the risk of being mistaken for cartel militia if they were spotted. He chose the latter, preferring to remain invisible. No one was likely to be on foot in the vicinity but it was possible that a plane could fly over. He instructed the others to move under the cover of the nearby trees, get into camo-gear and start putting the Jackdaws together – with the vinyl wraps removed.

Waiting. There was always the waiting. Often more draining than activity as the mind attempted to needlessly analyse every feasible eventuality. Shearman sat entirely motionless, staring up the hillside at the equally static little creature that stared back at him. A local rodent, grey, fat and fluffy; like a cross between a squirrel and a rabbit. Neither had shifted their gaze for a while and Shearman had begun to view the contest as an omen of the mission to come. A tap on his shoulder made his head twitch around and he cursed quietly. Riley had come with the suggestion that he should take a recce down the hillside with Morris. Shearman agreed but told him to keep it to an hour, maximum. When he looked forward again, the viscacha had disappeared. He wondered how they might catch the little creature if they started getting hungry.

They all heard the dull slap of rotor blades approaching from the distance. They were hidden from sight and wearing their camouflage fatigues but the helicopter seemed aware of their location. The dark-green Mi-17 swung right over their landing point, revealing the lettering EJERCITO DEL PERU stencilled in white letters along the length of its flank. Heat haze shimmered behind the engine exhausts. The barrel of a mounted machine-gun protruded from the open side door. The aircraft lowered into their landing zone until its big wheels bounced on the ground, the hidden patrol watching intently as several soldiers dismounted and took defensive positions facing outwards. Shearman recognised the SAR-21 assault rifle and the M249 squad-automatic-weapon, both of which he knew to be carried by 4SF – their hosts.

Satisfied that this was the expected supply drop, he took a deep breath and walked out of the security of the brush with his hands held high in the air. A man spotted him immediately and swung his rifle onto target. It was impossible to hear but he could imagine the shouted warning. He made no attempt to approach the aircraft for fear of being gunned down. Behind the soldier, the last man out of the helicopter was wearing civilian clothes. Shearman was relieved to recognise Tom Daniels. One of the men hurriedly grabbed Daniels by the shoulder and pointed in Shearman's direction. Daniels responded with a vigorous nod and then ran over, bent double to avoid the brunt of the rotor wash. He took Shearman's hand and gave it a solid shake.

'Glad you could make it, Calvin. How do you like your hotel?'

'I'll book somewhere else next year,' Shearman quipped. 'I'm glad that you've showed up.'

'I can move around freely at the moment so I came along for the introduction – in case the chopper made you nervous.'

'It definitely did that. You've bought some gear for us?'

'Come take a look.'

Daniels waited to greet the other three SAS men before leading the way to the waiting Mil. The pilot kept the engine throttles open and the rotors spinning, ready to lift-off rapidly with only a pull on the collective-pitch-control lever, her head turning continually, scanning, alert for danger. It was impossible to communicate any further over the screaming roar of the turbines. The SAS men joined the Víboras in ferrying the provisions down under the cover of the nearby trees at a run. Daniels trotted alongside Shearman until they could examine the shipment properly.

'You've got tents, water, rations, camo-net, everything you need. There's an encrypted radio you can use to contact General Torres – instructions are taped to it – but don't switch it on unless there's an emergency. The six metal crates are the assault gear. You'll need to get them hidden up. We've already had a strong warning about carrying weapons.'

Shearman simply nodded.

'Carver will be dropping the next patrol later today, then two more runs tomorrow,' Daniels informed the sergeant.

Shearman pulled a folded sheet of paper from a pocket.

'McCowan's sending Dylan out here. I've got his flight details for you.'

'Dylan! *Why?* Does he want to get him killed?' Daniels gaze bounced between the sheet and Shearman's face.

'To continue the training. We're not good enough yet, apparently. McCowan said he'd be safe here for a few days.'

Daniels looked around then pointed to the west.

'There are major cartel operations just over there. The air force patrols this area and won't consider us friendly. How safe does that feel to you?'

Shearman looked sceptical, but there was little he could do about it.

The four SAS men waved their thanks as the utility helicopter departed with Daniels back aboard, then they set about the task of caching their haul. Shearman was at last content with the situation. Now they had everything they needed to survive, including the weapons to defend themselves if necessary.

* * *

By the time the Eurocopter returned, a makeshift camp had been set up under the dense foliage of a coniferous thicket. Eight two-man tents were erected, and a camo-net was suspended over a central area. There would be no fire built at Outpost, but under the net they felt it safe enough to use a small burner for tea and heated up ration meals. The raid equipment had been hidden a short distance away. Shearman's men ran over to help unload the next group's heavy Jackdaws, dialogue being suspended until the new arrivals were brought to the camp. Carver was kept waiting for the minimum possible time and within just a few minutes he was airborne again. As the drone of rotor blades disappeared into the distance, dusk was beginning to fall.

With the newcomers came the buzz of adrenaline, typical of active operations. The helicopter flight had been exhilarating; the views incredible. Arrival at the remote mountain camp had done nothing to quell their excitement. Unlike Shearman's group, they were spared the tension of waiting unarmed in potentially hostile territory. Squadron mates made the most of the opportunity to catch up, recounting the details of their journeys and sharing opinions on the training, but talk about the mission itself was avoided. Half the assault team were still absent and such conversations would inevitably need to be repeated. There would be a thorough planning session at a later point. Shearman sat with a mug of tea, quiet and pensive, evaluating the assault team choices privately in his own mind. O'Neil, Wade, Madan and Taz – these were the first group from Mountain Troop. As with the Mobility men, each had been chosen for the specialist skills they would contribute to the mission.

Sergeant O'Neil was the son of a Lancashire livestock farmer, and a man who had grown up accustomed to working long, hard days in adverse conditions. He was intelligent and mentally tough – one of very few people to make it through the notorious SAS selection process without being seen to struggle. It was not that he was fitter than the other candidates; his natural disposition simply didn't allow him to consider giving up. He was a specialist medic, extensively trained and experienced in the field. All of the SAS men had attended a basic medical course, and at least one within each patrol would be further qualified; but O'Neil was most so, and would direct the others in the event of a casualty.

He was a serious man, sobered by memories of the horrific injuries he had witnessed and deaths he'd been unable to prevent. A combat veteran of several conflicts, he was three years older than Shearman at thirty-eight. Each of the two sergeants held authority for the eight-man section from their own troop, and between them they would orchestrate the movements of the four patrols. Shearman was decisive and confident in command, but would happily share the load with a man of O'Neil's calibre.

Delta Four – the patrol responsible for conducting the vehicle ambush at BLUE-1 – would be led by Corporal Renford Wade, who had attended an advanced demolitions course that would stand him in good stead for the task, as well as the destruction of the airstrip gun emplacement. Wade was the smallest man on the team, short in height and wiry. The black Londoner had a lively, upbeat manner and was a quick worker whose eagerness for activity sometimes bordered on impatience. Wade maintained the highest possible level of physical fitness, and regularly tested his ability as a marathon runner – a discipline in which he was fast and consistent. Delta Four needed to penetrate the furthest into the enemy camp to reach their designated target, and once there would require the longest interval to set and bury their charges in the dirt of the track. It was critical that they remained unnoticed throughout this infiltration. Wade's compulsive determination would no doubt be instrumental in getting Delta Four to their objective in the shortest possible time.

Madan was a Nepalese national who had joined the SAS from his parent regiment, the Royal Gurkha Rifles, who are an elite force in their own right. Every year, the Brigade of Gurkhas selects only the foremost candidates from a large number of applicants, then puts them through an extensive three years of basic training. As a result, every soldier within the unit is highly committed and capable as a minimum standard. Madan had served in Kosovo and East Timor prior to his transfer to the SAS, and had been promoted to lance corporal during his service since. He was one of D Squadron's specialist linguists, able to communicate in several Asian languages, but had been chosen for Operation CATHODE because his dependability and professionalism were ideal qualities for an unsupported mission.

Tarek, or Taz, was the last of the new arrivals: a tall and strongly built man with a kind smile and courteous manner. His Egyptian born father had been awarded UK citizenship during a long career in the Arabic section at GCHQ – the British government's communications analysis centre – where he decrypted and translated intercepted communications from the Egyptian embassy. Here he had met Tarek's mother, and the couple were duly married and later blessed with a child. Tarek had grown up fervently proud of his British nationality and his parent's contribution to state security. As a youth, his intention had been to pursue a similar vocation. Enlisting in the Intelligence Corps, he had worked diligently and tirelessly, completing every task to the best of his ability – efforts that would ultimately steer him to a place within the SAS.

He felt little sentiment towards Egypt, a country he had never even visited. His unusual name and command of Arabic were the only significant links to his lineage. But his fluent tongue and appearance had proven advantageous on Middle Eastern deployments, allowing him to move openly without attracting attention, even in crowded locales. The newly badged trooper had operated covertly for long periods in Iraq, sometimes crossing borders to countries where the Army's activities were less well publicised. It was the skills he had honed during this clandestine role that merited his place on the current mission. Taz was chosen for his prowess with a sniper rifle.

Shearman's travel companions had also been selected for their specific skill sets, in addition to their previous experience with off-road motorcycles. Match's portfolio included a series of modules on secure communications. It was a standard format within the SAS to have one such man assigned to every four-man patrol, along with a medic, a linguist and a demolitions expert. Match was keen and capable; he had already unpacked the Peruvian radio unit, familiarising himself ready for when the need arose. Shearman had seen action with the twenty-nine-year-old trooper and knew him well as a friend. He would be solid under fire.

As one of the newer members of D Squadron, Riley had been included to increase his range of experience. Short and stocky with shaggy auburn hair and a full beard, he was renowned for his fearlessness – a man who simply lacked the necessary imagination to perceive himself to be in any kind of danger. In his service to date, he had shown himself to be focussed, pragmatic and appropriately aggressive. Shearman considered Riley capable of fulfilling a successful military career, and suspected that he wasn't the type to find satisfaction in civilian life. He was assigned to Delta One as the second designated marksman.

Finally, of the eight team members currently at Outpost, Welshman Iain Morris was the only man yet to have been deployed in action. A younger member of the unit, he had been proficient during training and had qualified as a forward air controller – the specialist responsible for directing airstrikes around a busy battlefield. As no air support would be available during the forthcoming mission, this ability would not be called upon; but it is the policy of the SAS to give their troopers combat experience as quickly as possible. By positioning Morris within a team of seasoned operators, his learning process would be greatly accelerated. He would carry munitions for the vehicle ambush under Wade's command, and therefore was highly likely to run into some close-range contact.

* * *

Two lookouts were stationed on watch throughout the night, rotating on two hour shifts so that everyone got a few hours' sleep. It was eerily quiet during those dark hours, and only the occasional shuffling of nocturnal creatures alerted their attention. At 06:00 the team rose, and soon the first rays of sunlight reached into the valley below them. They boiled water for tea and made breakfast from ration packets, then sought ways to keep themselves busy for the few hours until Carver was expected. If things were running to schedule, the next group of four would be inbound from Bogota, Colombia, and due to land in Cusco shortly.

The first priority for O'Neil's men was to assemble their Jackdaws. They gladly accepted some assistance from the Mobility members, who were mechanically proficient and had just recently completed the task themselves. To fit inside the flight cases, the bikes were packed with their wheels, handlebars and cranks removed. Reassembling them wasn't complicated, but each bolt required tightening to a precise torque setting with a calibrated wrench, and the drive-belt had to be correctly tensioned to operate smoothly.

Next, a safe running loop was marked, snaking down the hill and back without being overly exposed to sight from the air. The assault team would be stationed at Outpost for some time and needed to keep up their fitness routine. They took turns, running in pairs, completing several laps of the loop at pace.

By 09:00 they had begun a stocktake of all the equipment delivered by the EP helicopter, carefully checking each item as they went. Surprise malfunctions or breakages could prove disastrous if they occurred in action, especially during the insertion phase when silence was essential. It was a further hour and a quarter before the Eurocopter touched down and unloaded its next consignment of passengers, two of whom were unexpected.

The first was Elana Govrin, who it seemed had been given permission to participate in the raid in an unprecedented act of international cooperation. She would replace the injured Bryce as a spotter for one of the Delta One snipers. Shearman contemplated this supervention for a moment, suspecting there was purpose behind her presence. Her own unit, Sayeret Matkal, used a similar format to the SAS. On her return, she would be able to provide an in-depth analysis of the methods and tactics used in the covert assault. Her inclusion had likely been sanctioned in order to gain operational intelligence. What Shearman wasn't so sure of, was how she would fit into their carefully planned team structure.

The other surprise was McCowan himself, who had stepped in after the final training accident to make up the team numbers. Carr's thumb injury had turned out to be worse than expected, rendering him incapable of riding the bike. Shearman had concerns about this switch. McCowan had participated in some of the basic Jackdaw lessons – mostly to understand what was being asked of the troops – but was nowhere near as competent as the rest of the detail. He said there was plenty of time to practice before the raid, especially seeing as Dylan was now en route to resume the tuition. In truth, Shearman knew that the SSM was just capitalising on an opportunity to take an active role in the assault. McCowan was a man who led from the front. And in this case, it seemed that he simply couldn't bear to miss out on the action.

Accompanying Govrin and McCowan were the two remaining Mobility Troop men: Hugo Haynes and Jonah. Shearman found Haynes to be an odd character. Often quiet and always softly spoken, Haynes rarely displayed any discernible emotion. He was slightly plump and below average in height. Wispy grey hair surrounded a bald patch that dominated the entire upper part of his head, and his skin was so pasty white that people might think he had never been outside. Round, metal-framed glasses completed an appearance more akin to an eccentric scientist than a special-forces soldier. But his military accomplishments were both numerous and enviable.

He had previously held the rank of sergeant with his parent unit, the Royal Engineers, but as with all non-commissioned officers he was relegated to trooper on joining the SAS. The ranking procedure is then very slow within the regiment; members must be willing to strive without expectation of reward. Haynes was not concerned with the matter of seniority. He had passively made his way back to corporal over a long period served. Regarded as the squadron's foremost expert in technical, high-risk demolitions, it was his responsibility to guarantee destruction of the all-important primary target – the mobile missile launcher – without killing his own patrol in the process.

Jonah was the youngest man on the assault team and had served just one year since passing selection. A single deployment in Northern Ireland in an intelligence gathering role was his only previous operational experience. Jonah was yet to see combat, but was quick-witted and fast on his feet. Shearman was confident he would perform well once the shooting started. The Mancunian was also the best qualified linguist for the mission, being the only fluent Spanish speaker; not that there was much scope in the plan for conversing with the enemy.

* * *

Carver had not arrived and was at least an hour overdue. This wasn't especially remarkable: the team at Outpost had no way of even knowing whether the airline flight had departed on time. Shearman, McCowan and O'Neil were in a state of unease, nonetheless. When the Eurocopter did finally reappear, shortly before sundown, their relief was immediately apparent. Shearman first realised something was wrong when Daniels got out of the front passenger door, which didn't leave room for the other four men.

'We've got problems,' Daniels shouted over the roar of the aircraft.

'What's going on?' McCowan demanded.

Daniels turned to Carver and ran his finger across his throat, instructing him to kill the engines.

'I'll fill you in when this thing winds down. We need to get her secured and under cover.'

Shearman turned around and waved towards the others. Once he had their attention, he pointed at the helicopter then drew an upside-down U shape with his hands. Jonah and Taz were soon lugging over a long roll of camo-net.

Daniels opened the rear cabin door, allowing Dylan to get out, then extracted some bags of gear to be taken over to the camp. The young civilian cast his eyes around the bleak, gloomy mountainside that would be his home for the immediate future, his reaction lacking the enthusiasm of the military personnel. Dark smudges beneath his eyes indicated that he was feeling the effects of jetlag. The temperature was dropping rapidly and he wrapped his arms tightly around his torso to fend off the chill. He kicked at stones on the ground, wearing an expression of abject dismay, and waited for someone to tell him what to do. Sulking in silence, he was eventually escorted under the cover of the makeshift camp with his bags carried for him.

Ten minutes later, the aircraft was camouflaged, with the rotor blades tied down to prevent them turning in the wind. Two men were posted on sentry duty while everyone else gathered expectantly around the seating area, where the burner was boiling water for tea. McCowan and Riley smoked cigarettes. Daniels enlightened them.

'Dawson's patrol got rumbled at customs. We don't know how it happened. Derrick contacted me when they didn't materialise after the flight landed. I was on my way to the airport at the time, to collect Dylan and take him to a hotel until we could bring him up here. Then I got a call from Torres confirming that they'd been held and questioned.'

'Bollocks!' McCowan vented his frustration, then blew a plume of smoke into the air. 'How soon can we get them released?'

'Torres has already squared it. They're being collected and taken to the Mountain Brigade training camp. Once they realised they wouldn't be able to talk their way out of it, they said they were part of the TDU. Trouble is, the shit has now hit the fan with Joint Command. Customs rang them to verify our permissions. So now they're all under house arrest – Dawson's lot and the TDU team. Ballesta, the Head of the Joint Command, is demanding to know why they were posing as civilians.'

'What happened to the Jackdaws?' Shearman asked.

'It seems that nobody has realised their significance. Hopefully, Joint Command will assume they were just stage dressing. Customs identified enough of the other kit to give the game away, though. It will all be returned – or rather delivered to the quartermaster at War Mountain – but we can't hide the fact that our boys were coming in for a parallel operation. They may even go back through the CCTV footage and identify the rest of you. Then they'll be on to our helicopter.'

'I didn't file any flight plans, obviously,' Carver offered. 'With the route here through the mountains, we can't have been logged on radar. This position is safe.'

'That's one bit of good news,' McCowan said. 'But you can't go back to Cusco now – you'd be nabbed in no time. You're stuck here with us, mate.'

'Oh, that's great,' Carver replied sarcastically.

'There's no way Dawson's patrol will be allowed anywhere other than on a flight back home,' Daniels resumed. 'We can't bring any more men up here for the moment, and even if we could, we only have twelve Jackdaws. So you guys need to weigh up whether the operation is still possible with the team you have here.'

'Can we contact anyone at *'War Mountain'* to find out what's happening there?' McCowan mouthed the epithet with theatrical disdain, even though the use of such nicknames is commonplace within the military. 'I mean, it would be handy to know that our boys aren't being lined up in front of a firing squad while we're here having a fucking camping holiday. I take it that using the radio is out of the question.'

'For us, yes; but Torres said to stand by to receive every hour, on the hour. He'll get a message out when he can. Comms instructions were taped to the radio, I believe.'

'Yeah, I've been through them,' Match chipped in. 'I'll take care of it.'

'And what the hell is wrong with this brew?' McCowan spewed a mouthful of tea onto the ground.

'It's the altitude, Ken. The water boils before its warm enough to bath in,' Wade informed him.

'Well that's just bloody marvellous.'

Shearman mentally ran over the ramifications of this new turn of events. Corporal Dawson – the Delta One patrol leader – and Troopers Young, Barrington, and Lovell would not participate. Each man had been tasked with a specific role to fulfil during the raid. With just twelve remaining soldiers with which to prosecute the mission, their carefully laid plans would be stretched to the point of breaking. Bad weather was forecast, and now they were sailing close to the rocks.

Chapter Fourteen

Tuesday, 26 July
Lima

The episode had begun earlier that afternoon with a phone call forwarded by one of the Joint Command receptionists – an enquiry from AVA Customs relating to a British Army training operation. The call was only brief and Luis Oneto had already mentally recounted its content many times over. He sat in his plush leather chair, feet resting on the dark-hardwood desk, deep in thought. The caller had sounded expeditious and authoritative, while still respectful of Oneto's office. He dwelled upon the exact wording of the conversation as if searching for an elusive clue.

'Captain Scorza at AVA. We have four British men detained here, found to be carrying some unusual items – military equipment. They claim their army is working with Mountain Brigade under General Torres. Is this something you're aware of?'

'There's a British party working with Torres currently, but we weren't expecting any more arrivals. When you say you found equipment, do you mean weapons?'

'No weapons, but my men found a night-vision device on a routine search, concealed within a binocular case. This was a little suspicious as the men carried sporting gear and are dressed in civilian attire. They made no attempt to declare military status initially. On further inspection we found that each of them carried the same item, as well as combat overalls.'

'What kind of sporting gear?'

'Off-road bicycles, helmets, that sort of thing. Looked pretty normal until we found the other stuff.'

'Did they give you an explanation?'

'They said they're not on active duty yet, but are here to relieve a group of men returning home shortly. They claim the bicycles are for recreational use in their free time. Allegedly, they always carry their own night-vision units for reasons of accountability and hadn't thought it a problem.'

'The British issue night-vision to men who aren't on duty? I don't buy that – these things are expensive.'

'No, we didn't like it either, sir.'

'Is Torres aware?'

'We've attempted to contact him but are still waiting for a reply. What do you want us to do with them?'

'Hold them there until you hear from Torres. Only release them into his custody. They're his problem; he can deal with them. I'll make some calls at this end to find out what they are playing at. Thank you, Captain.'

'Understood. Goodbye.'

Oneto had considered this development for nearly an hour before taking any further action. President Mendez himself had authorised Torres requisition of the British services, much to the consternation of congress and the defence minister, but the surreptitious arrival of additional soldiers seemed to indicate something else altogether. His mind gravitated towards the most obvious possibility. *Covert action, maybe…against one of the cartels?* He wanted to find out for certain, and ideally before anyone else became involved.

Ballesta was in the adjacent office and had expressed a desire not to be disturbed. There was sufficient cause to ignore this request. Oneto rapped loudly until he was commanded to enter. He sat without invitation and loosely explained the details of the phone call, mindful to keep his inflection neutral, as if simply reporting a routine matter. Having no military rank, Oneto's options would be severely limited without Ballesta's involvement, but he still didn't wish to arouse any more interest than was absolutely necessary. Auspiciously, the admiral seemed neither surprised nor especially concerned.

'It's more or less as I expected. These 'instructors' have intended from the outset to attack the Del Bosque cartel under the guise of conducting an exercise. By confining them to the Mountain Brigade training area, I've disrupted their plan. So now, to carry out this unsanctioned operation, they are attempting to sneak in other men.'

Oneto disliked Ballesta, finding him arrogant and egotistical.

'Then Torres must be involved. What's his motive?'

'Plain revenge. He's bitter about that botched raid where he lost the helicopter. He thinks he can make amends with a strike against Del Bosque, and wants the SAS to conduct it for him so he doesn't get more of his own men killed. The very concept is ridiculous – cowardly, even. What kind of general rents a foreign army to do their dirty work? If he can't maintain control of his region, then he should be replaced.'

Ballesta sounded relaxed but spoke with absolute confidence, as if he'd known all along that these events would transpire. Oneto, however, remained unconvinced. Torres had an exceptional service record and a string of successful operations in the VRAEM under his belt.

'Then we'll be putting a stop to this, Admiral?'

'I have a solution in mind already. You say the detained men carried no weapons – then they plan to use those already brought in by their team of instructors. Tomorrow, I'll go over there and personally ensure that *all* of the British equipment is locked down. It can stay that way until Torres gives me an explanation. I'll have the Beechcraft take me to Cusco in the morning. You could speak to the minister in the meantime. I'm sure he'll be delighted to hear about this charade.'

Oneto was niggled by the admiral's self-assurance but the exchange had proven useful. His understanding of the situation had been sufficiently improved for the time being. Turning the conversation to other matters, he chatted energetically for a further ten minutes, just to disguise his interest in the British. On return to his own office, he immediately pressed the button for the receptionist.

'Get me Captain Scorza at AVA back on the line, please.' He waited a few minutes for the connection to be made and for Scorza to be summoned to the phone.

'Yes?'

'Captain, it's Oneto again. Can you do something for me please?'

'What is it?'

'Can you get someone to check back through the video footage of your recent arrivals. I want to know if any other groups of men have come through already, with equipment like the ones you've detained. Also, ask the British men if anyone else has come or is coming. Let me know what they say.'

'Very well. I'm not sure if we'll find anything useful but I'll put someone on it. I'll let you know, even if it is nothing.'

'Thank you.'

Oneto cut off the call and leaned back in the chair, lifting his feet to their usual resting place. He felt that Ballesta was wrong: if a second British team had entered Peru, then it would not be difficult for them to acquire weapons. Torres could send modern, well-serviced assault rifles from any of his bases. These SAS men wouldn't be fussy about what tools they worked with. He was confident of that.

* * *

He was in no rush to attempt the journey home, despite the late hour. The Joint Command building was located on Jirón Manuel Corpancho, Santa Beatriz district, and the traffic would already be heaving. Instead, he was preoccupied with the events of the afternoon. There was no reliable way to determine their significance and he couldn't rule out the possibility of a misunderstanding. He doubted that Torres would reveal his agenda to Ballesta, but the old fool's appearance in Cusco might at least buy some more time. It was nearly 6:30pm when the return call came.

'Put him through,' he answered quickly, swinging his feet off the desk.

'Oneto.'

'They all used the same big rectangular cases, for the bicycles,' Scorza explained. 'We found them easily on the video. Three groups of four, this morning and yesterday, all men apart from one woman. Are these people criminals?' There was urgency and excitement to the customs officers' voice.

'No, not at all,' Oneto placated. 'They have legitimate business here but there's been a serious breach of protocol that we'll need to address. Could you do one more thing for me and find out how the others left the airport.'

'We already have. A helicopter was waiting to collect them in each case, registered to a local charter firm based here in Cusco. An American named Derrick Carver is the pilot and owner. Air traffic control has no destination given on the first three occasions, other than an initial northerly heading. The helicopter was also here this afternoon. After we detained the four men, it first returned to a local aerodrome then left the city shortly after, again heading north.'

'Captain, you have been a great help. I cannot thank you enough. We will handle this now. Goodbye.'

Oneto's mind raced. The British *were* attempting a covert action. Exactly what, was still a mystery. A team of twelve had already successfully infiltrated, possibly joined by others using different means. The woman was a baffling development – women weren't normally used for combat roles. *A specialist possibly, but in what? Something to do with the cocaine? A chemist, a horticulturalist?* One thing was certain: they wouldn't charter a civilian helicopter just to fly to their hotel or one of Torres' bases. They were in hiding somewhere – in the mountains.

Scorza's efforts had narrowed down his current options. He could put in a call to the Fuerza Aérea del Perú, alert them to the presence of a group of unknown hostiles, maybe even imply a connection to the Shining Path terrorist group. Jets would be scrambled. But they wouldn't find anything, and he would be held accountable for any misinformation given. No, there was a more practical way to deal with these unwelcome British.

He made his way out of the building, nodding to the impeccably uniformed guards who flanked the ornate entrance set in the cream and red facade. His car was in one of the nearest bays and within two minutes he pulled out into the evening traffic. He drove for a few blocks, passing the national stadium, then retrieved the spare mobile phone from his glove box. He switched on the device and waited a few moments for it to load up, then dialled the only stored number. The phone rang several times and was answered.

'La Rosa.'

'It's Luis.'

'Ah, Luis, to what do I owe this pleasure?'

'There are a team of at least twelve British commandos – special forces – here in Peru to conduct an unknown covert action. Torres is involved. They were taken north from Cusco in a civilian helicopter operated by a charter pilot named Derrick Carver. We don't know where they went.'

'Derrick Carver! I use that prick!' La Rosa's angry, shouted voice was loud through the handset. 'If he's involved, I'll castrate him. I need to know where our guests are staying, as quickly as possible. Call me immediately when you learn more. I'll pay Carver a visit myself. I appreciate the call, Luis. It will not go unrewarded. And I was beginning to think you'd lost faith in our arrangement. Send my regards to your mother.'

Oneto switched off the phone and returned it to the glove box. He had a bad taste in his mouth but was sure it would wash out with a couple of beers. He would stop at the local bar for an hour or so, before returning to his comfortable town house and doting family. The traffic was thinning now. Without realising, Oneto had pushed down hard on the accelerator.

Chapter Fifteen

Wednesday, 27 July
Outpost

It was no use. He was warm enough in the sleeping bag but the ground beneath was hard and lumpy. Dawn sunrays were squeezing between the overhanging branches to penetrate the thin nylon of the tent. He would not be able to get back to sleep; it was time to face facts and get up. Dylan wasn't exactly overjoyed to be at Outpost in the first place, and then there was the constant military procedure. He'd been told to go nowhere alone and to let someone know when he needed the toilet. He'd been given a password to shout if challenged by the camp lookouts. This fuss had already become tiresome. But he did realise that he may as well make the best of the situation, seeing as he was already there and had no way of leaving. And after all, the location did have some good riding potential. He resolved to get on with the job at hand, and to try and enjoy himself while he was at it.

He crawled, blurry eyed, out of the tent to find Wade heating up a trio of foil packets in a tin of water. A few of the others were sat around under the net, spooning food from mess tins.

'How does all-day breakfast sound, Dylan? And a cuppa just coming,' Wade offered.

'Urgh, okay I s'pose. Can I have coffee?'

'You're not at the Hilton, Dylan,' McCowan commented. 'Speak to Hugo. He'll have brought some decent coffee; better than that crap in the sachets, anyway.'

Dylan was mostly silent as he ate, deep in his own thoughts. He added three sugars to his coffee and poured in whitener until it turned anaemic and tasteless. It was still too hot to drink comfortably.

'I'm going to need a few guys for a couple of hours,' he stated.

'What?' McCowan asked, more curious than incredulous.

'You want me to teach the guys how to ride this local terrain, right? What am I supposed to do, send them down the hill until they get stuck in the undergrowth? I need to mark out a trail.'

'Well, seeing as you've awarded yourself a field promotion, why don't you give the orders as well.' McCowan chuckled at his own jest.

'No problem.' He stood to gain an audience.

'Right then, listen up,' Dylan grandstanded in a deliberate parody of McCowan. 'I need six volunteers for brush-clearance operations. You won't need your weapons, but machetes and digging tools are essential – a mattock if you have one.'

'Cheeky little shit,' McCowan muttered, but did nothing to countermand the request.

Dylan's volunteers, including the restless Elana Govrin and the kukri-wielding Madan, were ready in three minutes.

The air was thin and fresh, the sky bright and clear. Raucous chattering birdsong filled the forest below. Dylan gazed down the incline assessing the terrain and felt it had promise. The slope was steep, littered with rock, and easily extended far enough for his purposes. They had enjoyed the benefit of trucks and helicopters in the Beacons, but here the heavy Jackdaws would need to be pushed back up the hill after each run.

Without doing any work at all, it would be possible for a rider to weave their way between the trees for a few hundred metres, seeking out the easiest path and avoiding tricky areas, but this would do little to advance the team's ability. The concept Dylan had in mind was more or less the opposite. He would make his way down the hill on foot, finding the most challenging natural obstacles to steer the trail into. At his direction, the volunteers would clear away any encroaching brush, then delineate the route with cut sticks.

He had repeatedly been told to teach the team to ride slowly and safely; the terrain was far too treacherous for high speeds, anyway. Instead, he would arrange the route to be as technically demanding as possible – a plan that also promised to provide maximum entertainment for himself, as his time would need to be spent performing repeated demonstrations. He wished he had his own bike – the one that McCowan destroyed – which would have skipped over the rocks with finesse, but the Jackdaw was not entirely without merit. He admitted to himself that it was probably even a superior machine when it came to riding slowly.

He led the trail over the top of a large boulder, with a fair drop and a hard landing on the other side. He noticed how the soldiers didn't bicker like his friends would have. There was no constant arguing over who did what and how it should be done. They worked together and got on with the task at hand. Some areas he left wide open with no marking – the riders would inevitably end up on a different line each run, adding to the difficulty. But when he found a steep staircase of jagged rock, he funnelled the route right into it. The feature would have made a professional racer look twice, but his volunteers didn't object.

This was another thing he noticed about the SAS team: no one, except McCowan, ever questioned his methods. If he told them they needed to ride down the trunk of a fallen tree, they would attempt to do it, even though it was clearly unnecessary. It wasn't as if the soldiers were gullible or stupid. Dylan reasoned that they must be so used to being bossed around that they no longer thought for themselves. He was glad that he hadn't made the mistake of enlisting in the army, not that it had ever been a likelihood. He couldn't find a suitable fallen tree anyhow.

As the work party made their way deeper into the forest, the ground became progressively wetter. Dylan marked the line close to the boles of the biggest tress, which would force riders to negotiate their networks of prominent roots. The roots were covered in algae that made them as slick as if they'd been greased. The lie of the slope was off camber in patches. Touch the brakes or roll too slowly and the bike's wheels would slip right out from underneath. These sections would need to be approached with conviction and momentum. There would be hard falls when things went wrong. The route would be challenging for everyone, their instructor included. He vowed that he wouldn't allow himself to crash, especially if anyone was watching – he wasn't going to give McCowan that satisfaction.

The going was becoming increasingly difficult; too much machete work was required. Their progress had slowed for little extra result. It was darker under the thicker canopy and Dylan had already spotted some alarming looking insects. Somewhere, the snakes he'd been warned about would be lurking. He announced that they would finish the trail up where they were.

The practice track fitted the bill perfectly and had not taken that long to complete. It would give the team the maximum range of new experience and keep him busy at the same time. He was undoubtedly going to overrun his original contract and would need to discuss his extra fees with Daniels or McCowan. He wasn't exactly in a strong position to negotiate, stuck miles from civilisation without even access to a phone. He began the climb back up the hill to take the first group out for a test run.

He knew that the army riders would not be egotistical about their successes. There would be no celebrations at the end of the course. They would repeat the task over and over until they were certain they could do it with reliability. Whenever they struggled, he would demonstrate, and with twelve Jackdaws available, it was unlikely that his personal riding would be interrupted by mechanical failures. He doubted that the soldiers had considered that eventuality properly. He knew there wouldn't be a bike shop for miles.

* * *

'No FAP markings, the colours are wrong – it's a cartel plane.' Madan viewed the distant passage of the Super Tucano through ruggedised binoculars from his position under a low conifer branch. The light attack aircraft was three kilometres away across the valley and had no chance of spotting them. The inhabitants of Outpost had gone to ground as a precaution. McCowan and Daniels lay either side, each with their own glasses.

'Probably the same one as earlier,' McCowan speculated. 'So are they looking for us, or is it coincidence?'

'Our op-sec has been tight. No one knows we're here except Carver, and I'm sure he wouldn't want to get himself shot at,' Daniels answered impatiently.

'He didn't expect to be staying here though, did he?' It was the second time that a potentially hostile aircraft had been spotted that morning, and tensions were beginning to rise. 'It's gone now anyway. We'll get back to work,' McCowan instructed.

'He comes back, I shoot him down,' Madan stated, leaving Daniels unsure if he was joking.

'Don't kill the pilot, Mad. We need him alive for questioning,' McCowan played along.

'Hmm, sorry. Not possible. The plane gonna catch fire.'

'Then do us all a favour and shoot him down elsewhere.'

Madan had an intense manner about him much of the time. Even when brewing tea or preparing rations, he would appear to the observer as if he were doing so under battle conditions. His fervour was never tempered by the risk of death or injury, bad weather or hard toil. In fact, the only situation guaranteed to rattle him was being told not to do something, such as when operations were cancelled, which usually precipitated a bout of heavy cursing. Despite this, he was not without humour and had a habit of cracking one-liners at inopportune moments. Cultural differences often prevented his jokes from being fully appreciated by the other men, and in some cases, Madan would erupt in laughter at something that was said in full seriousness. But his unflappable enthusiasm eased the strain in high stress situations. Every man in the squadron would happily work with Madan for that reason alone. The Nepali had a fixation with chewing cardamom seeds, which he claimed calmed his nerves, along with a list of other, somewhat optimistic, medicinal benefits. The squadron joke was that the seeds actually contained a natural amphetamine and that Madan spent his days high as a kite, or possibly even hallucinating.

Most of the assault team had spent the morning practicing their Jackdaw handling on Dylan's course, which now snaked over root and rock for more than a kilometre down the lightly wooded mountainside. They no longer jogged. The exertion of wrestling the machine over the rocks and through the tight switchbacks, then pushing it back up the hill again was more than enough exercise. Dylan himself was fully engaged with giving instruction and demonstrating techniques, the sense of purpose having lifted him from his previous state of melancholy.

Daniels thought it prudent to familiarise himself with the Jackdaw as a contingency. A rapid exit from Outpost might become the team's best option if they drew the attention of an aircraft, and the quicker the equipment could be hidden the better. He broached the subject with McCowan, who possessed an ingrained inclination to prepare for every possible eventuality. After a short discussion, he was given consent to participate in the practice sessions. There were only enough bikes for the assault team members but Daniels was told he could borrow one from whoever was posted on lookout. He stood at the top of the marked track, legs astride the hefty frame, readying himself for a trial run. He hadn't undergone any of the previous training and the technical difficulty of the descent before him was formidable. He felt relatively confident, regardless.

Unbeknown to McCowan, Dylan or any of the detail, Daniels had some history with mountain bikes.

He had previously mentioned to Dylan that he'd done some cross-country racing as a younger man. What he hadn't mentioned was the competitive level or his success. It didn't seem relevant to the Jackdaw programme and he was in the wrong company to brag. In fact, he had held the title of Combined Forces Champion as an officer cadet and had stood on the podium at several amateur events. He attributed his former achievements to a high level of physical fitness rather than innate riding skill, and doubted this would count for much on the unconventional Jackdaw. He'd never even attempted the kind of dramatic stunts that Dylan was so proficient at. However, the bikes he raced were only equipped with rudimentary front shock absorbers and no rear suspension at all. There were no disc brakes and the tyres were hard and narrow. Using the equipment available in the early 90's, charging down bumpy forest tracks through slimy mud took bravery and balance. Daniels had both in adequate supply.

The route had been marked with sticks laid flat or poked in the earth, some arranged in pairs to form gates. Branches had been cut and cleared to open the sightline down the intended path. Daniels stood up and pedalled hard to get the bike moving, glad of the opportunity to try the thing out. And what a machine it was. Bumps were soaked up effortlessly; the feedback from even the roughest ground was minimal. The big soft tyres clawed for grip at every turn. The weight of the Jackdaw was double what Daniels was used to – probably more – but the extra bulk gave stability and helped to keep the wheels on track, even when he made mistakes.

He thumped gracelessly over a drop, steadily gaining confidence as he progressed down the hill. He was far slower than the well-practiced assault team but managed to stay in control. *Bit rusty, but I'm still upright.* He approached a frighteningly steep series of drops that the lads had nicknamed 'The Staircase', where Dylan stood close by to observe. It was a tricky section, even for the others.

Daniels slowed early so that he didn't skid over the edge. Then with two metres to go, he released the brakes to maintain enough momentum for balance. He looked for the easiest line, trying to keep his limbs loose. His breathing deepened as he stared down the steep chute, his brain partially paralysed just by the sight of it. He felt the tickle of adrenaline. *Don't tense up, don't tense up!* He bumped down the rocky steps with only the lightest dabbing of the rear brake.

Drop; slight turn; drop; over the rock; avoid the edge; roll; drop; down. Daniels had safely negotiated the most dangerous obstacle. *Nailed it!*

His system was flooded with hormones. He attacked the rest of the trail with abandon, at least until a poor line choice sent him tumbling over the roots. He picked himself up, finding a few minor knocks and grazes, then continued. His arms and legs were already tiring; he was long out of practice. Errors became more frequent but he didn't care. He made it to the bottom and was still in one piece. *Not bad for a first run.*

Daniels was astounded by the performance of the Jackdaw. For the first time, he could fully appreciate its potential. The bike rolled swiftly and smoothly over slippery roots and jagged rock that would soon break the ankles of a walker. The machine would be an encumbrance if attempting to hack through jungle, but on open ground, paths, or vehicle tracks it would excel. He set about the long and arduous endeavour of pushing the bike back up the hill. For the excitement of the run down, it had been well worth the effort.

After ten minutes, Daniels shoved the bike back past The Staircase, sweating and panting from the exertion. Dylan called over from his vantage point.

'That was impressive, Tom, and a touch curious. What are you not telling us?'

Daniels simply gave him a smile.

Back under the camo-net, Daniels was summoned to join McCowan and the two sergeants. They were discussing the battle plan as they had done countless times previously in the briefing room at Stirling Lines. They crouched around a rough-scale representation of the enemy encampment, laid out from memory using sticks, rocks and gravel. The sticks marked the known routes and boundaries, the rocks indicated targets, and gravel was poured on to signify expected enemy strength at key locations.

'I've just been for a test run.' Daniels' face was still flushed from the strenuous hike. 'Wow – those things are capable. Worth the heavy price tag, I'd say. What's the score then, anyway?'

'With you stuck here with us, we've no line of communication to the boss.' O'Neil referred to Major Nolan. 'We need to keep him abreast of our situation.'

'You can send him a bluey,' McCowan quipped.

O'Neil didn't seem amused.

'We can't even get confirmation to proceed.'

'Nolan's still wet behind the ears; and anyway, he's not even in the country. We can judge the situation quite well enough for ourselves.' The SSM seemed unworried by the matter.

'Authority for you guys gets signed over to Torres for the duration of the mission,' Daniels pointed out. 'Were acting on behalf of the EP, not our own government.'

'Well then, that leaves us with two clear options,' McCowan concluded. 'Option one, is we abort the mission and try to get home without being arrested or getting the kit confiscated.'

'That isn't much of an option.'

'No. I think we all agree that we'd rather not run away with our tails between our legs. Option two: we carry out the raid as planned with the team we have here.'

'Can it be done with twelve?' Daniels asked.

'It *can* be done with twelve. It *has* to be done with twelve. The question is, *will* it be done with twelve?'

'If everything goes to plan, the numbers shouldn't matter. We just need to set all the charges without waking the camp up,' Shearman made light of the setback.

'Uh-huh. And if we can't, we'd still be in the crap with a larger force anyway.' McCowan finished the point for him. 'Okay, we've been right through this. The loss of Dawson's patrol doesn't really change anything apart from the degree of risk. Someone round up the guys, and get a brew on as well. I'm going to give the orders.'

Twenty minutes later, the Jackdaws were stacked under cover and the assault team had gathered around the makeshift map – minus the two sergeants, who knew the plan and had now taken the lookout shift. McCowan informed Dylan and Carver that they didn't need to attend the briefing, which he said only concerned the military personnel. The precaution seemed a bit pointless to Daniels. They already knew enough to blow the operation and there was nowhere else for them to go. They sat on a log fifteen metres away looking bored and chatting between themselves. McCowan had everyone else's rapt attention.

'If we're all here, I'll begin. We've taken the decision to press ahead with the raid as planned, subject to the final 'go' confirmation by General Torres. We are four men down, but still have the capacity to take out our allocated targets. However, we now have much less margin for error. If we're forced into a firefight, at any point, we'll be significantly outnumbered by cartel militia and could quickly become encircled. Each patrol must therefore carry out their specific tasks precisely and by the numbers. It's absolutely vital that we remain undetected throughout the entire mission.

'The insertion will go ahead as planned, using the Jackdaws to get within range of the plantation. We'll wear our personal radios, but these won't be used until destruction of WHITE is confirmed. We know the cartel use various comms equipment; interference from ours could warn them that something's going down. So that's complete radio silence until after we've disabled the launcher. Match will carry the general's high-frequency set, ready to invite him to the party at that point.

'The IR units on the Jackdaws will be switched off five kilometres from the target. In the unlikely event that someone at the camp has a night-sight, they'd see a train of our headlights coming down the mountain. Once within that distance, we'll slow to a crawl and make the final approach silently, with frequent stops to scan ahead.

'Obviously we've had to make some changes to the patrol format. They are as follows: The Delta One marksmen – Taz and Gav – will now be led by Elana, who will spot for both and coordinate movements.' To Daniels, it seemed appropriate that Govrin was free to make her own tactical decisions, since she was being asked to operate in an unusually high-risk environment. She was a fire-team leader within her own unit and unquestionably capable of the job. McCowan continued, after a pause for comment.

'Sergeant O'Neil will lead Delta Two, which will now include Match and myself. Delta Three: Cal, Hugo and Jonah. Delta Four: Ren, Iain and Mad. All targets and objectives are assigned to each team as before. Any questions so far?'

'Do we have an ERV?' Wade asked, referring to an emergency rendezvous, which would be used as a meeting point if the plan went awry. He was working his way through his twice-daily routine of stretches as he listened.

McCowan answered soberly. 'We can designate an area to regroup if things get noisy, but unless we complete the objectives there won't be a viable exit from the target location, I'm afraid.'

'I have an idea for that,' Daniels interrupted. 'Carver's been there before. He knows the camp.'

'So what? He can't fly anywhere near the place.' McCowan looked niggled that such matters had been discussed without him, but he didn't raise the matter.

He was unaware of Daniels leverage over the pilot, or that Carver was a paid CIA informant.

Daniels called Carver over. 'Derrick, do you know where that river ends up – the one below La Fábrica? We've seen canoes in the satellite images that can only be for taking people downriver.'

'Yeah, it meets a bigger river about ten miles downstream, then eventually joins up with the Apurimac.'

'Is there anywhere down there you can land the chopper?'

'Along the larger river, sure. There are some gravel beaches, a few rural settlements.'

'Then I'll go with Derrick and set up an extraction point somewhere safely out of range. We'll take the medical supplies in case anyone's injured. If you get in trouble, you can use the canoes to head downstream until you see the helicopter. It's a long trip but the river would be inaccessible to militia on foot. You'd be safe enough.'

McCowan nodded. 'Okay, that sounds good. Then the ERV is the riverbank to the south of the airstrip, where the canoes are kept. You've all seen the pictures.

'Now, each team needs to get their own charges checked, packed and ready to deploy. When that's done, I want to see some weapon drills happening with these Jackdaws. No firing, obviously, but we haven't even tried riding with the carbines in the holders yet. We need to practice stopping the bikes and getting weapons up to firing positions as quickly as possible, then stowing the weapons and moving off again. Reloading, stoppage drills, fire and retreat; everything you do normally needs to be done when standing over those things. We don't know how much time we have, so get to it.'

Daniels had to hand it to McCowan: he was thorough, professional and confidence-inspiring in the face of difficulty. The squadron sergeant major had no intention of giving up. Despite some forced amendments to their plan, Operation CATHODE would go ahead. Daniels felt a boost to his resolve simultaneously with the first few spots of rain on his skin. He looked up to see scattered cloud rolling in.

* * *

It was only really a light drizzle and it didn't last long. The raid had been planned for August as rainfall is lowest in this period and there are fewest storms. An untimely downpour could make the insertion more difficult and potentially prevent the EP helicopters from flying, leaving the SAS team stranded and without reinforcement. However, this brief shower was of seemingly little threat to the mission.

Dylan and Carver took cover in one of the tents for the duration, while the military personnel continued their routines. McCowan, Govrin and the Mountain Troop members rehearsed firing drills on the Jackdaws. The Mobility men practiced on Dylan's course. The rain had made the track more treacherous, especially where the surface was covered in slippery roots. The riders were now splattered in wet mud from head to foot. Everyone found the riding more difficult but there were no complaints. If it rained during the raid, they would still have to keep to the insertion timetable. After a short while, Dylan was compelled to leave the comforts of the dry tent and offer some assistance to the Mobility men. After he performed a full-speed demonstration of The Staircase, completely ignoring the reduced grip conditions, the team began to regain some confidence.

Daniels watched McCowan's group practicing stopping the bikes and getting to prone positions as quickly as the action could be performed. Then they worked in fours, assuming defensive formations while still on the Jackdaws. The first man would pull to a stop and raise his weapon, being careful not to allow the wheels to skid noisily; the second and third men would stop behind and cover the left and right; the fourth rider would stop sideways behind them to cover the rear. It didn't take long before these routines happened like clockwork. Sometime after midday, the teams swapped roles in the training tasks.

It had occurred to Daniels that Dylan and McCowan hadn't argued for a while. But when it came, it came from nowhere. McCowan had not spent enough time on the Jackdaw and it showed in his riding. Dylan declared that he wasn't sufficiently skilled to tackle the rocky chute and endeavoured to prevent him from doing so. However, at this late stage in the operation, inability to complete Dylan's course translated into inability to participate in the mission. McCowan flatly refused to entertain that possibility.

'Look, I know you're brave enough but it won't help you. These guys have been building up for a whole month. You'll just come straight off,' Dylan implored.

McCowan was lined up above The Staircase, its chunky boulders now slick and muddy from the spattering of rain.

'Dylan, I don't need you to tell me what to do, lad. You're just showing off because I didn't turn up for your lessons.'

Dylan tried to protest further, but McCowan rolled forward regardless. He stood up tall on the pedals, looking for the right entrance. *Way too fast*, Daniels thought as he watched McCowan approach the edge. A dramatic last-minute skid confirmed his fears but McCowan held on. Tipping over the lip, he dropped down into the chute. The bike nosedived disconcertingly over the back of a rock and immediately picked up speed. McCowan bucked and bounced with the jarring impacts, barely keeping hold of the handlebars. He snatched for the brake levers but the section was too steep for the tyres to offer any purchase. The Jackdaw slid out of control. He came off line.

His front wheel struck an outcrop of rock and twisted sideways. The bike upended instantly, launching McCowan headfirst over the handlebars. Those nearby stared, frozen, unable to prevent the inevitable. He fell through the air for three vertical metres before his helmet smashed into the ground. His body slumped flat onto its back, only to be struck by the rear wheel of the tumbling Jackdaw. Daniels, Dylan, the soldiers present sprinted over. McCowan lay still.

* * *

'Don't move him!' O'Neil snapped. 'He might have a spinal injury.' Once alerted, the medic had bounded down the hill to the scene of the accident. 'He's unconscious, but alive and breathing. His bowels have held which is a good sign. I want a neck brace down here and a stretcher; we'll need to be careful moving him. And get that helicopter fired up *right now*.'

Wade, Madan and Taz ran off up the hill to fulfil O'Neil's instructions. Daniels ran behind to locate Match.

'Match; get the general on the radio, or anyone else who knows what they're talking about. Tell them we've got a severe neck injury. We need a hospital that's equipped for this.'

'Shit! Got it.'

Match was at the radio in two minutes.

As the camo-net was tugged off the Eurocopter and the restraints freed from the rotors, Carver climbed inside. He began flipping switches, ensuring that the fuel pumps, hydraulics and control systems had power and were activated. First came the electrical whine of the motors. Carver checked his readouts on the bank of small rectangular screens. Then came the roar as he fired the first engine. The four-bladed rotor began to turn.

From the radio, Match received his answer. He ran out to the helicopter to relay the instructions.

'You need to take him to Hospital Militar Central in Lima. You can land on site there. Torres' man will call ahead and tell them it was a training accident.'

'That's got to be three hundred nautical miles,' Carver replied quickly. 'There'll be nothing but vapour in the tank by the time we get over the mountains. I'll have to refuel at Ayacucho. That's a three-hour trip with the fuel stop.'

Four men carried McCowan on the stretcher, with O'Neil accompanying alongside to keep his head stable, now supported by the inflatable brace. Daniels opened the rear clamshell doors so the stretcher could be slid right in. O'Neil shouted to Carver and Daniels, over the noise of the turbine.

'I need to go with him in case he vomits, he'll suffocate without attention.'

'No one else,' Carver replied. 'We're real tight on fuel.'

'Okay, let's go. As fast as you can,' O'Neil demanded.

Daniels grabbed Carver's arm before he reached to fire the second engine.

'I know I'm asking a lot, but can you get right back here after you've dropped them at Lima? We're washed up here. We're going to need an exit.'

'Sorry; not gonna happen, buddy.' Carver shook his head ruefully. 'By the time I get back, it'll be pitch dark and I'll be out of fuel. This cloud is getting worse. Weather forecast ain't great, either – we're in for some high winds. Best if I set down, re-prep the aircraft and be ready to move again at sunrise.'

'Good man. You'll be compensated for this.'

'Don't worry, you'll know about that when you get my bill.'

Daniels jumped down and closed the cabin door as Carver fired the second engine. The rotor picked up speed and O'Neil took his place beside McCowan's head. Minutes later the craft was airborne, climbing rapidly. The Eurocopter crested the ridge and disappeared from sight.

* * *

'I didn't speak to Torres himself but he relayed the message,' Match explained. 'He said stand by to receive instructions, on the hour, every hour, as before.'

It wasn't long before sunset. A few of the team had gone to the tents to get some rest before their night shifts on lookout duty. Most of the others were stood around in the open, discussing their options. Dylan was nearby, cleaning mud off the Jackdaws one by one.

'Okay, so we have to assume that Torres will extract us, but we need to be prepared in case he has other plans in mind. We're in no shape to proceed at present.' Sherman's disappointment was barely concealed. As the remaining sergeant, he had command of the unit. 'We'll get the gear packed up and sit tight for the moment, until we hear different.'

The surrounding faces reflected the same downbeat mood.

'He won't be coming to get us.' Haynes voice was quiet and dulcet but still caught everyone's attention.

'Sorry, Hugo?'

'Torres lost twenty men because of that missile launcher; how would you feel? He won't be quitting this mission.'

'Hugo's got a point,' Shearman conceded. 'But we're going to be holed up here for a while, at least until the political issues are resolved and we can get some reinforcement. We'll keep up whatever drill routines are practical to retain readiness but no more riding the Jackdaws for the moment. We've no logistical support now. We can't handle another injury.'

The sound started as a whine but rapidly deepened in pitch.

'Get down!' someone screamed.

The harsh drone of the turboprop split the air as the aircraft whipped past just above the treetops. The Super Tucano's skin was messily streaked in makeshift camouflage, devoid of insignia. The range was so close that Shearman caught a glimpse of the pilot's helmet in the glass bubble cockpit. He cursed at being caught in the open.

'*Shit!* Where the hell did that come from?'

Travelling fast and low, the cartel aircraft had only given a few seconds warning of its approach.

'Take cover, quick,' Shearman shouted unnecessarily. The men were already running. 'Get those bikes out of sight.'

Daniels grabbed Dylan by his overalls and pulled him down the hill, shoving him beneath the foliage of one of the denser conifers and following him under. He pushed the young civilian down flat and crawled on top of him to protect his body. The others had scurried out of sight in the panic, spreading in all directions. The exposed Jackdaws had been slung haphazardly into bushes. No one attempted to retrieve a weapon; there was little point. Eleven hundred rounds per minute from the aircraft's twin machine guns would soon saturate their position with incoming fire if the pilot saw muzzle flashes. Their best chance was to hide, and pray that they hadn't already been spotted.

They watched in dismay as the aircraft slowed and entered a wide banked turn.

'He's seen us. Stay down! *Stay down*!' Wade called out.

They hugged the ground in silence, nobody moving an inch. The aircraft flew out of sight over the lower slopes of their mountainside, performing a slow circle that would bring it back around over the camp from another direction.

Shearman lay by the edge of the landing zone under a small bush. A pointed rock protruded into his ribcage but there was no way to change position without breaking cover. He was forced to endure the discomfort. He listened to the hum of the plane louden steadily as it came around for a second pass. The point of the rock caused a spreading numbness that soon intensified into pain. Beads of sweat broke out on his forehead. He gritted his teeth, frozen in the agonising position as the aircraft approached from behind. Low branches prevented him from turning his head enough to look. The roar grew louder. He waited for the crackle of machine-gun fire, the whoosh of rockets… nothing. The plane passed directly overhead. *Is there a bomb?* He pressed his head down into the dirt, closed his eyes and counted the seconds. *One, two, three, four, five*… nothing.

'It's coming back around,' came a warning from lower down the hill.

Sherman rotated his body so that the rock stuck into an alternative part of his torso, his face soaked in sweat from the exertion of trying to brace some of his weight. The springy branches pushed down firmly on his back. Time passed excruciatingly slowly. To his front, he watched the aircraft enter another lazy circle. He groaned and gasped but held his position. The Super Tucano passed over the camp. Once again, no bullets, no bombs. It performed a final circuit further up the hillside then accelerated away to the west. It was gone.

'He didn't get a fix on us,' Shearman announced when the soldiers were gathered back together. He winced as he rubbed his bruised ribs, still breathing heavily. His face was covered with a mix of sweat and dirt.

'He must have seen something though. Maybe caught a glint then circled to reacquire it,' Haynes countered. His combat overalls and sparse remaining hair were covered in leaf litter from his cover position. 'He gave up and left when he couldn't find the source. Probably didn't want to hang around with the light fading.' A few heads nodded as Haynes spoke.

'Out here, heading west toward cartel territory, the sloppy paint-job – it was definitely the enemy, and looking for us it seems,' Shearman concluded.

'If he did see something, he might come back at dawn with a full tank,' Haynes warned.

'Agreed. We have to assume that this location is now compromised. It's vaguely possible that cartel militia could turn up here on foot; so we'd better be ready to defend ourselves, just in case.'

'The pilot couldn't hope to find anyone flying around these mountains at random. That would just be a waste of fuel. If they're looking for us, then they already know we're here.' Haynes shook his overalls to rid them of debris.

'Then maybe we have had a security breech after all,' Daniels conceded. 'Dylan can't stay here. We need to get him somewhere safe at the very least. We'd better get Torres back on the radio.'

'It looks that way,' Shearman agreed. 'But we'll be safe enough overnight. They won't move on us in the dark. Not through that forest. Match, get on the radio, and tell them we need the General himself this time.'

'Do you lot actually have *any* idea what you're doing?' Dylan yelled; his cheeks flushed red in anger. The intrusion of the flypast had evidently touched a nerve. 'I mean, *seriously*, what am I even doing here? Hiding out up a bloody mountain while you lot play soldiers. Now you don't even have transport. This whole stupid situation is a mess.'

'Okay, Dylan. You're right – you shouldn't be here.' Daniels made a futile attempt at consolation. 'We'll sort things out, I promise. You'll be on the first helicopter out. We're going to arrange that right now.'

Dylan's head hung down to his chest, the energy of his tantrum dissipated. He shrugged, puffing out the remaining air from his lungs, then turned and headed for the tents.

The military personnel huddled around the radio, glum faced and silent. McCowan's accident played heavily on their minds. Even the two lookouts had moved in to hear the outcome for themselves. Match got the connection up, entered the relevant key code and sent his first message, directly requesting the general. The digital scrambler would encrypt his voice before transmitting. Once the response was received, Daniels took the mouthpiece to do the talking. There was a wait of a few minutes while Torres was summoned. No one spoke.

'Outpost, are you receiving?'

'Yes, General.'

A brief pause occurred between each message as the radio units processed their signals.

'The assault must take place tonight – it will be our only chance. By tomorrow, I'll need the president's intervention to overrule Admiral Ballesta. The Defence Minister will become involved and congress will be made aware. Even if our mission is not postponed indefinitely, the enemy will learn of our plans. My helicopter will be with you in two hours. Be ready.'

'General, we're down six men here. We need to be reinforced by our training team if we're going to proceed?' They waited with bated breath, impatient for the answer.

'This will not be possible. Ballesta is here now and your troops and equipment are locked down. Transport to the target will come from elsewhere and will be masquerading as a logistical flight.'

'Ten men is too small a force for this operation. The odds of success or even survival will be low. You're asking my team to take an unreasonable risk.'

The moment of silence was long.

'Your men will be risking their lives if they proceed with this mission. My men have already done so and paid the price. We are at threat every day that this missile system remains functional. It must be destroyed or others will continue to die. I cannot order you, Lieutenant, but you came to Peru to demonstrate your abilities. Now I ask you to demonstrate them. There is much at stake. You have two hours to be ready.'

Torres signed off with his last comment and the radio fell silent.

Heads hung low. Darkness had crept into Outpost, its occupants barely able to see each other under the camo-netting. The burner would no longer be lit. The risk of its flame advertising their position to an unseen enemy was now too great. Shearman spoke up.

'You all heard the man. Who says we go and who says we abort?'

'We go.' Wade was first to answer and did so with assertiveness.

'Aye, we go,' Haynes confirmed.

One by one the remaining six SAS men agreed, 'We go.'

Govrin was last to reply. *'Of course* we fucking go. I'm sick to death of all this *training.'*

'I agree, we go.' Shearman concluded. 'We have no contact with the boss for approval but we're deployed at Torres' disposal. We can assume that our previous objectives still stand. We're not safe here, anyhow. Sooner we finish this the better.'

'I can take McCowan's place,' Daniels suggested. 'You're already short-handed; you'll need help to carry the gear. I know the plans, I'm trained with a weapon, and it seems I can get by on the Jackdaw. And besides, it was my job to put this whole thing together. I'll be the one responsible if it all goes wrong.'

'Okay, Tom, that's appreciated,' Shearman acknowledged, 'But what do we do with Dylan?'

'He can stay on the transport after the drop-off and it can take him back to whatever base it came from. He'll be safe there with the EP. We can work out how to get him home if we're still alive tomorrow.' Daniels got a brief laugh for the comment.

Shearman shook his head as if to rid it of an unwelcome thought.

'We're up shit creek here, but we can turn this situation around if we stay focussed. We're playing on our own terms, attacking in the dark. They're not going to know what's hit them. Let's break out the assault gear and get set to move out, before things get any worse.'

Chapter Sixteen

19:25
La Fábrica

After the long walk down the snaking southern road, Coniraya finally joined the throng of activity amassed at the western extent of the airstrip. He'd been told to make his way there as quickly as possible, then report to the duty-officer, Augusto, for orders. He hadn't rushed.

A few of the vehicles had been moved out from their covered positions and now stood in the northwest corner of the grass runway. The big tractor was parked adjacent to a smaller unit with an attached trailer, and these were flanked by the two pick-up trucks. The fire was burning as usual and Augusto stood beside it talking with three other men. The flickering orange glow reflected in their faces as Coniraya approached. A quad bike sat idling behind the group with a small trailer of its own. He stepped up close enough for his presence to be noticed.

'Concha, where the fuck have you been? We've been waiting. Go with Miguel and put flares down both sides of the runway, every thirty paces like before. And put a line across the end, every five paces. Don't light them; just stick them in the ground then report back here. Miguel will drive the ATV.'

Coniraya looked in the trailer to see two large bundles of the usual red marker flares, then stared down the airstrip with dismay. He would have to walk the entire length twice, with Miguel driving slowly beside him on the quad. He decided to be polite as he didn't wish to be taunted for the whole round trip. He nodded acknowledgement, pulled a few flares from one of the bundles and marched off into the darkness. Miguel would catch him up.

It was an annoyingly repetitive task. After an onerous half-hour, Coniraya completed the return journey seated in the quad's trailer. Augusto was still chatting to his companions by the fire, making some point about how their airstrip was sheltered from wind in the bottom of the valley. It was a bit gusty, but Coniraya knew it would be much worse for the guards up at the top of the plantation.

'Well done, Concha,' the duty-officer said patronisingly. 'Go get yourself a beer from the back of the pick-up.'

Coniraya perked up instantly at the mention of beer. There was a dearth of alcohol at La Fábrica and he didn't wait to be asked twice. He walked briskly over and helped himself. Someone must have been in a good mood that evening as two crates of brown bottles sat on the rear flatbed, one of which was nearly empty. He stood close to the pick-up while he gulped down the tepid liquid, hoping to grab a second unnoticed. In this respect, he was out of luck. There was some squawking from Augusto's radio, followed by a clipped conversation in Spanish. The duty officer waved Coniraya over and pointed to the back of the ATV, which Miguel had already remounted.

'Go light them all now. Go; hurry.'

Coniraya lit a flare in the fire then sat cross-legged in the trailer. Miguel would drive close to the positioned flares, so that he could light each in turn from his flame. They would burn for roughly twenty minutes but it would take nearly half that time to light them all. They sped around the airstrip perimeter then returned to the campfire. The quad was then tucked up alongside the other vehicles. As soon as the engine was switched off, Coniraya could hear the distant resonant thrum emanating from further down the valley, gaining steadily in volume.

The cliff path would offer a bird's eye view of the approach, but the vegetation surrounding the airfield blocked the line of sight from where he stood in the corner. Augusto was laughing loudly and Coniraya wondered if he was drunk. He thought about making a grab for another bottle but the noise was rapidly escalating and he knew there wouldn't be time. The drone reached a crescendo as the big dark shape swooped overhead, momentarily blocking out the night before it bounced down hard on the runway. The sound from the turboprops instantly changed pitch as the blades reversed thrust. Coniraya thought that the pilots must be crazy. One day, one of them would overshoot the runway and crash into the trees in an explosion of noise and fire. Not this time though. The giant craft came to a stop with forty metres to spare.

The instant the transport stopped moving, the shouting of instructions started. The big tractor trundled down the runway to turn the aircraft back around for take-off. The other vehicles would collect the cargo. Coniraya jumped on the back of the pick-up at Augusto's direction, then it accelerated down the airstrip towards the idling craft. Four other men rode on the rear bed of the truck, preventing any move on the beer. For the moment, there was work to be done.

The dull, light-grey skin of the Antonov An-12 was scarred and weathered – she was thirty-seven years old. A veteran of the Indo-Pakistani War of 1971, the aircraft had seen more military service than any member of La Fábrica's militia and had been used both as a bomber and a troop transport. The twin rear-facing cannons now sat defunct in their tail turret, accompanied by the angular glass windows of the gunner's position. The sixty-tonne plane seemed disproportionate, barely fitting on the small grass airstrip, but it was designed for exactly this purpose – heavy payload, tactical supply drops using short, unmade runways.

Coniraya stood beneath the wide fins of the tail, lit a cigarette, and watched the loading ramp lower to the ground. He was surprised to see a line of four military jeeps rolling down from the hold one after the other. This wasn't normal. Following the 4x4s, a crowd of men tramped down the ramp, about thirty in number. Coniraya was bewildered; he had assumed this was a regular supply drop. These men weren't the usual militia types either. They wore camouflage-pattern fatigues and proper equipment webbing. Rucksacks were carried and fancy looking rifles. They almost looked like men from an official army. He stood staring as they passed him.

'You want me to smoke that for you?' One of the soldiers snatched the cigarette from Coniraya's mouth, putting it between his own lips as he strode past. Coniraya was left speechless, his mouth agape.

'Get up there and unload the crates, Concha.' He heard Augusto bark from behind him.

'Who are these men?' He turned and asked.

'Mercenaries – professionals – come to protect the camp.'

'But it's our job to protect the camp,' Coniraya appealed pathetically.

'No, Concha, it's your job to unload the fucking plane. Now hurry up; the pilot wants to take-off immediately.'

Chapter Seventeen

20:00
Outpost

The transport was due. What was left of the assault team sat huddled around the equipment crates, static and silent. No outstanding tasks remained with which to fill the time. The air temperature was just above zero and a frigid wind had picked up, cutting through their clothing and causing an occasional shudder. Just a fine sliver of new moon hung low in the night sky, and a thin mist further diminished the visibility it might otherwise have offered. It occurred to Daniels that these conditions would not be ideal for the incoming pilot.

They waited in full readiness for deployment, faces smeared with camo-cream, body armour and belt-kits worn. Night-vision units were mounted on helmets, locked in the raised position and switched off. Each soldier carried their own munitions pack to prevent any possible mix-up during transit. Only the two marksmen wore holsters for the SIG Sauer 9mm pistols, the rest of the team opting to carry extra assault-rifle magazines instead. The handguns would be all but useless at the expected engagement ranges, and they did not have suppressors for noise reduction.

The others were accustomed to wearing this gear, but Daniels had to fiddle around to get his straps tight and comfortable. The weight of the webbing alone was significant when packed with water, rations, medical kit and ammunition. He carried ten magazines – short-filled to facilitate location and reduce spring stress – each holding twenty-eight 5.56mm rounds. With no secondary weapon to fall back on, the chances of stoppage had to be minimised. Shearman handed him two M75 fragmentation grenades, supplied by the Mountain Brigade quartermaster, and he stuffed them into his spare pouches. The body armour already restricted his movement before he had put on the backpack. He began to question whether he could operate sufficiently, and what he'd got himself into.

'We'll have to abandon O'Neil's objective – the cocaine store. We don't have anyone to carry the charge,' Shearman informed him.

Daniels shook his head. 'I promised Torres we'd take care of it. He was very specific: it's his second priority after the launcher. Elana has no pack. She could take it as far as the plantation and I could carry both to the targets from there. It's only a short distance.'

'No, that's not realistic,' Shearman stated flatly. 'You're already looking weighed down. It's not a critical objective. It can be taken care of once we're reinforced.'

Daniels dropped the point and changed the subject. 'We need to get a message to Carver.'

'Possibly, but later. We can't afford the security risk right now.'

The tents, water containers and camouflage netting were stacked up ready to load onto the transport first, along with the crates filled with spare equipment. Then the Jackdaws, each fully checked and mounted with its infrared lights. Most of the bikes had C8 carbines stowed in their forward holders with the stocks fully collapsed, although a different method was required to carry the two HK417 long rifles. These were more than a metre in length with the suppressors fitted and had been strapped to the sides of the marksmen's Jackdaws, an arrangement that made riding more awkward and meant the weapons were inaccessible in a hurry. Hence, Taz and Riley had chosen to carry pistols to avoid being caught unarmed in a surprise contact. It wasn't an ideal solution, but it would have to suffice.

The dark, cylindrical body and long tail boom of the Mil emerged out of the swirling mist and swung into position above Outpost's landing zone, accompanied by the roar of its engines and the slap of its blades. The Mi-17 – one of the world's most successful transport and utility helicopters – was ideal for this kind of operation, but it was double the size of the Eurocopter and precise positioning was required to land in the small space. The ungainly craft dropped abruptly and set down heavily onto its three wheels, its pilot forestalling the risk of being blown off target. The rear clamshell doors hinged apart. Dim red lights illuminated the hollow space within.

They shuttled the superfluous materiel to the helicopter first, then went back for the Jackdaws. Dylan carried no gear but pushed the spare bike over and was directed aboard. Within a few minutes, the aircraft was loaded and Outpost abandoned. The cabin was empty except for a row of padded fold-down seats lining each side of the fuselage. Daniels and Shearman took the seats nearest the front by the flight engineer. Others took the seats further back or chose to sit against the equipment crates on the flat floor. Daniels recognised the diminutive form of the same female pilot that had flown their initial supply drop, now wearing night-vision goggles along with her co-pilot.

Once again, rotor speed was maintained, the Mil held on the ground by the pitch of its blades. With a nod from the engineer to say the doors were closing, she pulled back on the collective lever, simultaneously twisting the five blades to the lift position and increasing engine power. The eight-tonne machine leapt rapidly into the air, its twelve new passengers grabbing for handholds. Then the craft pitched acutely forward, accelerating and gaining the momentum it would use to climb over the adjacent ridgeline.

The full strength of the wind became apparent the moment they crested the col. Every few seconds, the Mil was blown dramatically, forcing the pilot to manoeuvre aggressively to counteract. The passengers had to grip on wherever they could with their packs shifting around them on the cabin floor. Daniels clung on to his seat and stared through the porthole beside him. Visibility was practically zero, even when he tried using his NVGs. He wondered whether the pilot could see any better. *At least we'll be difficult to spot,* he consoled himself. He leaned forward and tapped the leg of the flight engineer to gain the man's attention.

'What's our flight time?'

'Maybe one hour. It is difficult to say.' The crewman shrugged his shoulders, answering in broken but intelligible English. 'We must stay low and take a long route. With this weather, it will be slow.'

Daniels sat back down next to Shearman.

'We'll be shaken to pieces by the time we make the drop-off.'

'If we make the drop off,' Shearman replied.

* * *

The aircraft continued to buck and roll sickeningly as it made its way through the bleak mist. Daniels noticed that a prolonged shouted exchange was taking place in the cockpit between the pilot and co-pilot. The flight engineer stood braced in the doorway, his knuckles white from their tight grip on the handholds.

'What are they arguing about?' Daniels asked him.

'He says we must fly higher or we crash into the mountain. She says we stay low or get shot down.'

Daniels checked his watch. They were only twenty minutes into the journey and conditions seemed to be worsening. Forward progress was slowing. The jerking of the helicopter was increasing in violence. A loud shout came from the pilot and the helicopter pitched over hard to the left, sending the passengers and Jackdaws tumbling. Then the Mil swung back to level and the displaced troops scrabbled back to their side of the fuselage, shoving the bikes back to an upright position as they went.

It was Wade that called out. 'Shit! Right hand window.'

Daniels looked through the porthole to see a large outcrop of rock just a few metres from the extent of the rotor blades. The aircraft was right on top of it. The pilot delicately steered forward and away from the protrusion, adjusting for the crosswind as she went. The atmosphere in the cabin had become thick with tension and nausea, the outlook turning more pessimistic with every minute that passed. But the howl of the twin engines prevented the team from discussing their predicament. The cabin lights had been switched off and they could barely see each other's faces. They were less than halfway through the journey and it struck Daniels that they would be lucky to reach their destination. He weighed up the implications of the helicopter crashing. Nobody would survive. He grabbed Shearman's arm and shouted.

'We need to get Dylan out when we land. He'll be safer on the ground with us than in this tin can.'

'I hear you, but we're heading into a firefight. We can't take him with us.'

'He can take the spare Jackdaw and ride behind as far as the plantation. We can hide him up there somewhere and collect him when the target's been cleared out.'

'We can't take a civilian on a combat insertion, Tom. Apart from his own safety he'd be a liability for us.'

'We use local guides and translators in war zones. What's the difference?' Daniels gained confidence in the idea. 'Let's see what *he* thinks.'

Daniels shouted over to Dylan, who was sat on a roll of camo-net looking queasy and terrified.

'Dylan, do you want to come with us when we get off? You can you ride the spare bike. We'll find somewhere safe for you to wait until we've finished our business.'

'*I don't care* where we go! Just get me out of this *frigging death-trap!*' Dylan bawled his reply.

Daniels turned back to Shearman and nodded.

'I'll take him with me. So long as nobody starts a shooting match, we'll head straight to the ERV. Then, if it comes to it, I can send him downriver in a canoe. Maybe he could carry McCowan's pack as well.'

'Oh, right. So we'll be court-martialled for drowning a civilian rather than getting him shot. You're off your rocker, Tom.'

* * *

Cold air cascaded down the mountain slopes at night, driven by the force of gravity. The Mil hit a downdraft and dropped, provoking desperate shouts from the cockpit. Daniels stomach lifted to his ribcage and stayed there. The whine of the turbines raised in pitch as the pilot applied maximum power in a futile attempt to maintain altitude in the thin, turbulent air. Daniels saw nothing but the same foggy void through the porthole. He leaned forward to see out of the cockpit windshield. A wall of dark granite emerged from the gloom ahead of them. They did not have enough height to clear it.

Instinctively, the pilot stamped on the right-hand pedal, bringing the nose around, then flicked the cyclic stick fully over. The craft banked at a steep angle, and once again, men and equipment tumbled across the cabin. The pilot pulled back hard on the stick, swinging the machine away from the looming face of rock, a stream of shouted profanities launching from her lips as she urged the Mil to maintain forward speed. Without it, they would fall from the sky. A meagre few metres was all that separated the helicopter's undercarriage from the jagged teeth of the bluff. She eased the Mil back into level flight, travelling parallel to the ridge, then gradually accumulated enough lift to pull up and over. It occurred to Daniels that a lesser pilot wouldn't have made it this far. Torres had assigned his best people to this operation.

'How bad does this get before we're forced to abort?' he asked the engineer, who relayed the question to the pilot. She cursed loudly and started laughing, then gave her answer. The engineer handed his headset to Daniels. Apparently she wished to reply personally.

'Mr Daniels, we can abort this mission when we hit the mountain. Otherwise, conditions are the same in every direction. We are just below the enemy radar horizon – we cannot fly higher without risking detection. But don't worry, we are nearing your drop-off point. You will arrive safely. For us, it is still a long journey, we are at risk of hypoxia, and I have just overloaded my engines.'

Daniels thanked the pilot sheepishly and returned the headset. Shearman was waiting to speak when he sat back down.

'You're right. We need to take him with us. This thing's on a one-way trip.'

'I'll get him kitted up fast.' Daniels leaned over to bellow some instructions at Dylan, then plunged rearwards, wobbling as he struggled to keep balance. He began frantically rifling through the supply crates for the required items. Dylan was already wearing combat fatigues to reduce his visibility at Outpost, but now he would need webbing to carry water, basic first aid and some ration packs. Daniels beckoned to Haynes, the nearest man, to help him find the necessary body armour and spare NVGs.

'What the hell are you doing?' Haynes asked Daniels.

'Getting Dylan off this helicopter.'

Haynes looked dissatisfied with the answer but simply nodded. He deftly located the required kit using a small torch. A few minutes later Dylan was geared up like the assault team – minus the weapons – and wearing McCowan's demolition pack. Haynes fitted him with a personal radio, attaching the aerial and adjusting the single earpiece and throat mike, but he firmly taped the radio's power switch in the off position to prevent any accidental transmission. Daniels sat next to Dylan on the camo-net, staring him directly in the eyes while he explained.

'Listen carefully. You remember our diagram we made on the ground?' Dylan nodded. 'After the plantation, we go into the forest and down a footpath. There will be some canoes on the beach. This is our ERV – emergency rendezvous. We'll get you there safely. If there's any problem, you can get in a canoe and paddle down the river. It might be a bit bumpy, but not like white-water rafting or anything. You'll be fine, okay?'

'What's in this backpack, Tom?' Dylan asked suspiciously.

'It's a demolition charge, but don't worry. It can't go off unless the wires inside are connected. It's totally safe to carry; I promise.'

Dylan glared furiously at Daniels, slumping down in the camo-net with his arms folded over his chest.

'If for any reason you do get approached by someone, put your hands up right away. Just tell the truth, answer any questions, say that you're a mountain bike…'

'Tom!' Dylan interrupted. 'Give it a rest. No one is going to catch me.'

Daniels smiled as sincerely as he could under the circumstances, then moved back forward to Shearman. The flight engineer held up two fingers – two minutes to drop-off point. *Thank fuck.*

'Daniels,' Shearman pulled him in close so he could talk into the MoD man's ear. 'Too many people have died already because of this bit of hardware. More good people are risking their lives right now. Torres has put his career on the line to go ahead with this gig. We can't be the ones to let the side down, mate. Whatever goes down tonight, that missile launcher gets taken out permanently – whatever the risks are.'

Daniels nodded soberly. He wondered how a simple defence-sales package had turned into a suicide mission, but he knew Shearman was right. If they didn't succeed they were as good as dead anyhow. Capture by Del Bosque didn't even bear thinking about. The Peruvian military leadership would have little choice but to disavow them. They would be explained away as mercenaries working for a rival cartel.

The Mi-17 slowed and settled into a hover, the engineer holding up one finger – one minute. Simultaneously the team stood, tightened their backpack straps and grabbed their Jackdaws ready for disembarkation. The engineer threw the switch. Cold air blew in as the rear doors began to hinge open. One of the helicopter's wheels contacted the ground and dragged sideways, causing the craft to list dangerously. They would not be able to set down completely – the crosswinds were too high. Instead, the pilot held position as best she could and shouted into her mouthpiece. The engineer conveyed the message – *this is as close as we get* – then he swung his arm and pointed out of the rear of the cabin. The aircraft hovered within two metres of the uneven ground, drifting and swaying as the pilot wrestled against the wind. To jump out and be passed a Jackdaw would risk being subsequently flattened by the drunken Mil. They were forced to deploy on the bikes, as they had done in training.

The first pair clicked down and activated their night vision, then lifted their bikes onto their back wheels. They stood side by side at the rear opening, then a second later were gone. The next men took position immediately as the first pair pedalled to get clear. Two by two, the soldiers hurriedly exited the aircraft. Dylan went in the second-to-last pair, completing the dismount gracefully and without hesitation. Daniels had to admire the younger man's nerve. He grabbed his Jackdaw but before joining Shearman he turned to the engineer and shouted.

'Tell her, tomorrow, it will be gone.'

The engineer relayed the message and Daniels saw the pilot nod slowly. He hadn't attempted the helicopter dismount before.

'This is easy, right?' he asked Shearman.

'Sort of.'

They shoved their Jackdaws out of the helicopter, into the darkness.

Chapter Eighteen

21:22
Drop-Off Point

Half the assault team had fanned out to secure the drop-off point, ditching their bikes and wielding their short assault rifles. The Mil made its precarious exit. Dylan watched the dark silhouette dissolve into the opaque night sky through his night-vision goggles and was overwhelmingly relieved that he wasn't still aboard. It was gone in moments; the visibility was poor in general and non-existent beyond about eighty metres. Then there was little to see but the barren stony ground and the rise of the peak above them. To Dylan it looked as if they were stood amongst the ash of a gigantic fire grate. It was cold – unpleasantly so – due to the biting wind and the thin, dampening mist. He huddled over the spare Jackdaw shivering while he waited for the others to sort out whatever it was they were doing.

By now he was utterly fed up with the war games, far beyond the point where he wanted the whole escapade to be over. He could vaguely comprehend why the soldiers needed to master riding these fancy bikes in the mountains – an army took pride in those sort of abilities – but he couldn't understand why they would do so in a location where they weren't entirely welcome. This was especially baffling as the whole party could have ridden freely in the Andes as tourists, provided they weren't jumping around in camouflage overalls and carrying weapons.

It was obvious enough that some kind of shady operation was taking place, and that the timetable had been brought forward by unforeseen events. As a result, he'd become entangled in a way that was never originally intended. Carver had made the matter sound almost glamorous – a spectacular plan to rein in an arrogant drug cartel with millions of dollars at their disposal. But Dylan knew there had been genuine danger on at least one occasion; he could tell that much from the team's mood. Even so, he wouldn't be completely surprised if Daniels turned around and said the whole excursion was an elaborate exercise. Big laughs; pat on the back; time to go home. The accidents had been real enough, though. He wondered if McCowan would be okay and if the programme had really been worth it.

Nevertheless, things were as they were, and now it turned out that a long descent stood between them and their ultimate destination. The ride down had potential to be a spectacular experience and might even justify the discomfort of his situation to date. This possibility was all the motivation Dylan needed to put in a final spate of effort. All the while he was riding the bike he would be in *his* element. He'd put in a lot of hard work training the team, and endured weeks of constant bossing around. He'd travelled halfway around the world just to hide in a tent, and then been made to suffer that hellish helicopter journey. Now he was owed the opportunity to tackle the mountain beneath them in a manner of his own choosing, before being delivered safely back home to the UK.

Haynes had advised him to conserve his NVG batteries in case they ran out during the night, but he could see more or less nothing without them. Supposedly the run time was shorter at low temperatures. Jonah had previously told him that the unit should last until dawn, so he opted to leave it switched on. He listened to the muffled thump of the departing helicopter fading below the sound of the buffeting wind. A few metres away, the few who hadn't taken defensive positions were clustered around a map, shining their red-diffused pencil torches. A discussion was taking place as to their exact location. After a few minutes, Daniels trotted over.

'How are you doing, Dylan?'

'I'm fucking freezing.'

'We all are. It'll be better once we're moving. We need to push up to the top of that saddle; our objective is down the other side.'

Dylan nodded. He couldn't really see where Daniels meant but he got off the Jackdaw and began to plod upwards anyway. He was glad to get moving in the energy-sapping conditions. It transpired that they were heading for a low point between two huge peaks, through which they would pass to cross over to the southern side. It was a fair distance and pretty steep but the prospect of a hike didn't faze him. Racing downhill tracks as youth, every run had been accompanied by a long push back up.

With one hand on the handlebars and one on the seat, he leaned into the machine and trudged up with his head down. Progress was slow and his breathing laboured in the thin air. When the incline became more severe, he held both brake levers and pulled himself forward a couple of steps, then shoved the bike ahead as far as his arms would stretch. His rate of ascent was comparable with that of any of the SAS men. By the time he reached the top he was no longer cold.

He tried to get actively involved in the next navigation discussion, even though there didn't seem to be all that much to talk about. Their destination was south of their current position, or as he saw it, directly down the mountain. The ancient path they intended to intercept crossed from east to west somewhere below them. They couldn't see it, but they had to come across it if they headed due south. The matter in debate was whether they would recognise the path in the dark. No one asked for Dylan's input but he decided to speak up anyhow.

'I can lead. I'll get us onto the path; no worries.'

'Dylan, you can't lead here, mate,' Shearman answered impatiently. 'We're not in friendly territory and we can't afford to be seen.'

'But we're still miles away from this plantation place, right? If we get spotted, what difference does it make what order we're riding in? At least if I lead, we'll get to the footpath in one piece.'

'That's a no, Dylan,' Shearman reiterated.

'But none of you are capable of picking the right line down – be realistic. I've been watching you stumble around for a whole month now, remember. The journey will take ages, there will be crashes and someone will get hurt. Meanwhile, I'll be riding at the back wondering what the hell you're doing. *Or*, I can get us down to the footpath safely.'

The risk of another injury was already weighing heavily on Shearman's mind, and the time window didn't allow them the option of travelling on foot. To a certain extent, Dylan was right; their best chance to make good and safe progress was to let him lead. But Shearman had a responsibility to protect the civilian and worried that Dylan might do something to give their position away. The prospect of an element that he couldn't control made him acutely uncomfortable. He tried to think of some stronger logic for forbidding the suggestion.

'Maybe Dylan could ride up front for a bit, while we're still a long way out,' Daniels suggested.

'To be honest, if we get in a contact before the plantation we're screwed anyhow,' Shearman conceded. 'This whole show rests on how quiet we can be for the final approach. A smooth run up to that point could prove a crucial advantage. You want to make the call, Tom?'

'Let him do it.'

'Okay, Dylan, then it looks like you're up. But pay attention: we all stay together, we stop every couple of kilometres to get our bearings, we don't do *anything* crazy, and there's no fucking around – you understand me? We've had enough accidents already. If someone gets hurt here, there's a good chance they won't be going home. Got it?'

'No problem; got it.' Dylan replied confidently, and for good reason. He was the only rider qualified to navigate the treacherous terrain without losing control, and he knew it. Even if he didn't start off in the lead, he would have been asked to take over as soon as someone hit a problem. *Now,* was his moment.

The twelve bikes stood line abreast with their riders poised atop, ready to peel off one-by-one from the left-hand end. They made final tightening adjustments to their straps and checked that the weapons were secure in the rubber-lined holders; nothing could afford to come loose. Each and every team member could taste the adrenaline, but Dylan felt a different emotion altogether. He imagined he was stood in the start gate, awaiting the marshal's countdown. The compelling drive; the focus; the red mist. He was about to contend a mammoth Andean mountain in the pitch dark, kitted out with awe-inspiring military hardware. A whole team of elite soldiers would be following behind him. These events would never be repeated – could never be. The next hour would be the defining race run of his life. He would deliver his masterstroke. A cold sweat clung to his body under the overalls. His palms felt prickly inside the gloves. The air almost seemed to sparkle, then he flipped down his NVGs and the effect was lost. He took one last deep breath and launched his Jackdaw down the desolate, fragmented slope.

He stood up tall, riding slowly but purposefully, providing a textbook example for the others to follow. Wide sweeping lines guided the team around the larger boulders and fissures, their wheels chattering incessantly over the smaller undulations. He slowed right down before the more challenging areas, so that the line of riders would bunch up behind him while he demonstrated the required technique. The team didn't need to watch their surroundings or maintain their bearings; each member simply copied the actions of the rider in front. Using this method, Dylan led the team without a hitch. Before long, they rolled onto the traversing pathway, plainly visible as a worn and flattened line across an otherwise untouched landscape. He only paused for a quick look behind and a headcount; there was no need to wait for confirmation to continue. He'd saved them time already and they'd only just got started.

On the smoother surface of the path he allowed his rate to increase, slowing down early for obstacles so that he could release the brakes going through them. The Jackdaws cruised near-silently along the pass, their soft-rubber tyres compliant, moulding to the shape of the rock beneath. Dylan rode with precision and poise that were near poetic; his wheels didn't skid by even the smallest amount. The caterpillar of trailing riders followed effortlessly in a tight line, their positions highlighted by the IR units. He made the next head count over his shoulder, without stopping.

He picked up the pace further. The team were keeping up easily and were in perfect control – he was wasting time by riding slowly. Applying less brake before each corner, the ground began to flow more rapidly beneath the bike. Loose stones skittered from the path of his wheels, occasionally ricocheting off the Jackdaw's dampened frame with a dull ping. The line of the path remained clear enough through the green ochre of the night-vision goggles but the surrounding terrain blurred into a monochrome moonscape. The rush of cold air chilled the exposed parts of his face. He opened up on a straight section and felt the shuddering of the wheels through the breath in his chest. *Forty miles-per-hour,* he judged. Easing back down, he took a glance around to see the train of riders still close behind. *No problem.*

Scanning ahead through the wispy remnants of cloud, Dylan could see the zigzag pattern of the trail below – a series of traverses linked by hairpin corners. The slope was steep but relatively even. There were just a few big boulders and patches of slender grass in places. The more direct route looked viable enough. He made a right-angle turn to bear straight down the hill, cutting out the windings of the foot trail.

Immediately the concentration requirement stepped up a level. He was forced to read the ground quickly, with a jump or turn necessary here and there to avoid troublesome patches. Constant gentle braking became essential to prevent his speed from increasing beyond control. His adrenalin level began to soar. *Now, this is real riding.* He bumped across the meandering path on its next return. He could no longer look over his shoulder but his line choice had been perfect; the others would still be behind. He hit a choppy patch – too late to slow down – and made a quick choice. His tyres weaved nimbly through a chicane of rocks, tighter than it looked through the night-vision viewer. *Whoa! Steady-up there.* He rejoined the footpath at the bottom of the incline and allowed the Jackdaw to coast to a halt atop a small ridge. He looked over his shoulder to the next man behind him. Shearman was breathing heavily but otherwise looked in fair shape.

'Nice work, Dylan. That was spot on.'

'Bit narrow through that last bit; sorry.'

'It's fine. We all got through.'

The soldiers formed up and scoured the area for signs of human presence, Haynes and Govrin using handheld night scopes. There was no other movement. Visibility had improved significantly since their departure from the cloud layer, but the plantation – their first expected visual reference – was still out of sight. The night-vision equipment revealed their immediate surroundings with reasonable clarity, but at longer distances, the moonless night provided too little light for the devices to amplify. They could see that the jagged scree was giving way to a more regular blend of dirt and gravel. This softer surface would be welcomed by the riders. Lactic acid had built in the muscles of their forearms, which now swelled and ached without exception. After ten minutes of silent observation, Shearman instructed Dylan to proceed.

'Okay, let's move off again. Just as you were, but keep it slow. We're still a long way out. Stop again in three more kays.'

The path they followed was historically used by Quechuans for passage over the mountains with animal trains, thus it snaked around to avoid the steepest inclines. Maintaining a southerly direction was becoming a confusing process and it wasn't long before Dylan opted to take his own route. At the crest of a ridge, he left the path altogether and took the fall-line down an abrupt face. His velocity increased rapidly but the Jackdaw's supple suspension kept his wheels under control. The momentum he accumulated carried him over the next rise without the need to pedal. *Easy. I'll stick with that approach.* He rode right to the edge of the next drop before he saw it – a sheer face of a couple of metres before the gradient continued again. With no time to find an alternative, he launched from the lip and thumped down onto the slope below. For the first time since their departure, he noticed that weight of his backpack and webbing were a significant hindrance. One by one, the train of riders followed. Behind him, Shearman wasn't appreciative.

'Hey! Dylan, reign it in. No crazy stuff!' A few similar exclamations accompanied the series of thumps from behind.

'I didn't know it was there,' Dylan snapped defensively. He felt that his navigation had been more than adequate so far, especially given the difficulty of the terrain. *It wasn't that bad, anyway.* He continued to pick his way through the petrified maze, sticking to the softer dirt where possible. Then finally the hillside opened out before him. The decline was near vertical for a short section, running seamlessly to flat over a stretch of about a kilometre. *Now this is what we need.* There was a long, shallow climb following the downslope. Dylan had no intention of pedalling all the way up it, whatever the others thought. The going looked smooth enough – no large boulders or ruts. He made his decision, and tipped the bike forward over the edge.

The rush of acceleration robbed him of breath.

Freefall.

There was a long moment of silence. The ground below seemed to rush up to meet him. Then the weight returned to his wheels. The judder struck with violence, escalating until it surged though his grips and pedals. The airflow filled his ears with a deafening roar. Still he accelerated, despite the easing gradient. The night-vision image disintegrated into a streaky green mess. He could see nothing. He squeezed the frame of the Jackdaw tight between his thighs and clung onto the grips. The wheels kicked frantically from impacts he couldn't avoid. His hands were going numb; he didn't know if he could hold on. It was far faster than he'd ever ridden. The noise, the blurring, the vibration – complete sensory deprivation. He was paralysed, unable to input any control. He shut his eyes.

The Jackdaw scooted onto the flat section, gradually slowing from the air resistance. The night-vision image eventually coalesced into a coherent picture. Dylan could function again. He hunched down low on the bike catching his breath, resting his shaken body while he coasted up the climb. With just a few turns of the cranks, he reached the crest. He spun around to check for the others, already knowing what the result would be, dread taking hold. There were no other riders behind him. *Oh fuck! Now I'm in trouble.* Looking ahead, he realised that the sprawling and sinister cartel facility was somewhere just below him. A cold shiver ran up his spine.

Chapter Nineteen

22:38
Mountain Path

Sonco stomped determinedly up the ancient caravan trail that wound like a ribbon around the shallower contours. The plantation was now a few kilometres behind him and the rolling slopes would soon give way to steeper inclines. He needed to cross over the ridge to reach the next valley and the journey would be long and demanding, especially given the weather and the darkness. But he had no choice. His daughter was pregnant and now she was sick.

He wasn't due to take leave for another two weeks and the unscheduled trip would not be sanctioned by his employers. Hence, he was forced to sneak away during the night. He disliked the Del Bosque cartel, anyway. It was not from choice that he worked for them. His family possessed a smallholding, part of a remote settlement – the place where he was now headed. Many years past, the militiamen had come. They were little more than armed bandits. Every family in the village was instructed to grow cocaine for Del Bosque. None of the inhabitants were brave or foolish enough to argue. Within a few years, the men had all been transferred to duties at La Fábrica, leaving the young and womenfolk to manage the settlement's own crops.

But Del Bosque did pay, and with fairness and regularity. Once per month he was permitted to travel home for a few days with his wages. The militiamen would soon rob him of this money if the cartel's laws did not forbid it, and few men would dare to break those rules. Three times a year, after the harvests, a truck and trailer would come to the settlement to collect the dried leaves to be taken elsewhere for processing. The village women were always paid by volume and the price never fluctuated. The reality was that coca provided a more reliable income than any other crop his family had grown.

He could not afford to wait for two more weeks to see his daughter. His family needed him. One of the camp's guards, a particularly uncouth individual, routinely taunted him about being the father of his daughter's unborn child. But recently, the man's mood had turned grave as he warned Sonco of the girl's deteriorating condition. So now Sonco was compelled to make the journey without permission. There would be consequences, but to hell with them. Most likely he would just be shouted at and docked some pay. He wasn't physically imposing or rebellious in his attitudes – the militia would achieve little by beating him to set an example. The farmers were the cartel's bread and butter; excessive brutality was never good for morale. Sonco knew the plantation far better than any of the sentries. Slipping past unnoticed had been child's play.

What he saw ahead of him was utterly mystifying. There shouldn't be anyone else on the mountain at all, let alone someone so strange. He had come within twenty metres before noticing the unusual figure in the darkness, and then his eyes had taken a while to focus. To start with he wondered if his imagination was deceiving him, but now that moment had passed. There really was a stranger before him on the hillside, standing as still as a statue over what appeared to be some kind of bicycle. It looked like a motorised scooter but Sonco couldn't discern where the engine was. The stranger wore a belt of pouches around his waist and had padded patches on his arms, legs and torso. Most curiously, he wore a helmet with a square box mounted right in front of his face, though which he stared into the black void of the night. Sonco was reluctant to believe that this stranger was real.

He quickly dismissed some unlikely possibilities: native, tourist, military; none of these made any sense. One of the camp guards with a new toy? This was more likely, but the only way the scooter could have come was on one of the transport planes; he would have heard of its arrival. Routines ran like clockwork at the plantation. News of anything out of the ordinary spread like wildfire. There were no secrets at La Fábrica.

So the man was a mystery. He could almost pass for one of the spacemen said in the stories to have visited their ancestors. Sonco was sure all cultures had such tales and was also sure that there were no spacemen. Besides, he looked more like a costumed fool at a carnival. Whoever he was, he must be seriously lost. It would be more or less impossible to arrive at this location by accident – it was difficult enough to access on purpose. It defied all logic that someone could just turn up here. He would need to offer this spaceman some navigational assistance.

Sonco called out a gentle, inquisitive greeting. The man's head flicked around like some terrified, hunted animal. He spoke again, this time in Spanish – something placatory. Sonco felt a hard slap, as if someone had struck him in the body. There was no one else there. Then he felt burning in his chest, spreading, intensifying. A sudden spasm seized hold of his insides, preventing him from drawing breath. The stranger hadn't moved but was staring at him, now with his mouth hanging open. Sonco saw the stony ground rushing upwards to meet his face.

Chapter Twenty

22:51

Four Kilometres to Target

'Good shot!' Haynes said calmly. He was laying prone on the rim of the bluff, watching the scene unfold below through a handheld night-scope. Govrin crouched next to him with an identical device.

'What's happening down there?' Wade asked. The distance was too great for his NVGs to reveal any detail.

'What's happening?' Haynes answered. 'They followed Dylan down this escarpment and now they're spread out all over the place. Sod's law, that's when we get a contact. Dylan's over a hundred metres from the nearest man. Luckily Gav's taken care of it. That was some quick work to get his rifle off the bike and make the shot.'

'The dead man… I don't see a weapon.' Govrin sounded concerned.

'Might have had a radio though, mightn't he,' Haynes countered.

'He could be a civilian.'

'Oh well, too late now.' Haynes seemed unfazed. 'Couldn't risk him getting a shot off.'

'Why have we stopped? Shouldn't we be down there?' Match, the most skilled of the trainees, had been riding at the rear to minimise the chance of the last man falling unnoticed. Now he had come forward see what the hold-up was.

'I'm sorry; it was my fault,' Govrin confessed, sounding frustrated. 'I heard Jonah curse as he reached the edge and thought I was about to follow him over a cliff. I panicked.' She had watched the five preceding riders vanish downwards like parachutists exiting an aircraft, then snatched her brake levers and skidded to an abrupt halt on the lip. The train of following bikes had bunched up at her rear.

'It's not as bad as it looks. Just point straight down and the bike will roll. I can take the lead.' Match offered. The face was near vertical to begin with – a slab of sheer rock the height of a house – then the surface gave way to gravel and transitioned to a more manageable gradient over a hundred or so metres. There would be no possibility of using the brakes. The route barely looked viable. The first four riders had followed Dylan blindly, without realising the danger.

'No,' Haynes interjected. 'She was right to stop – this is madness. Cal should never have let Dylan lead. We need to stay here until they've formed up; then they can count our headlights and confirm that no one's got lost.' Haynes was the most experienced soldier present. His suggestion was accepted without further comment.

'Then we'll need to find another way down. I can still take the lead,' Match offered.

'So be it,' Haynes concurred.

Govrin's forearms and thighs burned from the intense descent. Dylan had made good time – they were comfortably ahead of the expected schedule – but the fast pace had taken its toll on her physically. The terrain itself had not been exceptionally difficult, but constant concentration had been required to avoid making a costly mistake. She spoke up.

'No, it's okay, Match. You need to cover our rear. I can lead us down to their position. I was caught off-guard but I'm fine now.'

'We're set to move off again as soon as they get their act together down there,' Wade confirmed. 'In the meantime, I'll take a recce along this ridge on foot. There might be an easier way down.'

When the four men below had re-formed, Haynes signalled Shearman by toggling an infrared headlamp. The Morse coded signal conveyed the message: *hold position, we are en route.* The frontrunners would adopt defensive positions around Dylan until the rest had caught up. Nine more minutes passed before the unit were reassembled.

Govrin coasted to a gentle halt by Jonah, who was crouched providing protection for Dylan and the Jackdaws. The crest of the rise was featureless and offered no cover. The six riders following her wasted no time in spreading out into a defensive formation. Shearman, Riley and Daniels had already fanned out on foot to ensure there was no one else lurking around. Dylan sat on the dusty ground with his knees pulled up and his head slumped down between them. The dead man lay where he fell a few metres away.

'How are we looking, Jonah?' Govrin enquired.

'We're okay. Luckily, the guy was alone. He didn't shout. No radio.'

'What about our position?' Govrin kept her voice low.

'Good. We're two kilometres from the target and right on the coordinates. The plantation is just below us. The others should be back shortly. What happened to you?'

'We didn't like your route.'

'Let's just say it was exhilarating. You definitely made the safer choice. You have to hand it to Dylan, though. He said he could find the fastest way down.'

'How's he doing?'

'He just saw a man get shot in front of him. He's in shock, but I think he'll be okay. He also got a serious bollocking from Cal for leading us over that cliff. He'll be feeling some backlash from the adrenalin now – trust me, I am. He's been told to switch off his goggles for the moment; that's why he's staring at the floor.'

'*Pffft,*' Govrin hissed her disapproval. 'He shouldn't even be here.'

Crouching down by Dylan, she rested a hand on his shoulder and spoke gently.

'Hey, you just did a great job for us. We wouldn't have got here otherwise, or at least, not for a long while.'

'Shame Calvin doesn't see it that way,' Dylan replied sulkily.

'He doesn't mean it. He's just very tense right now because he's responsible for all of our safety, and this is a dangerous situation. From now on you need to be more cautious.'

'I've already been told. I'm riding at the back the rest of the way, with Tom behind to keep an eye on me.'

'That's not what I meant, Dylan. Listen to me carefully. This is not about riding bikes anymore. From now on you must watch *everything* that's happening around you, check where we are, listen for instructions, and make absolutely no noise. We just want to get you home safe.'

He lifted his head and sat up straight.

'I understand, Elana. Thanks. Don't worry, I'll be fine.'

* * *

Match took the lead for the final approach to the target and employed an entirely different riding technique. They travelled at a smooth crawl, noiseless and invisible as they weaved through the patchy vegetation. Navigating a route to avoid the ruts and fissures became a painstaking process. The ground was scattered with enough hidden boulders to have made it a minefield for a parachute insertion. Infrared illuminators were doused, forcing riders to rely purely on their NVGs, and this made it tricky to read where the bumps and dips were. The Jackdaw's soft-treaded tyres were excellent for absorbing sound but it still took absolute focus to avoid making a noisy mistake. Govrin found this silent phase even more taxing than the previous rapid descent.

The tendons of both her forearms already felt strained, but she refused to let the discomfort affect her performance. Having been assigned command of Delta One, she now held responsibility for the clearance of the plantation landing-zone. This was the crucial first step of the mission that must be conducted without raising the alarm. They rolled ever nearer to the point where she would assume control. A knot began to form in her stomach.

Her role was to locate targets and direct the two marksmen, who would then neutralise these threats with their suppressed rifles. It wasn't realistic for the snipers to use rifle scopes in conjunction with their night-vision goggles, so the two HK417's were fitted with separate Hensoldt night-sights. This meant that the marksmen would have a restricted field of view when aiming, and no awareness of their immediate surroundings. Govrin would monitor their near-field area, allowing them to focus solely on their marksmanship. It was also essential that the enemy were removed in the right order – if a sentry saw a compatriot fall and fired a warning shot, the mission would fail as a result. This entire task had to be coordinated without using the radios. She could feel the pressure mounting.

They came to a halt amidst a thicket of dense vegetation on the hillside above the plantation, finally dismounting the Jackdaws. Govrin was glad to give her aching arms a rest, and thankful that she would be operating on her feet from now on. Shearman indicated that he would accompany Delta One on an observation of the fields below while the rest of the unit secured a temporary lying-up point. They selected an elevated vantage point from where Govrin could memorise as much of the plantation layout as possible. The team had all studied the satellite imagery but it gave little detail and was taken from a high-angle perspective. Now she looked for reference points that would clarify her whereabouts on the ground. She would need every advantage to navigate the area swiftly.

The plantation stretched for over two kilometres east to west, and was roughly one and a half north to south. Its entire perimeter was bordered by a wide headland and the interior divided into blocks by crude vehicle tracks. It was apparent from the height of the plants that the crop was most established at the western end. A man could walk upright in cover between the tallest rows. Each block became sequentially shorter heading eastwards, and at the farthest extent Delta One would need to crawl to remain invisible. The entire crop was planted in furrows around thirty centimetres deep that ran horizontally across the breadth of the field. These would provide shelter for a soldier lying prone but would also make movement more difficult. The team would need to use the flatter vehicle tracks to cover distance quickly, where they would be reliant purely on darkness for concealment.

During her vigil, Govrin thought back to the briefing sheets that were issued at Stirling Lines. La Fábrica was unusually large for this type of facility – the cultivated area was in excess of three hundred hectares. Its audacity was testament to the cartel's confidence in their defensive arrangements. The report stated that cocaine farming across South America produced an annual average of five kilos per hectare. But in Colombia, aerial herbicide sprays had been used as part of a US-sponsored eradication scheme, and this brought the aggregate figure down. No crop-dusting aircraft would ever survive a visit to La Fábrica. It was therefore assumed that the facility could potentially achieve double this yield. By centralising their operations, Del Bosque were also able to refine their techniques to generate the maximum quantity of processed product. The gross output was therefore suspected to be in excess of three tonnes of pure, high-quality cocaine per year. This was a multi-million-dollar enterprise.

In the northwest corner of the plantation, sat an armed guard in a white plastic chair, to the south of the team's lying-up point but obscured from them by vegetation. A second could be seen walking away from him eastwards along the northern headland. Govrin could see neither the eastern nor the southern headland from her vantage point but it was assumed that the roaming sentry would pass through these locations on a clockwise route around the perimeter. Taz was first to make out a third sentry with his rifle scope, moving north up one of the vehicle tracks. McCowan's plan had been to sit tight and analyse the enemy movements. Now Delta One agreed that it seemed favourable to press home their time advantage.

Govrin would move her patrol to a position above the north-east corner, keeping ahead of the patrolling guard. After removing the sentries currently visible, they would then enter the plantation and work back towards the west. Shearman would return to the lying-up point and assign someone to keep tabs on the guard in the plastic chair; when the man went down, he would know that the area had been cleared. It would then be safe for the mission to proceed. The team would then split up to pursue their individual objectives while Delta One shifted their focus to keeping the LZ secure.

* * *

They crouched, concealed by the low brush, forty metres from the headland. A fourth militiaman stood on station, facing away from them. Govrin gave concise instructions as they waited for the roaming guard to catch up. It was an unusual format, having two shooters for one spotter, but she intended to make good use of the arrangement. The roaming guard would perhaps stop to chat, providing two stationary targets. The marksmen would hit both guards together on her mark, while she ensured that no witnesses arrived in the vicinity. The HK417 rifles were fitted with suppressors and sixteen-inch accurized barrels – known as the 'Recce' format – and were chambered with 7.62mm subsonic rounds, boat-tailed to reduce drag and susceptibility to crosswind. The 200-grain ammunition offered plenty of impact energy, but headshots would still be required to guarantee the departing sentries' cooperative silence. Delta One crouched motionless in the dark, watching the slow approach of the ambling guard.

'Ready,' Govrin whispered. Both men already held their rifles up in the shoulder. The guard only had a few steps to go. Govrin watched for the instant he stopped, scanning her head from side to side for other movement.

'Now, go!'

Phut, phut.

The muffled reports were almost simultaneous, and the two lifeless sentries slumped to the floor.

'Nice! Shift the bodies.'

They hustled down the slope to the headland, Taz covering while Govrin and Riley dragged the two limp corpses into the brush. The other patrolling sentry was now visible some distance away between the rows of shorter plants, moving southwards in what appeared to be an inner-field circuit. He hadn't heard a thing. They moved quickly down the eastern headland and then west to intercept. Govrin kept her eyes on the southern headland as Riley took the man at eighty-metres range with another clean headshot. The deceased guard was left where he fell between the short, bushy coca plants.

Delta One moved west along separate paths, stalking like cats through long grass, spaced a hundred metres apart and pausing at every junction to confirm sight of each other. It was soon established that no enemy remained in the eastern half of the plantation. To their front the crop was high enough to conceal a man and they would need to progress with less haste. A guard was sighted on the southern headland, stationed by the entrance to the track designated GREEN. It was assumed that the RED route would be similarly manned. Govrin instructed Taz to hold position and monitor their rear, while she accompanied Riley to remove the lookout to the south. Riley would then loiter close to the GREEN entrance to prevent any new arrivals from turning up; she would return to Taz and continue their sweep to the west.

They crept in close for the kill and a third discreet round spat from Riley's rifle. As soon as the man dropped, Govrin dashed over and dragged his body into the undergrowth. The marksman moved hastily to an angle where he could see directly into the tunnel-like passage, then backtracked to a safer range of ninety metres. He lay prone in a furrow and trained his weapon on the point where further enemies might appear.

Govrin sprinted back to Taz on the central track. Time was critical now – every minute that passed increased the chance of an unseen sentry entering the area. The coca plants surrounding them were above head height – it was impossible to be certain that no one was nearby. She was forced to make a snap decision: they would prioritise speed over caution.

They snaked along the remaining vehicle tracks at a run, checking all four directions at each crossing. Reaching the western headland without encounter, they then moved south to locate the expected guard at the entrance to RED. There wasn't time to re-check the southern headland. Govrin prayed it was still clear and gave the order for Taz to fire. She left the body – anyone who arrived to find it would be killed immediately anyway.

Taz adopted a position covering the RED passageway entrance, while Govrin made north for the final guard in the plastic chair. Her suppressed carbine wasn't loaded with the subsonic rounds necessary for a completely silent takedown, but if all had gone to plan the nearest listeners would be surrounded by dense forest two kilometres away in the main camp. To rely on this assumption was risky, but it was the quickest solution available.

She closed silently to within forty metres. The man in the chair was unquestionably awake but slouched lazily and staring at the cigarette he was rolling. He had little chance of seeing her in the pitch black of the night. She held the C8 tight to her shoulder and crept forward, slowly, gently. She saw movement behind her target. A dark clad figure slipped out of the brush and cupped a hand over the man's mouth. A long, hooked knife flicked around in the other hand and sliced savagely into his throat. It only took a few seconds of this butchery before the flailing body went limp. Madan had employed his kukri.

It is an accepted fact within the military that killing a man with a knife will not normally be a noiseless process. There will be screaming, gurgling and thrashing that will create far more sound than using an appropriately quietened firearm. But Madan was not a normal man. For a Gurkha the kukri is sacrosanct. Each man not only trains to fight with the weapon, but maintains it meticulously to ensure effectiveness and readiness for use. To Madan, the waste of such an opportunity would have been tantamount to blasphemy. And in choosing this course of action, he had solved Govrin's final problem. The plantation was declared clear.

She had barely managed to discard the body when the other Delta units scooted down the headland on their Jackdaws. They didn't stop for confirmation – the starting gun for the mission had been fired. Now she needed to return through the crop to a position where she could cover the rear of the two marksmen.

A crossroads of vehicle tracks offered a clear view east and west behind her two men, and also a sightline towards the southern headland – the anticipated direction from which enemy would approach once the mission went loud. She wriggled into a ditch below a coca bush, just to the side of the track, where she recovered her breath from the rapid run. With her first objective accomplished smoothly, the immediate pressure had abated. Her team only needed to keep the area secure for as long as it took for the general's forces to arrive. There was a noise behind her. Then another. Footsteps on the dirt. Suddenly she was gripped by fear. *Shit! I've missed one!*

She did not dare turn her head but could clearly hear the footfalls approaching from her unguarded rear. She had just come from that direction and seen no one. *Was there someone asleep somewhere?* She could roll over, locate the target and shoot, but the offender could easily get a shot off. A rifle could be trained on her back already. She lay petrified, frozen in the ditch, praying that she hadn't been noticed, knowing that she was done for otherwise. The footsteps stayed even and progressively became louder, in competition with her thumping heart. *Step, step, step.* She could hardly breathe. The walker was right on top of her – surely the soft hum of her night-vision unit would give her presence away. Her pulse pounded deafeningly in her ears. *Step, step, step.* The grind of a boot on stony ground, right behind her. Then to her left. Further to her left. Beside her. The guard was walking past.

She needed to move fast. She slowly turned her head to reveal a lone sentry now two metres past her, rifle slung over his back. If he made it to the southern headland, he would see the main group. She could shoot, but now she was closer to the main encampment and there could be someone within earshot along one of the passageways that led to the clearing. *Oh hell!* She gripped her rifle tightly by the foregrip and the base of the extendible stock. In one smooth movement, she pushed herself to her feet and took five long, smooth strides toward him. The guard heard enough to pause his step and his head began to turn, just as Govrin smashed her rifle butt into the base of his skull with all the force she could muster. He grunted, then his knees buckled and he tumbled face forwards onto the floor.

She jumped flat onto his back, dropping her carbine, trapping his rifle between their bodies. The guard was partially stunned but still conscious. Her left arm wrapped around his neck and gripped the crook of her right elbow. Her right hand angled backwards to push his head forward into the brutal choke hold. She squeezed as hard as her sore arms would allow and felt him begin to thrash around in panic. She spread her feet out wide to keep stable; his writhing would not dislodge her. The scissor-like grip on the man's neck constricted his carotid arteries, starving his brain of oxygen.

Training had taught her that he would black out within moments. She squeezed even harder as the body became limp, counting the seconds. Lactic acid filled her arms and she gritted her teeth against the pain. Her count reached ninety and she could squeeze no more. She released the guard's head, letting it flop forward into the dirt, her arms so numb they would hardly move. With no small effort, she rolled the man over, checked his neck for a pulse, then put her ear to his chest. No heartbeat, no breathing. The guard was dead.

After retrieving her assault rifle and checking the stock for damage, she dragged the man's body out of sight and collapsed exhausted on the ground beside him, the beating of her heart still quick in her chest. She remained still for a full minute until her breathing was under control, then rolled onto her front and crawled back to her previous position in the furrow, resuming her duty covering the rear of the two marksmen.

Chapter Twenty-One

Thursday, 28 July, 01:44
La Fábrica

They had come to a halt on the headland near the southwest corner of the plantation, close by the mortar pit – the target designated RED-1. Daniels, the last rider, pulled his bike in beside Dylan. The soldiers had already dismounted and were crouched, facing outward, their weapons held up, scanning side to side for enemy who weren't there. Carefully and quietly, the Jackdaws were wheeled off one by one into the undergrowth and hidden out of sight. Shearman snapped out orders in brisk, whispered tones.

'Ren, head down GREEN and get eyes on the camp. See if you can suss out a safe route through. Be ready to grab us when we follow up shortly.' Wade turned without further word, signalling by hand to Madan and Morris. The three men promptly peeled off, departing eastwards along the southern headland, their creeping figures merging into the brush. Daniels feared for a moment that Riley wouldn't recognise them as friendlies, but Shearman was busy giving instructions and in no mood to be interrupted.

'Match, size up that mortar and make damn sure it's not wired. Hugo, Jonah, cover Match and watch Dylan. Tom, you're coming with me for a quick recce.'

Shearman turned and slid smoothly into the dark passageway, adopting a crouched stance, while Daniels mimicked his movements in tow. It was impossible not to be nervous; their sluggish progression only amplified the suspense. Daniels breathing felt shallow in his chest but he tried to stay focussed. Step by step they inched through the eerie tunnel, weapons raised, stocks extended and pulled tight into their shoulders. It was so dark that they could barely see a few metres, even with the aid of the night-vision goggles. The inky blackness could hide an enemy almost until they stumbled into them, and still they might not be spotted themselves. But there were no militia to be found. They advanced unchallenged down the track until it reached the western end of the encampment.

Shearman and Daniels found themselves within the immense clearing. Its highest branches formed a vaulted ceiling twenty metres over their heads. Its farthest extent was way beyond their visual range. The space within was both surprising and impressive in equal measure, but they had neither the time nor sufficient light to scrutinise the details of its construction. However, the scale alone gave an indication of the cartel's commitment. Countless man hours, skilled engineering and expensive equipment had been required to create this facility.

There was a sizeable structure close to their position – the workstation for cocaine refinement. A stout timber frame held a tarpaulin roof over several rows of wooden bins and tables. Thick plastic sheeting covered parts of the floor. Assorted apparatus hung from the framework or was stacked on shelves. A brief inspection revealed plastic containers holding sulphuric and hydrochloric acid, potassium permanganate powder and ammonium hydroxide. Larger drums held chemical solvents: acetone, kerosene – the former would be conveniently volatile. They moved through the production facility and progressed further into the clearing, moving slowly, checking every angle. To the south was an open-ended hut with a large overhang – storage for the processed cocaine, now designated RED-3.

They continued eastwards until reaching a tall wooden shed with full-height double doors at one end. Shearman gave cover while Daniels eased open one door to take a quick peek, praying throughout that the hinges wouldn't squeak. The shed contained a tractor, horticultural equipment and mechanical maintenance tools. A pair of heavy metal ramps sat on the floor, suggesting that the shed was used for vehicle servicing. There was no human presence nearby. The western end of the clearing was deserted.

But further to the east there *were* signs of enemy presence. Lanterns hung around a covered seating area; figures were dotted along the benches. Adjacent was a huge marquee. Men could be seen milling around both these structures in numbers. Daniels noted that some of the militia appeared to be wearing camouflage fatigues, although the monochrome image of the viewer made it difficult to discern any real detail at distance. Shearman took his arm and squeezed it tightly, then pointed to a shape close by at the clearing's edge. Daniels couldn't make it out initially, until Shearman eventually whispered a one-word explanation: *hammock.* After a few more minutes of silent observation, others became visible dotted along the edge of the tree line. They could move in no further, but Shearman was already content that they had seen enough. Soon they carefully retraced their path to the mortar pit.

Match had made an interesting discovery.

'There's a whole crate of one-oh-seven in there – white-phos *and* HE. We can't put the charge in with it, Delta One would get rained with shrapnel, but I've checked thoroughly and I'm sure it's not rigged. I reckon we can move it.'

'How heavy?' Shearman asked.

'Two of us will manage.'

Daniels voiced the inherent suggestion. 'We're counting on RED-2 to thin out the enemy, right? So the bigger the bang the better.'

Shearman nodded once to acknowledge.

'Jonah and I will carry it down there, then provide cover while you set both charges. We can't go through the camp to reach our targets, so once you're done we'll backtrack via here. It's coming up for 02:10 now. Set RED-2 and RED-3 to blow at 03:00 precisely – that's fifty minutes from this point. Match, rig the mortar to blow five minutes beforehand at 02:55. It'll only be a small pop, but it should still be loud enough to draw the militia toward the production area. We'll just have to hope the farmers aren't too keen to get involved. That doesn't give Delta Four much time to get into position. Hugo, get over to GREEN asap and tell Ren to get moving, then wait for us there. Go now.'

'Got it.' Haynes turned and jogged off along the southern headland, dispensing with the stealth of movement employed by the others.

Their watches had already been synchronised back at Outpost and now each unit had a precise timetable to keep. Shearman and Jonah lugged the heavy ammunition crate out of the rear of the pit, allowing Match to place the charge that would decommission the mortar. The task took him just forty seconds.

'Done,' he declared.

'Okay, Match, the western camp is empty. Get across to the other side of the clearing and sweep the exit route for Tom and Dylan. If there's anyone on the path or the beach, take them out.'

Match surprised Shearman by moving off in the wrong direction. He blundered into the vegetation for a moment then came out with his Jackdaw.

'I'll be quicker with this.'

He swung a leg over the frame, pushed off and cranked a few turns of the pedals. Both bike and rider vanished spectrally into the dark passageway.

'Good idea,' Daniels agreed. 'Dylan, go grab our two bikes and follow me closely on foot. No noise.'

Dylan, who had not spoken for the last two hours, simply nodded.

Daniels spearheaded the group moving down the track, his carbine at the ready. Shearman and Jonah followed a few yards behind with the heavy box of mortar rounds, their breath labouring audibly. On reaching the clearing, Daniels led Dylan to the westernmost extent – the farthest point from potential trouble – then kept watch for any movement while the crate was lugged over to the tractor shed. The SAS men deposited the crate inside and took covering positions – Shearman outside the doors, Jonah by the cocaine storage hut.

'Dylan, leave the bikes here and take your backpack over to the hut by Jonah,' Daniels gestured towards the cocaine store. 'Just leave it inside, in the middle of the floor somewhere obvious, then come straight back here and wait for me. I'll be five minutes. Okay?'

'Okay.'

Daniels jogged over to Shearman and slipped through the open door of the shed. The wooden building was full of tools, trays of ironmongery, a compressor and three fifty-gallon drums of diesel fuel, all of which would contribute to the lethal effect of the explosion. He saw that the ammunition crate had been pushed underneath the small tractor. He took a quick peek inside.

'Ouch!' he whispered to himself. *I'm glad I won't be standing near here.*

He set to work priming the RED-2 demolition pack, the largest of their charges – sixteen 570g blocks of American M112 C4 plastic explosive, individually wrapped in olive-green film. He inserted four pencil detonators into the putty-like material, each already attached by wire to the timer device. He checked his watch, set the timer, and counted down the last few seconds before clicking off the safety deactivation switch. He manoeuvred the charge pack underneath the old, rusty workhorse and placed it inside the crate. The shockwave from the C4 would obliterate the shed, peppering anyone nearby with a wall of deadly shrapnel. What additional effects the white-phosphorous rounds would bring about, he genuinely had no idea, but whatever they were it would not be good for the militia.

He was heading over to the cocaine store when he saw the first indication that the plan was going astray. Dylan sprinted away from the hut and back to the

Jackdaws, one of which he snatched up from the ground. Daniels scanned around in case there was an enemy present but could see no one. Shearman and Jonah still had their arcs covered. Daniels turned back to see Dylan mount the bike and pedal rapidly away in the direction of YELLOW – the footpath to the beach. *No Dylan, you're supposed to wait!*

Daniels could hardly shout after him with the enemy so close. *Something must have spooked him.* Daniels resolved that he would catch up with Dylan once his task was complete, and prayed that Match had successfully cleared the route through. The RED-3 charge needed to be set before he could follow. He sprinted into the small hut. *What the hell has he done here?* Dylan had left the charge in the middle of the hut as requested, but had tipped it out of its backpack instead of leaving the whole thing. The pressure of the situation had clearly become too much for the young civilian. *Never mind, it doesn't matter.*

He rigged the charge as rapidly as his shaking hands would allow, setting the timer to detonate simultaneously with RED-2. The whole room was stacked high with thick plastic packets containing dried, refined cocaine powder. He pulled a few down to cover the charge. At this concentration, the effects of the burning fumes would be far from euphoric – they would be highly toxic. Daniels guessed that the room contained over a tonne of product, worth millions of dollars on the street. Not for much longer. A quick head swivel to check that the vicinity was still clear, and he dashed back to his Jackdaw.

He rode urgently southwards, following the edge of the clearing, attempting to locate the entrance to the footpath. He desperately needed the IR units to find his way but could not risk using them inside the clearing. His tyres were making too much noise as it was. A dark patch in the brush revealed his destination and he heaved at the pedals with relief. Exiting the clearing, he toggled his light switches while riding, without slowing down. He had to catch Dylan at any cost.

The passage was narrow, windy and bumpy – intended for walkers. The ends of his handlebars repeatedly clipped tree trunks, bruising his knuckles though his gloves. He rode at maximum pace regardless, standing up and pedalling wherever possible. The Jackdaw juddered skittishly around a tight corner roughly hewn with rugged steps, then rapidly regained speed as the steep path straightened.

A narrow bridge came into view. No railings. No time to brake. Daniels pointed the front wheel at the far side and prayed the bike would roll straight. A quick glance to the side dented his confidence: the span crossed a several-metre drop into a rocky fissure. The bike wobbled as his steering became increasingly erratic. His courage was ebbing, his brain screamed at him to slow down, but somehow, he managed to keep up the pace. A flicker of infrared somewhere to his front renewed his resolve. He was catching up. Rounding another bend, he could clearly see the other bike's headlights – not that far ahead. Dylan was only coasting. *Is he exhausted?* Dylan's Jackdaw slowed up to a crawl and then vanished from sight altogether. *What?* A few more pedal-turns and Daniels understood.

Sticking out of the ground ahead were a pair of rounded wooden posts – ladder ends. There was a drop. The lights were still moving below, so Dylan was still on his bike. It had to be possible. Daniels kept rolling towards the edge and the pitch-black void that followed it. Only at the last moment did he see the ground appear far below. The landing was narrow with a wall of rock to the left. Daniels slammed down hard, the subsequent bounce glancing him into the rock face. A sharp pain bit into his shoulder. He gritted his teeth, fighting to ignore it, and began turning his legs to regain the lost speed.

His energy was flagging. Dylan was almost within reach but he couldn't afford to ease up. He skidded around the bumpy corners, no longer caring about the noise. A surge of adrenaline gripped him when he saw the other Jackdaw just twenty metres ahead. *I've caught him!* The trees were peeling away; the path was widening. Daniels let off both brakes and mashed the pedals for a final burst of speed. He was right behind. He opened his mouth to shout.

Dylan banked smoothly into a sweeping left turn, his inside pedal lifted to avoid it scraping the ground. Daniels realised his situation just a fraction too late. *Fuck...the cliff!*

He snatched at his brake levers but to no avail. He carried too much speed to make the corner. In panic, he squeezed harder, locking up both wheels. The Jackdaw wallowed into an ungainly skid, then went down hard on one side. He let go of the grips and desperately kicked the bike away, clawing at the ground in search of a handhold. The sheer edge slid beneath his body and slipped from his fingertips. Daniels caught a brief glimpse of Match crouched on the cliff top as he dropped, his stomach sucking in with a cold rush of fear. He tried to brace his legs. There was a metallic clatter as the Jackdaw struck the hard surface, then the ground hit him. The first impact slammed his knees directly into his chin. He was flung flat onto his back, knocking every gasp of breath from his lungs.

Momentum threw his legs over his torso, his head and shoulders whipping around after them. The back of his helmet smashed into the slope. Daniels' world went black.

Chapter Twenty-Two

02:39

Green

Shearman crouched on the dirt track, hoping he wouldn't have to dive for the brush. The bellowing roar of a massive diesel engine preceded the appearance of a quadrangle of powerful headlights sixty metres to his front. The bright glare whited-out his night-vision goggles, preventing him from discerning the shape of the machine as it drove through the clearing. It turned to the east, away from their direction, much to Shearman's relief. The growl of the engine slowly diminished and the lights retreated through the sparse vegetation. He waited quietly with Jonah until certain there was no further activity.

Their C8 CQB assault rifles were fitted with magnifying ACOG scopes – ideal for engaging targets at longer ranges in daylight. Positioned above each scope was a small red-dot sight that provided an instant close-range aiming point. Neither of these systems worked well in conjunction with the NVGs. Night-time aiming was therefore achieved using the Insight Technology AN/PEQ-2 laser, mounted on the upper-forward rail. The device had two individually switchable functions: an infrared illuminator, and a targeting laser beam that pinpointed the destination of any fired rounds. These emissions were only visible to those using night-vision equipment. Shearman had instructed his team to keep the units switched off until the shooting started, just in case any enemy carried night-sights.

As they reached the clearing, Haynes emerged from behind and rested a hand on Shearman's shoulder. The three men huddled together, remaining crouched.

'Was that what I think it was?' Shearman asked.

'Yep, 'fraid so, but there's worse news.'

'Go on.'

'There's a few guys in the bunker it just came from, along with a nasty-looking technical. Ren took a peek when he got here.' Haynes referred to an armed and armoured pick-up truck. 'We'll need to get rid of it first and there's no way of doing it quietly. The SAM's driven a little way east to a patch they've cleared of trees. It's doing radar sweeps of the sky. There'll be three crew plus the driver, so we can't do that quietly either.'

'Then we'll have to be loud,' Shearman declared. 'What about GREEN-1?'

'There's a lot of activity around the radio tent and lights on in some of the others. I doubt you can get close to it. But there's a generator providing the power, about thirty metres closer to us. They've probably put it there so the radio operator doesn't have to listen to it. That's your best bet.'

'And have Delta Four located BLUE?'

'They couldn't see it, but it must be over to the south. There's tyre tracks heading that direction. They've gone via the perimeter rather than run right across in the open. It will take them a while but they'll get there unseen.'

The clearing had been sited to exploit a flattish ridge, but on the far side the ground dropped away sharply. The point where BLUE emerged was hidden by the lie of the ground somewhere below them. Shearman could only hope that Delta Four had found the correct route; following tyre tracks seemed to rely on a dangerous assumption. Without locating BLUE there would be no escape from the clearing. He checked his watch – less than eleven minutes remained until the diversionary charge fired. They were running out of time.

'Which one first?' Haynes asked.

'We don't have time to fuck around. We'll sort the radio first, then storm the bunker just before the mortar charge goes off. If we attract some attention, the sound of the explosion will at least split the militia up.'

'Okay. What about WHITE?'

'We'll set GREEN-2 then rely on our NVG advantage for taking out the SAM crew. Anyone following us will get a shock when the bunker goes up. Then we leg it for BLUE and hope for the best.'

'Sounds okay,' Haynes agreed with his normal lack of passion.

'One other thing: I'm not taking a chance on the radio operator getting a message out. I'll set GREEN-1 to blow immediately after RED-1. Let's face it, it will probably kick off by then, anyhow.'

'Fine.'

The GREEN-1 target was housed in a tent, roughly five metres square, with light emanating from its doorway. A satellite dish and a tall metal aerial were adjacent. Several other tents were nearby, as well as three modern-looking military jeeps. A few men stood around smoking or wandered between the tents, some of whom wore camouflage fatigues and carried weapons. That was as much detail as Shearman had time to absorb, but enough to know that things would get very difficult if he was spotted approaching. His charge pack wasn't especially large – it would disable the radio but not all the surrounding men. It was also doubtful that these enemies would be close enough to the production area charges to be neutralised. The situation required a high-risk strategy. Nine minutes remained.

He crept through the shadows towards the hefty diesel generator, the monotonous hum of its motor comfortably covering the sound of his footsteps. Relieved to arrive unnoticed, he knelt behind the rusty hulk and formulated a simple plan: he would kill two birds with one stone. He adeptly primed the plastic explosive, matching the timer to his watch in a mere few seconds as he worked. He attached the pack low down on the motor housing, attempting to judge the centre point of its mass. Satisfied, he slunk back to the other two as fast as he could manage in a crouch.

They moved swiftly to the bunker entrance and formed up in a tight group, stood in the very spot where Wade had made his observations shortly before. Voices could be heard from within. Shearman glanced cautiously around the thick wooden prop that supported the entrance. The interior was lit with overhead bulbs, so he pulled his head back and flipped up his goggles for a clearer view. The garage had a ceiling height of several metres, its walls and roof shored with stout timber. It was easily sufficient to accommodate the mobile SAM. The earth ramp leading inside was rutted from the deeply treaded tyres of a large and heavy vehicle. This was undoubtedly WHITE's usual sleeping quarters.

At the bottom of the ramp, three men in camouflage fatigues were engaged in conversation, each carrying the distinctive AKS-74U assault rifle slung over his shoulder. These guys looked more professional than Shearman had anticipated – presumably ex-military. *Mercenaries.* On the right-hand side was the pick-up truck, and behind it a fourth man attended a workbench against the rear wall. There was no opportunity for stealth. Shearman was forced to place his bets on a bluff.

'We'll walk right into the garage, smile, say hello, then hose them down. Hugo, take the guy on the right. Jonah and I will take the group.' There were nods from both men.

They had all practiced relentlessly for this situation in the Killing House at Stirling Lines. Every movement was so deeply ingrained in their muscle memory that they could hit their targets without even pausing to take aim. But facing an armed enemy at such close range, the adrenaline was electrifying. Shearman's head felt numb as reason tried to force its way into his thoughts. He pushed any fears from his mind, refusing to dwell on them – *don't think, just do*. He couldn't afford for doubt to affect his coordination. Hesitation at this point would quickly prove lethal.

'Jonah, full-auto?'

'Definitely.'

'How long till the decoy charge.'

'Fifty seconds.'

'Let's go.'

Shearman let out a burst of deep, hearty laughter and walked down the entrance ramp, Haynes and Jonah line abreast, cradling their weapons loosely in their arms. The mercenaries' heads spun sharply around to face them, bodies visibly tensing. They were alert, wary. The man at the back of the room turned from his bench and stared. Shearman smiled and held his left arm high in a phoney greeting. Enemy hands reached for the weapons that hung on their straps. Delta Three strode deeper into the chamber, still smiling, their posture relaxed. The guards were silent, wide eyed, suspicious.

'Que tal?' Shearman called. An assault rifle swung towards him.

'*Now!*'

The SAS men fired in unison. Haynes kept walking forward, casually lifted the weapon to his shoulder and put four single rounds in his target. Jonah stopped dead, whipped up his C8 and emptied the magazine, fanning left to right across the group. Shearman dropped to a crouch, unleashing his clip in three steady bursts, one into each man. The mercenaries were riddled with bullets before they could fire a shot, their safety catches still on. Haynes' target fell into the bench then slumped to the floor. Shearman felt a moment of elation that the room was clear, but it was short-lived. Even suppressed, the sound of their gunfire was unambiguous, and distinctly audible outside the bunker. A chorus of shouts rang out in the clearing. The mission had gone loud.

The thump of the mortar charge echoed back from the mountainside. Militia voices momentarily fell quiet then intensified fivefold. Every fighter in the camp would have snatched up his weapon and now be looking for targets, their handheld radios squawking with frantic enquiries.

'*Jonah, rig it, hurry*,' Shearman shouted, sprinting back to the entrance to give cover. He heard a single report behind him as Haynes put a follow-up shot in the head of his target.

'Jonah, here,' Haynes indicated a point under the rear bed of the technical. Jonah ran over to him and swung the pack off his back, then got to work with the detonator sticks. The charge would be timed to coincide with RED-2. It didn't give them long.

A man in military fatigues ran out from the comms tent and started shouting in Spanish – one of the camp's officers. Shearman got the gist without needing to translate. *Is this an attack?* The operator got his answer. The GREEN-1 charge was loud at this range, its violent crack accompanied by a metallic pang. The mangled generator was ejected from a puff of smoke and flung, tumbling haphazardly across the thirty-metre gap to the radio tent. The three-hundred-kilo engine felled the unsuspecting radio operator then smashed into the aerial assembly, mauling the tent in the process. Shearman smiled, pleased with his handiwork. There would be no call for reinforcements tonight.

Militia fighters swarmed like angry hornets, interspaced with horticultural workers running desperately for safety. Men spun, pointed, grabbed at each other's shoulders; some even attempted to take cover. So far, they weren't certain which direction the threat came from. Shearman refrained from opening fire, but it wouldn't be long before the enemy organised themselves. Men were staring toward the bunker; Delta Three could expect incoming rounds at any moment. Jonah and Haynes appeared at the entrance. The charge was set.

'*WHITE, now*!' Shearman shouted. They flipped down their NVGs, activated their aiming lasers, and ran from the bunker to the east. Shouts behind them were immediately followed by the staccato crackle of gunfire. They didn't turn to look.

The missile crew had weapons drawn and were peering through the darkness in their direction, but the headlights of the vehicle were now facing south. The SAS men remained invisible as they ran towards the machine. Three minutes fifteen seconds remained. Relieved of his backpack Shearman's load wasn't heavy but he felt like he was running through water. Every step seemed to be taking too long. He heard the zip of a bullet passing close – fired from a distance, its whine indicating that it had slowed to subsonic speeds. A rifle round fired from nearby would pass with a spine-tingling snap. The sporadic bursts of incoming were still relatively light, the militia reluctant to fire near the launcher. Delta Three dived to a prone position at Shearman's command.

The SA-8 Gecko was the size of a bus, with six big wheels spaced far apart and thick ribbed-metal plating running along its length. On its back stood a turret with a huge dish on the front, and a smaller dish mounted each side. A pair of long rectangular boxes sat above the rear of the vehicle, angled skyward over the radar turret. Each could hold three surface-to-air missiles. The rumble of the twenty-litre diesel engine reverberated along the ground to their position. The heads of the crew continually scanned around, alert for any threat. The driver could pull away at any moment if he sensed danger. He stood upright in the cab with his head and arms protruding out of the roof hatch, his side window too small to offer a clear view. He was unaware of the infrared beam that had settled on his chest.

'I've got the driver,' Haynes declared.

'Okay. Three, two, one, go.'

Bursts of fire cut down the vehicle crew. Even their bodies seemed to fall too slowly. There were only seconds remaining.

'Move,' Shearman barked, and Haynes sprinted for the machine with green tracer rounds buzzing past like deadly fireflies. Shearman took position at one end of the vehicle, watching as more and more figures amassed at the eastern end of the camp from where they had just come. A bullet pinged off the armour plating beside him. Muzzle flashes. Enemy heads bobbing in and out of cover. Surely there could be no escape from this position. The headlights of one of the jeeps swung around to face their direction. Shearman could hear Haynes panting heavily, and he glanced up to see him positioning the pack beneath the missile tubes. Jonah returned fire and Shearman followed suit, but it was fruitless – they wouldn't hit anyone at this range. Shearman sent a volley of pointless shots down the beam towards the multitude of targets. He wanted to check his watch. The moment was taking an age. The timer expired.

The nine kilos of C4 plastic explosive that constituted the RED-2 charge detonated, instantaneously generating over 250 kilobars of pressure. The mortar crate and its contents were obliterated in a shockwave that travelled outwards at eight kilometres per second. Metals were shattered, then liquefied by the immense temperature, their molten fragments igniting pyrophorically. The diesel fuel was vaporised and the shed dissolved into a million supersonic splinters, followed in their departure by a hail of sizzling steel.

An instant later the RED-3 charge fired, creating a second flash that flickered across from the production area. The vacuums formed at the two epicentres were equalised by violent return shockwaves that wrenched the framework from the surrounding structures. A thick, billowing fog of aerially suspended cocaine powder thrust outwards, propelled by rapidly expanding gas, until it met the blazing white-phosphorous of the mortar rounds. The resultant dust explosion engulfed the western clearing in a squat, orange fireball, wreathed with the flaring vapours of diesel fuel and industrial solvent. The fireball rolled outwards, consuming every trace of oxygen in its path.

A belching tongue of flame spewed from the underground bunker, signalling the demise of the technical, throwing with it the incinerated bodies of men who had taken cover in the doorway. The remains of the tattered barracks tent rained down over the site. Scraps of camo-net dangled ablaze from high above the structures. La Fábrica was ripped apart.

'*Jeezus!*' Jonah whistled.

Shearman felt the shockwave ripple over him, even at 300m distance, followed by the noise of the double crump. It sounded as if the air itself had been torn like fabric. He watched the fireball balloon into the night sky, scorching foliage as it rose. Last to reach him was the acrid, intoxicating stench of burnt cocaine powder. It was unpleasant enough, but he suspected that the breezy air would dissipate the fumes too quickly for the effect to be incapacitating.

In the clearing, men stumbled around, retched, some dived for cover, but surprisingly many were still alive. This was the largest and most destructive explosion that Shearman had ever witnessed. Nobody could have survived at the western end of the camp. The reality became clear: their attempt to draw the enemy into the kill zone had not worked as planned. The sound of gunfire from the bunker had confused the militia, saving their lives in the process.

Shearman switched on his personal radio, confident that the rest of the team would now do the same.

'Go loud, repeat go loud.'

'I reckon they got that, Cal,' Jonah followed.

Enemy muzzle flashes flared up again. Tracer rounds whipped past, working their way closer, zeroing in on Delta Three's cover positions. Bullets pinged as they ricocheted off the metal body of the launcher. The cartel fighters might not have known what was happening but they had a good idea who was responsible. They refocussed their efforts with a sense of purpose, many abandoning their concern for hitting their own hardware. With the camp mostly destroyed, there was nothing left to defend; the infuriated militia now switched mode to assault.

'I'm done here,' Haynes shouted. 'Three minutes. Run!'

They sprinted south from the launcher, exposed to enemy fire, seeking the cover of the brush for their return west towards BLUE.

'All teams, come in,' Shearman shouted as he ran.

'Delta Four; in position.'

Thank god, thought Shearman. At least the route to BLUE had proven viable.

'Delta One; we have contacts approaching via the vehicle tracks, but we have it covered.'

As was expected, the marksmen were sufficiently effective in keeping the enemy pinned down.

'Match; Daniels is down.'

'Match, repeat that,' Shearman demanded.

'Daniels is down. He rode right off the cliff at the bottom of YELLOW. I'm trying to get to him now. There was a guard on the beach that I had to take first.'

'Where's Dylan?'

'Dylan's gone.'

'Gone where?'

'He went straight to the ERV and took a canoe. I found his Jackdaw dumped on the beach. He's buggered off.'

'I don't bloody blame him. Report when you get to Daniels.'

Shearman went ahead, skirting the perimeter of the clearing until locating the southern road that would take them to the airstrip. The enemy seemed temporarily unaware of their location but were becoming more coordinated in their efforts. Groups of men were forming up, others taking position to provide suppressing fire. Delta Three needed to prevent the militia from reaching the launcher where they would quickly find and disable the demolition charge. They lay flat on the ground, just to the sides of the track, the fall of the slope offering limited cover. The return fire would be deadly at this reduced range. Shearman took a deep breath.

'Pin them down.'

The three weapons spat out in short bursts, catching their targets from an unexpected direction. Jonah immediately brought down a running figure. Shearman aligned his laser on a cover position and waited for a man's head to pop up. The militia responded in kind. Haynes flipped up his goggles and aimed directly for their muzzle flashes with the red-dot sight. Delta Three's own muzzle flashes were reduced by their Surefire suppressors, denying the enemy such an obvious target; but enough of the militia were now aware of their location. A group of combatants were defilade behind the jeeps, laying down fire, while a separate party moved southward between the tents in a flanking manoeuvre. Shearman realised they were becoming trapped. They could suppress the enemy to their front for perhaps three more minutes before the flanking group nailed them. If they tried to get up and run, they would make easy targets. He scanned his head from left to right, looking for an exit route. The brush would be impenetrable after just a few metres. Dirt kicked up in front of their faces as an unseen gunner found his range. It was only a matter of time before someone got hit.

A single loud clap rang out from the east, followed by a flare of intense, blue-white light that shone like a firework. High-energy-composite rocket fuel had ignited in two of the four remaining missiles. Delta Three's position was bathed in bright light. Shearman and Jonah flipped up their goggles, now in full view of the militia. Gleaming enemy faces peeked out from their cover positions, momentarily mystified by the glare before them. Then a crescendo of fire erupted, causing Delta Three to press their helmets hard down to the floor. Shearman twisted his head eastward. The Russian missile launcher erupted, its turret blazing like a roman candle.

'Match, come in,' he shouted.

'Receiving.'

'WHITE is down. I repeat, target WHITE has been destroyed.'

Chapter Twenty-Three

03:06

Blue-1

Delta Four heard the V8 engine of the second technical revving aggressively as it made its way towards them up the snaking turns of the southern road, its tyres scrubbing noisily on the dirt and gravel surface. It came at speed. Wade had set two separate explosive devices at the third hairpin from the clearing, hidden on the inside of the corner and spaced five metres apart. It had originally been intended to use proprietary vehicle mines for the job, but these had not been available from the stores at the Mountain Brigade training facility. They had to make do with packs containing eight blocks of C4 plastic explosive, similar to the munitions used by the other teams. Morris and Madan had discarded the folding shovels they carried for burying the charges; the ground was too hard and there was precious little time. Instead, the demolition packs were hidden under cut brush at the apex of the bend. It was a crude and inefficient approach but Wade was still confident that the pick-up truck would not survive the ambush.

He temporarily ignored the radio chatter, his full concentration required for the timing. His left hand held a clacker-type detonator switch, with connecting wires stretched from the explosives to his position amongst the thick vegetation at the side of the road. The two charges were linked with det-cord – a flexible, linear explosive that ignites at a rate of seven kilometres per second. They would detonate simultaneously, turning the whole hairpin bend into a kill-zone. The technical would not be able to corner fast enough to escape.

Wade had positioned his team fifty metres down the track from the site of the ambush, and had climbed up the bank to a higher vantage point where he could keep out of view. The approaching pick-up illuminated the bend below them with powerful, roof-bar mounted spotlights. Its driver dropped a gear as he slowed into the turn, then swung out wide and railed the truck around. The roaring 4x4 beast had considerable power, its wheels spinning under high torque on the loose surface. A group of militia passengers rode on the rear bed, one of them manning the mounted .50 calibre machine gun. The truck's spotlights flickered over Delta Four's position, its occupants and outriders unaware of their presence. The driver floored the accelerator and the vehicle surged up the dusty track towards the ambush point.

Wade stood upright, abandoning caution – he needed a clear view. The technical had no rear lights but he heard the engine revs drop as it neared its last corner. He watched for the swing of the headlights and it came. He counted one, two more seconds then gave the clacker a firm squeeze.

With a solid clap and a flash of light, the truck was knocked over like a toy, the outriders flung violently from the rear. The vehicle came to rest upside down – the gun was out of action – but the crew might have survived. Wade was about to shout the order when he realised Madan had pre-empted it. The Gurkha sprinted up the road towards the upturned technical, its spotlights smashed but the engine still ticking over. Wade watched intently, his ambidextrous C8 rifle tucked high into his left shoulder, its laser activated. Madan closed to within twenty metres of the truck, then arced his arm over his head and dived to the ground for cover. Madan had thrown the grenade just beyond the upturned vehicle, right where the rear passengers would have fallen.

The Yugoslavian made M75 fragmentation grenade consists of a plastic outer body containing three thousand ball-bearings wrapped directly around a high-explosive core. At close ranges, the blast effect is similar to that of a shotgun, except spread around radially rather than pointed in a specific direction. After four seconds, the fuse resolved with a heavy thud. The ruptured tank of the pick-up had disgorged its full load of petrol, and the fuel ignited with devastating effect. The vehicle was instantly consumed, enveloped in a pillar of angry fire. A faint scream from the cab signalled the rapid demise of the only surviving occupant. If any of the rear passengers were still breathing, they would no longer be in a fit state to offer resistance. Madan sprung to his feet and sprinted back down the roadway from the flaming wreck.

'All teams, Delta Four. BLUE-1 vehicle ambush is complete and successful,' Wade announced through his neck-mounted microphone.

'Delta Four, we're at the top of BLUE and being engaged from the central clearing. We're retreating down the track toward you now.' Shearman's voice was ragged and desperate, his words shouted in bursts between stertorous breaths as if he was mid manoeuvre.

'Be advised: the technical is on fire. When you pass it, you'll be lit up like Christmas.'

'Ren, they knew we were coming. There's loads of them and they're professionals. We'll have to chance it.'

'Then we'll move south from the ambush point and clear the road ahead of you. If there's still an enemy presence at BLUE-2, we'll wait for you to reinforce us.'

'Copy. Match, what's happening?'

'I'm with Daniels. He's alive but out cold.'

'Get him to the ERV and into a canoe,' Shearman ordered.

'He's unconscious. If he falls out, he'll drown.'

'Go with him and get to somewhere safe. We're in the shit here. Delta One, is the landing site clear?'

In contrast to the replies of the other teams, Govrin's tone was still calm. 'LS-1 is secure at present but we have multiple contacts incoming. Ammunition will be a problem if this continues.'

'*Shit!*' Shearman's voice distorted through their headsets. 'They're using night-vision. Ren, we are coming at a run right now.'

Wade knew that Delta Three's NVGs would be impeded in the vicinity of the flaming truck, and their natural eyesight would lose sensitivity if they ran past with their goggles flipped up. The militia, however, would be able to see the running soldiers as clear as day. There was nothing he could do to help. If he didn't clear the path to the south, both teams would be caught in a pincer. He gave the order for Madan and Morris to advance down the dirt road. He followed behind, the only man still carrying an explosives pack – the charge for BLUE-2.

Delta Four negotiated the remaining hairpins and only encountered a single combatant, found pacing slowly up the road towards them. He was swiftly dispatched by Morris with two short bursts. The respite was short lived. The moment they reached the final corner they came under fire from below. There were two lines of plant vehicles flanking the track for the last fifty metres before the airstrip; remaining militia were behind these in good cover. Delta Four could advance no further.

'Ren, Delta Three. We're approaching the truck. We're going to deploy grenades behind us and run through. Is the road clear on your side?'

'Yes; the road *is* clear to our position,' Wade answered, speaking slowly for clarity. 'We are pinned down at the final bend before the airstrip. We have heavy incoming from the vicinity of BLUE-2.'

Wade heard a prolonged series of discharges above, then a brief pause before a symphony of assault rifle fire erupted. A significant enemy force remained and it was converging on their position. He prayed briefly for Delta Three's safe passage past the burning truck; a casualty at this point would be unsustainable.

Delta Four could do little more than keep their heads down – they would only waste ammo firing on the covered positions and they were way out of grenade range. The brush to the side of the track would offer concealment, but their progress through the vegetation would be so slow that they could swiftly become encircled. Then the cartel fighters would only need to flush them out. After a few minutes, Morris announced, 'Cal's lot are coming in behind us.'

The Delta Three soldiers came scurrying down the road in a running crouch until Madan and Morris leapt to their feet and pulled them into the brush. Shearman stumbled over to Wade's position.

'I'm all out of ammo,' He announced between heavy gasps for breath. 'The others must be low.' Haynes and Jonah had run first while Shearman hung back to throw the grenades. Shearman had then sprinted to catch up and needed a moment to recover. The two black men were in stark contrast – Shearman sweating, exhausted and covered in dirt from head to toe; Wade still fresh, clear-headed and relatively unsoiled. The junior man assumed control of the situation.

'We'll hold this corner. You cover up the road; we'll cover down.'

Haynes and Jonah adopted prone positions on either side of the track, facing up the hill and training their sights on the previous hairpin bend. They awaited the imminent appearance of their pursuers. Shearman felt helpless without ammo but at least could take the opportunity to get his breath back. Sweat stung his eyes; he tried to dry his forehead with the sleeves of his overalls. Wade's hands were delving into webbing pouches to supply Shearman with a few magazines when a clanking noise rattled on the road above them. The SAS men flinched, cringed, held their breaths. With a thump, the incendiary grenade flared like a flashbulb, spewing a plume of white smoke and bathing their position in bright light. Now they were visible to both groups of enemies.

'They're throwing white-phos; they've got height advantage – this position's done for,' Haynes declared.

'I'm out,' Jonah called.

A muzzle flash erupted in the vegetation above them, to no avail but worryingly close.

'They're coming through the brush – we have to move now,' Shearman warned. Wade responded with the only solution.

'Take our grenades and defend the rear. We'll put down suppressing fire and advance down the track.'

Shearman accepted the suggestion with a mixture of determination and dread. The militia below were becoming less frivolous with their ammunition and he prayed it was a sign they were running low. Even so, the situation wasn't hopeful – advancing without cover was more or less suicide. His hands shook slightly as he took more grenades from Morris. Both men's pulses thumped in their chests. Madan was on the other side of the track and Shearman signalled for his attention, wishing to ensure that he saw their intention.

The Gurkha smiled briefly. 'Looks good, yeah? We go now.'

Shearman was too dog-tired to play along with Madan's comic bravado. *To hell with him.* He scuttled back towards Jonah with the four grenades. Wade gave the order.

'Go, go, go!'

Delta Four sprung to their feet and bolted down the road, crouching periodically to send bursts of fire towards the enemy positions. The men fired in sequence, each waiting for the last to stop shooting before releasing his own rounds, so that fire was maintained during reloading. One by one the remaining grenades were deployed behind to dissuade their pursuers. Haynes walked backwards with his weapon held high, replying to muzzle flashes with single shots, his intention to kill rather than suppress. A trio of assault rifles blazed to their front and Wade felt a white-hot pain lance through his shoulder. This was the end – they were walking into a hail of bullets.

He could hear the desperation in his teammate's breathing between the clattering bursts of their suppressed carbines. Empty casings tinkled as they hit the stony dirt. He heard the clang as Madan jettisoned an empty magazine to the ground, then the clicks as he attached a fresh one and chambered a round. Frantic, unintelligible shouts of foreign language came from three points of the compass. His boots crunched on the floor as he persisted forward towards the source of the fire. For the first time that evening, Wade noticed how the wind rustled the leaves of the forest canopy above.

A flash between the vehicles seemed to momentarily extinguish the enemy muzzles. Wade's mind leapt to an optimistic explanation. *One of them's dropped his own grenade.* Moments later, a second discharge disproved that theory.

'Guys, it's Match. I'm on the airfield. I've put a couple of frags between the vehicles. Looks like your targets are down.'

'Move, now!' Wade screamed, and immediately broke into a run. Within seconds, the others followed at full sprint.

A volley of fire rang out from behind but they had already departed the danger zone. As they reached the bottom, a man stumbled forward with arms held in the air. Haynes took him down before anyone realised, he was unarmed.

'Sorry, chap,' Haynes muttered.

Partially buried and ostensibly immobile, the Brazilian made EE-9 Cascavel sat with its turret facing the runway. Wade felt his shoulder. A round had grazed though his camouflage overalls, cutting deep into his muscle flesh. It stung like hell.

'Give me one minute,' he instructed, then entered the armoured car through its open turret roof hatch.

When he emerged, he saw that Match had joined the group and was distributing some of his unused magazines. Their dash had earned them a respite from the gunfire above, but it wouldn't take long for the militia to catch up.

'Get over the other side of the runway. We'll find cover on the track to the beach. Let's go.' Despite the shoulder wound, Wade was quick thinking and capable. He remained in de facto control of the wearied unit.

'How much time?' Shearman asked.

'Four minutes.'

'Four?' Shearman stammered 'Why so long?'

'May as well give them time to get down there before she blows. I've put the charge in a stack of cartridges for that 90mm gun. I doubt they've ever fired the thing. There's box loads of them.'

'We need to get the fuck off this runway,' Shearman stated.

They lay prone on the dirt and expended their remaining ammunition keeping the enemy pinned down between the plant vehicles. Wade was reassured to hear the crackling fire of multiple rifles when the four minutes finally elapsed. His wristwatch held close to his face and a smile across his lips, Corporal Renford Wade chuckled softly to himself as the deafening metallic blast from the exploding armoured car annihilated the remaining fighters. His shoulder hurt no more.

There was no further incoming fire. Any militia members remaining alive had lost impetus and began retreating up the road. Wade couldn't control his fit of giggling for a few minutes. He cracked open a slow-burning marker flare and threw it as far as he could onto the grass runway. LS-2 was secure.

Shearman, now recovered from his earlier exertions, resumed command of the mission. 'Ren, you guys take Jonah and hold the airstrip. Hugo and I will go to Daniels. Match, lead on.'

'Yes, guv,' Wade replied, the smile still wide across his lips.

Chapter Twenty-Four

03:31
LS-1

Through her headset Elana Govrin had heard confirmation as each target was destroyed, one by one, until the second landing site was finally pronounced secure. The operation was all but complete. The problem was that the enemy were still steadily advancing on Delta One's location. It seemed that the entire remaining contingent of cartel fighters had formed up and were now attempting to assault the plantation. To begin with they had approached via the vehicle tracks – those targets had been swiftly dispatched by the marksmen. The threat posed had been so low that Taz had opted to put a round in one man's leg, then allowed his compatriots to carry him away. It kept a few of the militia busy and Taz saw no added benefit in killing the man. This relatively benign mode of combat didn't last long.

The sharpshooters hid in furrows between the straight rows of coca plants. They were invisible to the enemy but their own sight lines were restricted to just a few angles. The trouble began for real when the attackers changed tactic and spread out along the brush within the treeline, adopting too many positions for Delta One to cover simultaneously. Both snipers had retreated thirty metres to reduce their vulnerability to grenades. Govrin scuttled around in a crouch behind them, hoping to spot any ingress into the plantation.

'One-One, two breaking cover, twenty metres east of GREEN,' she warned.

'I see them.'

She watched one of the men drop, hit by a silent round, then pulled her own weapon to her shoulder and loosed off a burst to force the other man to the ground.

'Both targets are down,' Riley notified. 'I've hit the second guy on the floor.'

Riley's voice was still calm and level. As yet, he didn't feel threatened – so far. But Govrin herself became increasingly concerned. More and more tracer leapt out from the treeline to their south, and the bright glare of the rounds was overwhelming her night-vision goggles. She took cover temporarily in a furrow. If two or more groups rushed the plantation at once, they could easily be outflanked. They couldn't afford to fall back any further or they would lose control of the essential landing site. She got up, fired a few rounds, sprinted to a different location and dived back to the ground. This method would not suffice for much longer.

The scoped rifles carried by Taz and Riley were ideal for making precision shots but their targets were now invisible, concealed in the brush beyond the headland. They had begun the mission with just three twenty-round magazines each – the 200-grain ammunition was heavy and no marksman expects to fire that many rounds. Now they could potentially fire all of their remaining supply into the undergrowth without hitting anything. What Govrin really needed was a support weapon to lay down some suppressing fire.

A grenade detonated somewhere to her front, sending shockwaves rippling through the coca plants. Its loud report echoed off the hillside behind her. Her men were safely out of range but the action signified an attempt by the militia to flush them backwards before advancing into the plantation. They would soon be outmanoeuvred if they allowed that to happen. Govrin was grateful that they could now at least use their comms equipment.

'One-One, One-Two, use your grenades. We need to slow them up.'

'Throwing now.'

Two loud discharges sounded a few seconds later. Govrin could hear the patter of dirt as it rained down on the coca leaves to her front. The two grenades had landed just as close to themselves as the enemy, but they might have been enough to dissuade any gung-ho militiamen from sprinting forward. Another minute elapsed before the next grenade detonated, again followed shortly by a second, this time provoking a fearsome response from the treeline. Enemy muzzles flared simultaneously from multiple locations. A stream of bullets passed uncomfortably close to Govrin, shredding the vegetation above her. She pressed herself to the earth yet again as splinters of trunk peppered her prone body. She wriggled deep into the furrow and kept her head down.

'I'm pinned down here. I can't move or fire.'

'Same here,' Taz responded. 'One-One, we need an opening.'

'I'm free to move but I've got no shots. Hold on, I'll get to another position. *Wait,* there's a vehicle coming up GREEN. *Fuck!* Now I've got incoming. I've got to take cover.'

Elana could hear and feel the bullets zipping over her back. The volume of fire was steadily increasing. A series of grenade blasts – the enemy were preparing to storm the plantation. Her men had now run out. She felt a round thump into the ground not far from her. The furrow wasn't deep enough to offer complete protection.

'*Shiiit…*'

Govrin squeezed her eyes shut and waited for the inevitable hit. She didn't want to die *here* in this godforsaken place, so far from home. She thought about giving the order to break cover and run – to hell with the landing zone. With some luck they might be able to escape the plantation unscathed and crawl their way through the brush to the ERV. There was no chance. It would be hopelessly unrealistic – none of her team could even move. They were being overrun.

The onslaught reached a crescendo around her, the crackle of gunfire becoming a thunderous roar. It sounded like she was being run down by a train. Her eyes pinged open with sudden realisation. *That isn't gunfire!* She rolled over onto her back and peered through the foliage above her. She couldn't see anything but it had to be worth a try. She took a marker flare from her webbing, pulled the tab and threw it northwards, just behind their position. The flare attracted a fusillade of rounds from the treeline, then her suspicion was confirmed.

Noise and wind escalated in concert until the foliage around her was battered and torn by immense downdraft. The foreboding dark shape of the Mi-26 Halo loomed into view directly above the marker flare. The helicopter crew could see the gunfire emanating from the treeline and quickly deduced the mechanics of the battle unfolding below. Their response was immediate. A two-metre-long tongue of white-orange flame flickered out from the side door of the helicopter, accompanied by the unmistakable chainsaw whine of the six-barrelled GAU-17 Minigun. Govrin lay on her back, staring upwards, as a long stream of full-metal-jacketed ammunition lacerated the treeline at 4000 rounds per minute.

'The troops are here. Get the enemy off the LZ,' Govrin shouted. She rolled over and raised to a crouch, scanning for targets, just in time to see a running man felled with a silent bullet. The two sharpshooters were already up and firing. The Mil coasted forward, performed a turn over the eastern plantation, then ran back along the length of the headland with its other flank facing the militia. The second Minigun screamed as its rounds tore into the brush – the pilot had swapped sides, allowing the first rotary-barrelled gun to cool. The treeline fell silent.

Govrin stood up and moved away from the flare as the giant helicopter set down behind her, its bulk crushing the coca bushes beneath it. Its wheels met the ground, then a swarm of Víboras commandos poured out of the open rear doors. They looked fearsome enough with their black painted faces and SAR-21 assault rifles, but more importantly they were fresh and ready for the fight. Govrin pitied the remaining militia; they would be running scared now. The commandos briefly acknowledged her team members as they passed but did not stop to talk. They filtered quickly through the plantation in the direction of the encampment. The final soldier to pass tugged her arm and pointed towards the helicopter.

'Gavin, Taz, converge on the helo. Our job here is done.'

Chapter Twenty-Five

03:50
Apurimac Tributary

Dylan was terrified. He clung to the sides of the kayak with the oar gripped between his knees as it pitched and rolled like a rollercoaster in the dark. There was insufficient light for the night-vision goggles to amplify and he could see more or less nothing. Overhanging branches persistently attempted to knock him out of the boat, only becoming visible moments before he crashed through them. He lacked the necessary control to steer the craft away, and one such limb had cut his chin already.

His assault webbing sloshed around in the bottom of the canoe in a few centimetres of water. It occurred to Dylan that if he ditched, he would lose these survival supplies. He snatched up the webbing, removed the water bottle from its pouch, and drunk down the remaining contents in one go. He threw the bottle back into the boat along with the belt-kit – he didn't care about the other stuff. It never occurred to him that the river water might be safe to drink, or that there were purification tablets stored in his webbing.

He could hear the rush of approaching rapids and his apprehension rose with the sound. The perspective was confusing. The foaming white-water glowed pale green through the NVGs, but the rest of the river appeared like a sheet of dark glass. He frantically attempted to back paddle, to slow down, to steer; but the current was irresistible and his efforts only made the boat yaw as it entered the cascade. He clung on again, leaning hard to avoid being tipped out, cringing as the hull scraped over a series of rocks. The canoe dipped down, bobbed back up, then was level again.

There were more rapids just ahead. There seemed to be no end to them. The kayak had now orientated itself so that he was travelling diagonally and backwards. He would never stay upright like this. He paddled hard, first on one side, then the other, but his input didn't have the effect he intended. The boat was sucked through a gushing chute, now travelling completely backwards. His head spun around as he tried to see what was coming next. With a bump, the rear of the canoe jammed onto a rock and rose out of the water, halting his progress temporarily. He could hear the water churning behind him, but he had no idea how high the drop was. The front of the boat was steadily drawn around by the flow. *I'll be tipped over sideways.* He scanned around for a riverbank he could swim to, knowing immediately that he would never make it in the fast-flowing torrent. The kayak pivoted until the rear came free of the rock, then slid gently over the small fall, dropping less than a metre into the river below.

The bottom of the canoe was filling with water and Dylan had no way to bail it out. He would have to abandon ship at some point. The river flow was too fast for him to stop on a bank, even if he could get past the branches. He was utterly fed up, despairing of his hopeless predicament. He felt like shouting, so he did.

'I've hadda fucking nuff of this!'

His voice reverberated off the canyon walls, punctuated by the beating of his oar blade on the edge of the boat. The outburst left him feeling foolish but somehow better. But the relief was short lived. More rapids neared. *Not again!* It occurred to Dylan that he was sat right in the middle of the craft, and that maybe this wasn't helping. He moved to a wooden bench nearer the rear and soon found that his steering corrections were more effective. At least he could drag the oar and bring the bow around to point forwards. The river around him was gaining speed. Ripples appeared like chevrons pointing in the direction of the fastest flow. He gave up on fighting the current and allowed the kayak to be drawn in, restricting his efforts to keeping the craft pointed straight ahead. The boat bobbed around sickeningly as it scooted over the rapids, and rose up high over the standing waves, but this time it avoided the rocks. With a little technique, he realised, negotiating the river wasn't necessarily that complicated. *Alright then, maybe I can do this.*

* * *

Dawn. Dylan sat in the boat, his shoulders slumped, drifting with the current which had now slowed considerably. He was utterly exhausted and his chin was sore from the tree branch. Hunger gripped his stomach, despite him having eaten the last of the rations from his webbing. The glow of the morning radiated down into the shadowy canyon, its sides hewn sheer through layers of grey limestone. Dotted vegetation protruded from fissures, softening the walls of his prison with patches of deep green. Sporadic birdsong broke the silence. Dylan thought for a moment he had seen an otter. He felt that the location might be more beautiful if he wasn't so likely to drown.

He pulled the helmet from his head, along with the valuable night-vision unit, and irresponsibly flung them both into the river. There was too much water in the boat and his half-hearted efforts to flick it out with the oar were achieving little. Even if he managed to clamber onto a rock or climb up a tree branch, he would be trapped in the ravine until he starved or passed out and fell in the water. He was a passenger, unable to influence his own destiny. His only hope was that an opportunity to escape would present itself, and that he would have enough energy left to exploit it.

To start with, the hissing noise mystified him – it almost sounded mechanical – but soon it manifested into an enormous natural roar that echoed off the surrounding walls of rock. It was just like the gushing of the previous cascades but amplified many times over. He realised what the source was with dismay. Either there was a *real* waterfall ahead or gigantic rapids that would chew him up like a meat grinder.

There was a long bend in the river and the noise steadily increased as he floated around it. A small strip of gravel materialised on the outside bank. He stared for a second, then began rowing furiously. He didn't care if he was stranded; he would beach the boat there. His long sodden hair hung down over his face as he heaved the craft forward, his arms and shoulders so strained that he had almost nothing left to give. The canoe was now one-third full of water and it barely responded, but slowly he traversed towards safety.

Looking down he saw smooth, rounded, multi-coloured pebbles dotted amongst fine gravel, and small darting fish. The river was only thigh deep – he could jump out and walk to shore. His boat was drifting towards a beach that was much larger than he first realised. He stumbled out of the kayak, capsizing it and losing the webbing. His legs had been inactive for so long that they refused to move with any coordination. He waded awkwardly through the shallow water, so desperate to reach solid ground that his momentum overwhelmed the resistance of his unwieldy legs. He stumbled and fell, face first. Clambering back to his feet, his eyes caught a glimpse of vivid turquoise.

There was a hut; next to it an old, battered, rusty car. Dylan wondered whether the people he found there would be hospitable. He reached dry land and sank to his hands and knees, his head hanging down so that his wet hair trailed onto the gravel. He closed his eyes, overcome with gratitude, unwilling to let the reality of his new situation spoil the feeling. After a long moment, he got back to his feet, and saw the Eurocopter.

Chapter Twenty-Six

06:20
La Fábrica

The first glimmer of morning penetrated the forest canopy and reached into the clearing. The scorched and tattered remains of the camo-nets no longer obscured the pale blue sky above. Patches of dappled light moved sluggishly across the bare ground, illuminating the aftermath of the previous night's skirmish. General Juan Carlos Torres stood by the former site of the cocaine production area, now vacant of any equipment bar the blackened, truncated remains of an old tractor that was impacted into the ground as if it had been flung in the air and dropped from a great height. Its external appendages had been ripped from its body and were nowhere to be seen. He was looking for evidence of the cocaine storage structure, which was now absent along with its contents. A pungent chemical smell hung in the air – like burnt plastic. He concluded that he would need a forensics team to find a trace of the product amongst this scattering of charred debris.

He had arrived at dawn in one of the Mi-17s. At his instruction, the pilot had flown an aerial circuit of the facility before delivering him to the airstrip, allowing him to survey the scene from above. Little had been revealed from this preliminary observation. Wisps of smoke curled out of the forest canopy. Bodies were being lined up along the plantation headland by his men.

A commandeered jeep had awaited to ferry him via the southern road to the clearing. The scale of destruction along the route was truly staggering. The results could hardly have been different if the site *had* been bombed from the air. But airstrikes could not have guaranteed the destruction of the missile launcher, and other helicopters may have been lost during the raids that followed. Torres had not been prepared to take that risk again. The chosen method of action had been sufficiently justified. He wandered past the mess area and sleeping quarters,

214

neither of which had escaped the brunt of the explosive charges. The surrounding ground was littered with bodies – more than he would have liked. Thankfully, most appeared to be combatants. What was done, was done.

The commandos had secured the facility within an hour of landing, capturing and disarming all those who remained alive. There had only been a handful of rounds fired. The militia's resistance had collapsed once they realised they were outnumbered and boxed in. This suited Torres – none of his men had even sustained an injury during the assault. He reasoned that he was owed such a favourable result after the previous tragedy.

There was something strange apparent, however. More than half the fighters, both the dead and those captured, wore webbing and camouflage fatigues. His men had confiscated modern assault rifles, pistol holsters and even some night-vision equipment. Tatty denims and cotton shirts were the more regular apparel of the cartel militias. Some pointed questioning had revealed that these men were professional mercenaries – ex Bolivian Army soldiers flown over to reinforce the camp. This angered Torres for two distinct reasons. Firstly, Bolivia and Peru both had enough domestic troubles without the complications of foreign interference. Secondly, it indicated that there had been a leak, despite his efforts to minimise the governmental involvement in the operation's planning.

Torres strolled around the centre of the clearing inspecting the smashed radio tent, identifiable by its toppled mast. The contents of the tent were obscured by the misshapen generator that sat atop. A man's body was visible beneath the mangled hulk – the radio operator. He nodded in appreciation and wondered if such an artistic result could really have been achieved intentionally. The ways of these SAS men were most mysterious to him.

The tents that provided the cartel officers' accommodations were being searched by his men. He would come back later to see what had been found. Instead, he continued to the gaping mouth of the underground bunker, built to protect the launcher from airstrikes. The engineering effort was commendable, but also very worrying; the cartels had never attempted anything on this scale before. The whole facility was designed as a long-term asset, as if the law had no bearing at all. The hollow was now home to a few corpses and the charred remnants of a pick-up truck. Torres looked up at the ceiling and wondered by what method his men could bring it down. He intended to leave nothing usable at La Fábrica.

To the east of the clearing was the thing he wanted to see most of all: the accursed surface-to-air missile launcher. The crew had fallen close to the vehicle and had evidently been taken without a fight. The body of the driver slumped from its open roof-hatch. The wheels, undercarriage and front cabin were still relatively intact, but the missile tubes and radar appendage were disfigured and mostly missing. A gaping molten hole breached the body where the turret had once sat. A thin smile crossed Torres lips. This nightmarish episode was finally over. Never again would such equipment be allowed to fall into the hands of the cartels. Measures would be taken to ensure it. He walked around the outside of the machine three times, stepping between the bodies, then headed back to the clearing. The weight that had pressed on his shoulders so heavily since the beginnings of this affair had lifted. No longer would he tell himself that his men had died in vain.

Torres had to admit it: he was impressed. It wasn't so much the degree of destruction that he found incredible – he had given Daniels' team enough C4 to level a small town – it was the fact that the small unit had been able to access all of their objectives unimpeded. The timing of the charges had been orchestrated with extraordinary precision, allowing the SAS to mostly avoid a direct stand-off with the militia. Torres wondered if these British were charmed with good luck.

Men were dragging the generator free with one of the jeeps and a tow rope. They wished to investigate the radio equipment buried beneath. Items of potential intelligence value were being gathered for further analysis. Whatever else was left, his men would burn along with the coca fields. He had already given an order to employ the surviving plant equipment to plough up the grass runway, and then to sabotage the machinery used with explosives.

A Víboras master sergeant addressed him, the ranking NCO on the ground. A major and a captain were also on site and engaged at the airfield and plantation respectively. The master sergeant wore an expression of deep concern.

'General, we found a rifle in one of the tents – one of ours. It must have come from the crash site. I ordered a search for evidence of survivors. You had better take a look at this, sir.'

'What is it?'

'It's Manrique, sir. He's here. He's dead.'

Torres followed the man down a thin trail running south into the forest. They came to a spot where the rotten corpse of a man was propped against a tree in a sitting position, with his arms tied around the trunk behind. The combat fatigues were dishevelled, but recognisable as those of the 4th Special Forces. The master sergeant was right – it had to be one of the unit from the downed helicopter. The dead man's body was so badly decomposed that he could not have been identified without the dog tags that the master sergeant had already removed from his neck. Despite the state of deterioration, it was possible to see how the soldier's life had ended. A neat hole in the man's forehead aligned with a larger exit wound at the rear of the skull. The trunk behind was stained dark red with a coating of blood that ran down to the ground. Insect larvae infested much of the corpse. The smell was unbearable.

'There will be retribution,' Torres promised. 'Get some help and bury him here. His family must not learn of this. They have already attended his memorial service and that should be their final memory. Let them grieve in peace. We will dedicate our victory here to Manrique.'

Torres felt a burning fury as he marched back towards the prisoners, but he held his composure. The mercenaries, distinguishable by their uniforms, had their hands bound behind their backs with plastic ties. They had been made to kneel by the tents under the scrutiny of several armed guards. Torres knew he would get no useful answers from them. The militia men and agricultural workers were held in a separate group. Torres pulled a grubby, pathetic looking man from the floor.

'You're a farmer here, correct?'

The man wore a nervous expression, and lifted his hands in unnecessary surrender. His neck and shoulders hunched as he answered. *'Si; si, señor.'*

'You understand that the Ejército del Perú are not the enemy of farmers. Our fight here was with Del Bosque.'

'Yes, I understand.'

'I want you to help me with something, and if you cooperate I'll ensure that you're looked after. In a minute, you'll go with the master sergeant and tell him which of our prisoners are farmers and which are militia. Will you do this for me?'

'Yes, sir, I will.'

'Good. First though, come with me.'

Torres led the prisoner to the spot where Manrique's body was tied to the tree trunk.

'Who shot this soldier?'

'A man from Del Bosque came. A wealthy man in a suit. He had silver hair. I don't know his name. I heard that the soldier had been shot. That's all I can tell you.' Torres was silent for a moment as he mulled over this answer, but the man had said enough.

'Okay. Go now with the master sergeant and do as I asked. What's your name?'

'Coniraya, sir, but they call me Concha.'

Torres looked at him in mild bewilderment for a brief moment then shrugged it off.

'Your assistance will not go unrewarded, Coniraya.'

Torres summoned the master sergeant over from a group of men he was busy directing.

'I've seen enough here and there is other business to attend to. Ensure the destruction of absolutely everything before you move out – especially that bunker. I'll leave these matters in your capable hands. The captain will supervise the processing of the prisoners.'

The man acknowledged his orders.

'Now, have the driver take me back to my helicopter.'

Chapter Twenty-Seven
06:45
Lima

Louis Oneto rolled over and reached for the cell phone that sat vibrating on the antique wooden dresser, then squinted through blurry eyes as he fumbled to deactivate his daily alarm. An emblem on the screen notified him that he'd received a text message. He closed his eyes for a moment, laying back in the comfort of the handsewn mattress. Now that he thought about it, he had a vague memory of the phone beeping, possibly just before he awoke. His head swam and he began to drift back towards sleep, but he kept the phone gripped in his hand and forced himself to sit upright before it was too late. He blinked repeatedly to clear his eyes as he unlocked the phone. The message was from Ballesta. *What does that pompous jackass want now?*

He clicked open the message, read slowly, and immediately felt the blood drain from his face. The message was short and contained no detail but it spelt out a nightmare in the making. He stared at the two sentences on the glowing screen: *Get to the office immediately. Torres has conducted an operation.*

He re-read the words twice as if hoping they might change. *Shit! Shit! SHIT!'* The worst possible explanation also happened to be the most obvious one; he tried desperately to avoid drawing *that* conclusion. But speculation was futile. He already dreaded what he might find but the facts would only become clear once he reached the Joint Command building. A wave of anxiety, far more compelling than Ballesta's directive, urged him to get there as soon as possible. He scrambled out of bed and hurried into the bathroom, ignoring his mumbling wife.

Oneto lived in the exclusive La Punta district and needed to travel across the city to Santa Beatriz. He was on the road without breakfast, hoping to get ahead of the worst of the traffic – Avenida Venezuela would soon be busy. It was a long shot, but if he was quick enough he might be able to establish some of the circumstances of Torres' activity before he even spoke to Ballesta. Maybe then there would be an opportunity to take some measures of his own choosing, before it became unavoidable to follow procedure. Even just a few minutes prior planning might enable him to spin a lie for the admiral, contrived to steer him to a path that would limit the imminent fallout. Fear welled in his stomach – in the back of his mind, he knew it was already too late.

He fixated on the term *'conducted an operation'*. It could describe any number of events. Surveillance, intelligence gathering, or an arrest were possibilities, as was the worst-case scenario, a full-scale military raid. He had no solid basis for the reasoning, but it seemed highly likely that the mysterious, missing contingent of British troops were somehow involved. So Torres *had* been harbouring a clandestine plan all along, just as the old fool had suspected. But Ballesta's containment measures had only prevented the SAS instructors from leaving the training camp, and had allowed the second unit to operate unimpeded. The thought of an attack on Del Bosque left Oneto feeling cold to his core. It was now almost inevitable that he would face La Rosa's wrath.

His foot slammed on the brake pedal and the Mercedes convertible skidded, nearly running into the back of the car in front which had stopped at a red light. The driver angrily jammed on his horn then threw his hands in the air, prompting Oneto to wave in sincere apology. He realised he had no memory of the last few kilometres. His mind had been far away, whirling with futile speculation. It was only down to luck that he had made it thus far without a collision. Oneto told himself that he needed to get a grip; the impending crisis would be impossible to navigate otherwise. His nerves were already beginning to fray.

He cut aggressively into the lane for Jirón Manuel Corpancho, receiving another angry blast of horn for the manoeuvre. He had already forgotten the matter a few seconds later when he pulled into his usual parking space. Killing the engine, he snatched up the essential items: phone, suitcase, wallet. His chest felt tight as he pulled on his jacket, hurrying towards the entrance and its immaculately uniformed guard.

The hour was just before eight and the receptionists were not yet at their desks, and so gratefully he was able to march through to his office unaccosted. He switched on his computer which took an age to fire up, seemingly longer than ever before, despite his repeated and unnecessary clicking. When it did eventually come to life it revealed no indication of the matter that Ballesta had referred to. There was nothing of relevance in his email inbox, no mention from the usual news sources, no internal memo. He checked his answerphone to find four unrelated messages which he sat through impatiently. To contact Torres himself wasn't realistic; he would be obliged to speak to Ballesta directly as soon he made the call to the training facility. From that point onward his actions would be dictated to him. But he had no other choices. He clicked open his address book, found the number and dialled. He held his breath after asking for the admiral to be connected.

'Ballesta.'

'It's Louis. I'm at the office. What's happening?'

'What's happening?' The irate voice of the Chief of the Joint Command rattled out of the speaker. 'You mean, what's already happened. The good general now appears to have supreme authority to fight a war all on his own.'

Oneto felt an irritable urge to tell Ballesta to get to the point, but he held his tongue.

'Go on.'

'It transpires that our wise president has chosen to omit our office altogether and give his orders directly to the army. Torres has a mandate for this nonsense with the British. You won't believe what they've done overnight.'

'What *exactly* has happened?' Oneto shouted far louder than he intended, his fists clenched and pressed on his desk. 'Admiral,' he added as calmly as he could manage.

'They've wiped out one of the cartel encampments – killed everyone, by the sound of it.'

Oneto's chin dropped to his chest and his hands began to shake.

'Which one?'

'Torres is there now, claiming the victory for himself, but it's clear enough what the reality is. He's let the British do the dirty work, therefore avoiding further losses on his own record. The man's a coward in my view. I can't believe they've had this planned all along without...'

'Which encampment?' Oneto repeated, interrupting.

'That big Del Bosque one he's been gunning for. He's been hell-bent on revenge ever since he lost the helicopter.'

'La Fábrica?' Oneto pressed.

'Of course, La Fábrica. Where else? Where's your head this morning? They've destroyed the evidence already, burned everything: the cocaine, the crop. They've even dug up the runway which will make proper handling of the deceased unnecessarily difficult. There'll be a reckoning when he gets back here, ramifications, I assure you. I won't toll…'

The voice was abruptly silenced as Oneto stabbed his finger at the end-call button. He couldn't think straight with Ballesta's bombast rattling out of the speaker, and he no longer cared what his superior was saying. He stared into nothingness a thousand yards in front of him, tremors running through his body. La Rosa would hold him directly accountable for the lack of warning; or worse, he would be accused of personally arranging the raid as a deliberate insult. La Rosa was notorious for his violent temper and his cruelty. Oneto knew he would be made to suffer. His family would be killed, most probably in a gruesome manner. That kind of thing had happened before, to other unyielding officials.

There was no more time to waste. He had to stop La Rosa and there was only one way to do so. If communications had been cut at La Fábrica then it was just about possible that the cartel enforcer was still unaware of the raid. It was a gamble, but there was no other chance to save his family. He dialled his wife and spent ten frustrating minutes persuading her to keep their two children from school and take them to visit her friend in Punta Hermosa instead. He claimed that there was a generic threat from one of the cartels, but not to any specific employee. It was just a precaution, he reassured her, but a necessary one.

'Stay there until you here from me later, okay?'

He ended the call as soon as his wife had reluctantly agreed. There was no feeling of relief, but there was a glimmer of hope that the situation could be saved. Tears welled in his eyes. He took a deep breath. He would need to steel himself for what must come next.

Spinning the dial on his office safe, he deftly entered the combination, then swung open the heavy steel door. Inside was a stack of folders, a box of .38 Special ammunition and a short-barrelled, stainless-steel Smith and Wesson Model 64. The revolver was engraved with his name and had never been fired in anger. He took the box and began to feed rounds into the pistol's chambers. With three rounds loaded, he paused. His hands were shaking. Snapping the cylinder shut, he stood and retrieved his jacket, pulled it on and dropped the handgun into the right-hand pocket. The safe door remained open as he strode out from his office.

He hurried down the staircase in the hope that he could exit the building without running into a colleague. It struck him as odd that Ballesta hadn't attempted to call him back, and he wondered if the egotistical old fool was still didactically lecturing the dead phone line. The metal detector only covered the entrance lane and so he dashed past the door guard unimpeded, into the air of the busy morning.

His head spun immediately from the onrush of stimuli: pedestrians, traffic, a cacophony of noises, the sickly smell of exhaust fumes. Tyres squealed and a car horn blared as Oneto stepped out into the busy junction, oblivious to the danger. He turned to see a concerned look on the face of the door guard. The man called after him to be careful, then began to stride in his direction to give assistance. He would not make it in time. A chorus of horns now informed Oneto that his erratic behaviour was hindering the flow of traffic. He stood on the crossroads of Avenida Arequipa and Jirón Manuel Corpancho. The guard picked up his pace to a jog, but froze again as Oneto pulled the .38 revolver from his pocket.

He had a responsibility to protect his family, and that meant stopping La Rosa. There was only one guaranteed method. He must punish himself before La Rosa could do so, and in the most public manner possible. The cartel would no doubt attempt to take revenge against the military for the raid, and perhaps against some politicians, but he believed they might now overlook his family. It was all he could hope.

He pressed the barrel under his chin, squeezed his eyes tight shut and jerked the trigger. The report rang out along the bustling streets. A desperate denial was shouted by the dumbfounded sentry. The car horns fell silent. Louis Oneto's lifeless body slumped to the asphalt.

Chapter Twenty-Eight

09:07
Cusco

The black SUV slewed through the gates of the aerodrome at breakneck speed. Alfredo La Rosa fumed with anger in the rear. He'd heard rumours of an attack at La Fábrica through his government sources but nothing that satisfied as a clear explanation. He endeavoured to find someone who actually knew what had happened, and quickly. The other members of the syndicate would expect him to have the matter under control, and they were not men of patience.

To fly there himself posed too many risks. He had no idea if his men had control of the airfield, or whether a firefight was still taking place. It was possible that either side could shoot him down. If the army had taken the facility – a concept he could not readily believe, given the defensive arrangements – then he would be arrested immediately on landing. So his involvement was limited to less direct activities: calling in favours, leaning on people, even offering cash rewards for good information. He had already tried to phone half of his address book. So far, the effort had engendered no useful result.

And now it transpired that the man most qualified to enlighten him had recently killed himself. News of Luis Oneto's self-imposed demise had been broadcast almost immediately. He had heard the radio bulletins and knew that tv crews were already on site. *That coward, the scheming traitor... How dare he! The plantation was my responsibility. He must have been guilty – how could he have done this otherwise? Did he think he could get away with it so easily, that his family will go free while I am humiliated? Of course an example will be made; an example is always made.*

The SUV screeched to a stop beside the Eurocopter on the concrete apron. The helicopter had only recently reappeared at the aerodrome and La Rosa had come immediately he was informed. There was no sign of the mechanic carrying out the routine maintenance. *At least this man Carver will give me some answers, whether he wants to or not.* La Rosa knew that Carver had been ferrying British commandos. The pilot would soon be made to reveal the nature of their activities.

The driver killed the engine and exited the vehicle, along with the bodyguard who sat in the front passenger seat. Both men carried Steyr TMP machine pistols in shoulder holsters under their jackets. La Rosa could barely control his fury as he jumped out of the rear and swung the door shut, clutching his usual leather shoulder-bag.

'Wait here,' he ordered. 'I'll send the woman out. Put her in the car.'

He stormed through the outer office to find the secretary was absent from her desk. *Maybe I'll catch him with his pants down,* La Rosa thought as he barged through the door into the back office. He stopped still in the middle of the room and stared at the man behind the desk in front of him.

'Buenos días Señor La Rosa.'

La Rosa struggled to reconcile his expectations with the image before him.

'Allow me to introduce myself. I am General Juan Carlos Torres, commander of the Región Militar del Sur and 3rd Division. I'm glad that finally we meet in person.'

The office door slammed shut behind La Rosa and he turned to see that he was flanked by two muscular special forces soldiers, their faces obscured behind thick, black camo-cream. One snatched the shoulder-bag and placed it on the desk before Torres.

'I've seen your face in the newspapers, General, but I didn't realise you were in the helicopter charter business.'

Torres face set into a patronising smile, but there was no mirth.

'Not charter, Señor La Rosa. I'm here to audit the accounts, and you must be here to pay your bill.'

La Rosa glared aggressively into the general's eyes. 'I'm afraid that's incorrect. I have come to make a complaint. Despite a sizable deposit paid to secure Mr Carver's services, it seems he has double booked. And as for my bill, you will find that I settle my dues very quickly, General.'

Torres raised his eyebrows disbelievingly and let the implied threat hang in the air.

'The Del Bosque syndicate owes me a twelve-million-dollar helicopter, plus compensation for the lives of the twenty-two men who were killed when it crashed. Do you intend to settle this due, Señor La Rosa?'

'You are referring to my clients; I'm not responsible for their financial affairs. I simply provide legal counsel. So, if you don't mind, General, I came here to see Mr Carver and have other business to attend to. I don't have time for these cryptic games.'

La Rosa's flaring temper had no discernible effect on Torres' disposition. He remained impassive and answered in his own time. The two troopers stood still as statues.

'I'll be demanding payment from Del Bosque, of that you can be assured, but first we will discuss the matter of your own personal arrears. You owe me for the life of Sergeant First Class Raúl Manrique, Señor La Rosa.' Torres slowly tipped the contents of the leather holdall onto the desk to reveal a bottle of mineral water, two large bunches of keys, an envelope stuffed thick with dollars, an advanced satellite phone, an address book, a packet of paracetamol and a loaded Colt Anaconda .44 Magnum with a four-inch barrel.

'You used this gun to execute one of my best men,' Torres stated flatly, accusingly.

'You need ballistic evidence to make that kind of allegation, and in any case, I recently purchased that gun second-hand – the gunsmith will confirm it. I'm happy to explain my legal rights to you if you are not completely clear on them.'

Torres picked up the stainless-steel revolver from the desk. 'I'm neither interested in ballistics, nor especially concerned with the law. A soldier's justice would seem more fitting to me, and soon you'll discover that I'm free to deal with you exactly as I wish. Now, I've grown tired of your voice. If you would.'

Torres stood, prompting the two soldiers to roughly grab La Rosa and shove him through the doorway. He was manhandled past the reception desk and out of the building onto the concrete apron, where he saw that the SUV, its driver and the bodyguard had vanished. In their place stood four military 4x4's, surrounded by ten camouflaged men carrying assault rifles.

'Where is my driver?' La Rosa demanded.

'He has chosen to leave your employ, along with your bodyguard. It seems that they held temporary contracts and were required to give you no notice.' Torres pushed La Rosa from behind as the soldiers steered him toward the rear of one of the jeeps.

'You can't just kidnap me – there are laws. I have friends who can take your job for this.' La Rosa's face glowed red and his voice had broken into a shout.

'You're no longer in a position to make threats,' Torres said calmly, his cold eyes boring into La Rosa's. 'You'll remain in my custody until you've revealed to me every detail of the Del Bosque operation. Then I'll decide whether to send you to jail or put a bullet in your head myself.'

Torres slammed the door with such ferocity that La Rosa tumbled flinching toward the interior of the vehicle, only to be shunted back by a soldier who had climbed in through the other door. The general gave a hand signal to his men – *wrap it up* – and the troops boarded the jeeps. Torres took the passenger seat of the lead vehicle and the convoy set off.

La Rosa thought and hoped that the general must be bluffing. He had been arrested and questioned before, endured similar experiences, and had always been released in short order. This time seemed different, though – less like routine procedure, more like the arbitrary decision of a man with nothing holding him back. La Rosa was accustomed to people being intimidated by him. Yes, there were always a few foolish heroes who thought they could stand up to the cartels; their demise came quickest. But those with influence knew they were not invincible. They all had families. Del Bosque had a long reach and a longer memory. Why take such risks when it was easier to play along?

It was clear, nonetheless, that Torres was genuinely unafraid; La Rosa could read it in a man's eyes. There would be little to prevent the general from holding him indefinitely, without legal process, should he wish to do so. There would be no compromise this time, no bargaining, no concessions. The general was in a position of real power – *his* normal standpoint – and La Rosa knew that prerogative well. He felt an emotion, unfamiliar to him since his childhood. Now, it was he who was scared.

Chapter Twenty-Nine
23:45
Lima

Sergeant Calvin Shearman found that the rigid plastic chairs of the airport concourse offered little comfort, but at least he was out of the transport helicopter. The noisy, bumpy flight from La Fábrica to the Víboras barracks had been followed by a similar journey to Jorge Chávez International, with a lengthy stop at Hospital Militar Central en route. The relative luxury promised by the RAF Tristar laid on for their return to the United Kingdom seemed teasingly beyond his grasp in the final hours before departure.

The SAS team had endured a lengthy wait at La Fábrica while Torres' forces cleared the camp, and dawn had long since broken before they managed to hitch a ride out on the first returning helicopter. There had been no time for rest since. As the ranking NCO, the exfiltration process was Shearman's responsibility. He had spent nearly an hour on a secure telephone line to Major Nolan at headquarters, reporting their status and requisitioning the aircraft. Then the weapons and other martial materiel had been itemised, sorted, cleaned and carefully packed into flight cases for repatriation – minus the little ammunition that remained, which was left with the Víboras. He was dead on his feet by the time he took a seat in the terminal.

Wade's shoulder had been dressed temporarily during the wait at LS-2, then expertly cleaned and redressed by a Víboras medic. He would need no further medical attention until he reached the UK. But Daniels injuries were of more concern and had required a series of tests for which they had flown to Lima's military hospital. X-rays had revealed a tibial shaft fracture and a broken radial head, and now both limbs were set in casts. He sat two chairs away from Shearman, badly bruised and groggy from painkillers, with his crutches resting on the vacant seat between them.

While halted at Hospital Militar Central, the team were also able to collect the injured McCowan. He wore a stout neck brace and had been given a wheelchair, which was positioned facing Shearman and Daniels. Fortunately, there had been no damage to his vertebrae or spinal cord, but the ligaments of his neck were severely sprained. Despite spending a prolonged period under sedation, McCowan was cheerful and enthusiastic to hear details of the raid's prosecution. It had been agreed that no operational specifics would be discussed before the official debrief back at Hereford, but this edict had largely been ignored. McCowan displayed a mix of emotions: he was overjoyed that the objectives had been met without loss of life, but also deeply disappointed that he hadn't taken part.

O'Neil had been compelled to stay with McCowan during the series of medical examinations and had been awake for as long as the assault team. Now, he had fallen asleep a few seats away. The remainder of the assault team – excluding Match and Haynes – were scattered around the nearby benches, lounging or dozing, dressed in civilian attire and carrying rucksacks for their personal items. Taz, ever the gentleman, sat upright, hands in his lap, watching the concourse with detached disinterest. Riley, in stark contrast, was slouched spreadeagled against his rucksack on the floor and was snoring loudly. Wade was the most upbeat of the team members. He bantered and giggled with Madan and Jonah and was decidedly pleased with himself. Daniels and McCowan had both suffered concussions, and Shearman was on the brink of collapse with exhaustion; hence, their conversation was subdued in comparison.

'You say Hugo and Match have gone to join the TDU. Why?' McCowan drawled the question at a rate that reflected the speed of his thinking. It was Shearman who answered.

'They've gone with the Jackdaws. They'll be setting up a training module for the EP – Match teaching the riding skills, Hugo doing the tactics. Torres agreed on the spot to purchase all the raid gear: the bikes, the body armour, even our new NVGs.'

'It's his way of saying thank you,' Daniels explained. 'I made him certain promises and he expected them to be fulfilled. Now he's keeping his end of the bargain. He knows I came here to generate sales for this stuff.'

McCowan chuckled. 'So the one responsibility you actually had on this operation, negotiating the business arrangements, Calvin took care of while you were unconscious. Is that right?'

Daniels and Shearman broke out in laughter, hearty, albeit hoarse and restrained.

'Maybe you should leave the action to us lot in future, Tom. Then you'd have time to do your own job,' McCowan pressed.

'It's true,' Daniels held his hands up in submission. 'I was out cold for the whole thing. I didn't fire a single shot. Some commando I made.'

Shearman came to Daniels defence. 'But you did take care of the two biggest charges. We couldn't have gone ahead without you. You pitched in when it mattered and we appreciate it.'

'And so what did happen to Dylan?' McCowan asked.

'He rode straight to the ERV, took a canoe and rowed downriver.'

'Fuck off!' McCowan said incredulously. 'You're having me on.'

'Straight up. Luckily Match was able to get a message to Carver, otherwise Dylan might have turned up in the Atlantic.

'And Carver knew where to find him?'

'Those were the last arrangements we made before Carver flew you to hospital; he already had the landing site in mind. He flew straight there once he received word that the raid had gone ahead.'

'Dylan's a lucky little…' McCowan trailed off.

'It came as a shock to me as well,' Daniels admitted. 'The EP flight crew picked up the radio call just before we took off from La Fábrica. I'd only been conscious for a while and was still pretty dazed, but they gave me the headset anyway. Carver told me that he'd just picked up Dylan. Said he'd pulled him half drowned from the river – lucky to be alive. He gave me a proper dressing down over it.'

'Fair enough, really,' McCowan affirmed, as if he shared no responsibility for the way events had turned out. 'You can't just go shoving civilians into the firing line like that, can you? Where's Dylan now then?'

'It turns out that Carver owns a beach house on the coast; they've both gone there to lie low while Torres clears up and the dust settles. Carver said it wasn't safe for him to return to business at the moment, so he'll just bill us for the consequential loss.'

There was a chorus of laughter from the three men, much louder this time. Daniels continued once they had settled down again.

'I was able to speak briefly with Dylan. Said he was going with Carver and more or less told me to get stuffed; had enough of playing soldiers, apparently.

After all, he *is* a civilian – I can't make him come back with us. Carver suggested that I arrange a first-class flight home for him in a few days' time.'

'He went through a hell of a lot. All that stress must have taken its toll. He'll need a chance to recover.' Shearman seemed satisfied with Carver's decision. 'We should consider ourselves lucky that he made it out alive.'

McCowan nodded, inhaled deeply; his voice was regaining its usual tone of authority.

'Well, anyway, you can tell Torres he's welcome to keep the bloody Jackdaws. I never want to see those damned things again.'

Shearman could no longer control his laughter, which erupted in a prolonged fit until there were tears in his eyes. He felt a tinge of euphoria. He'd been awake for over forty hours, and for the last few his emotions had been soaring and diving like a funfair ride. This level of fatigue wasn't especially unusual by SAS standards, but the whole programme had been physically and mentally intense from the outset. There was still a long flight ahead. Despite his weariness, he felt a warm, deep satisfaction that he'd been part of Operation CATHODE. Repeated misfortune had pitched the odds against them but they had still managed to pull it off. He knew there would never be another mission like it, and that the stories would be told and retold whenever enough beer had been drunk.

But it was Elana Govrin who had the longest journey ahead of her. She sat exhausted with the others on the plastic chairs of the concourse. Initially she had seen no value in the Jackdaw training, but now its final accomplishment seemed surreal. What began for her as a training exchange programme had escalated into the most dramatic deployment imaginable. After the RAF flight to Brize Norton, she would return briefly to Stirling Lines to collect her belongings and sign her release forms, then make the five-hour flight back to her home country of Israel. There, she would undergo a series of meticulous debriefings over the course of a week, before receiving a promotion and command of a small but highly elite, specialist unit.

Epilogue

Tuesday, 9 August
England

Tom Daniels headed south on the Purley Way, feeling somewhat light-headed from the single glass of champagne. Fortunately, the automatic gearbox of the BMW allowed him to drive with his left leg in the cast. Tidewell and Pearson-Roberts, whom he had left at the restaurant, were evidently more accustomed to lunchtime drinking, and at the rate they were going would no doubt have already polished off a second bottle. Lunch at *Chez Morin* had been a jubilant affair. Even Didier had been persuaded to join in for one of the toasts, after some jovial arm twisting. *To the success of the mission. To Daniels safe return. To the substantial invoice being raised by the MoD.*

The minister and the lieutenant-colonel could not have been more delighted with the conclusion of the enterprise. But it seemed they were far less interested in the realities of the operation than they were in the opportunity to claim it as a success, announcing to the world in the process that the British Army were a versatile, deployable force with unorthodox capabilities. In theory, participation in the raid was deniable, but that wouldn't stop it from being advertised in the proper circles.

The Jackdaw had performed flawlessly. Its design was unique, ground-breaking and without competition. The machine certainly had impressed Daniels throughout the duration of the programme, but at what cost in terms of training, and with what rate of attrition due to accident and injury? How likely were there to be future operations with the necessary parameters to allow insertion via such a vehicle? Daniels' lunch companions were neither interested in these questions nor their answers. The Jackdaw had been proven in action, and that was all that mattered.

Daniels could see the point – it *was* his job to maximise the revenue gained from export contracts – but he couldn't help feeling that the legend had already superseded reality. Torres had ordered a further thirty Jackdaw units, along with all their associated kit, and this package came at considerable cost. If the approach were found to be workable, there was a possibility it could be adopted by the Ejército del Perú as a whole. And while the charter of the TDU was expensive, the fees submitted for carrying out the raid were astronomical. This revenue alone was sufficient to justify the endeavour, but interest had already been shown by two other countries, in both the equipment and the associated training. Operation CATHODE had been quite a scoop. The ultimate irony was that the Jackdaw would not be purchased by the British Army, with the exception of a small detail tasked with foreign training services.

Daniels had been glad to leave. He didn't share the genuine elation of the other two men and had put up a pretence for their benefit. He was content with the conclusion of his assignment but for entirely different reasons. Too much had been left to chance, too many lives put at risk. It had not been the usual game where sales targets and contracts were the pieces to be won or lost. This job had put him worryingly close to carrying a needless civilian death on his conscience. At least the headaches that had been dogging him since the raid had finally abated. He powered the BMW up to speed as he reached the M23.

He found an empty space in the car park of the Hooden Horse and pulled the BMW into it, ignoring the 'patrons only' sign. He didn't intend to stop for long and it wasn't practical for him to travel far on foot. The public house was conveniently just across the road from his destination. He collected his crutches from the rear seat and locked up the car, then hobbled along the opposite pavement where he could observe Dylan's shop without much chance of being noticed. A few changes were immediately obvious.

The shopfront had undergone a makeover. New signwriting displayed the Cycl-One logo in graffiti style lettering and it wasn't a bad job. Underneath the sign, through the front window, Daniels could see a pair of downhill racing bikes hanging on display – someone had acquired some expensive new stock. As he passed the side alley, he saw that Dylan's rusty old banger had been replaced by a VW Transporter van, not brand new but in fair shape and displaying the new shop logo in transfers down its flanks. The van would have cost a fair sum. Too much, Daniels surmised. *Dylan didn't buy that with the money we paid him.*

He limped over the road and back past the front of the shop, taking a glance through the window as he went. A flat-screen television hung on the interior wall playing an extreme sports video. The dowdy clothing displays provided by Dylan's exploitative business partner had been replaced with vivid stands of full-face helmets, knobbly tyres and suspension forks. He was relieved to see Dylan standing behind the counter fumbling with a mobile phone, his hair hanging down over his face. He was completely oblivious to Daniels' presence.

Of course, he had made sure that Dylan was returned home safely and paid his full fee. Now he wanted to see for himself that the young lad had settled back into his everyday routine. The possibility of post-traumatic stress had been a real concern. But it seemed that Dylan was doing fine. He was at last able to take control of his own business. Daniels wasn't sure whether he possessed the wherewithal to make it a success or not but at least now he had a fair chance.

Daniels pressed on past; he didn't want to stop and chat. He doubted that Dylan would be overly keen to speak to him anyway. But this personal visit was also necessary to confirm the suspicions that had been building slowly in his own mind, almost to the point of certainty, over the last few days of his recovery. It warmed him inside to see that Dylan's fortunes had improved, but the fact was that Dylan was doing *too well.* The sum of money paid to him by the MoD wasn't exactly enormous. Somehow, Dylan had earned himself a bonus.

Did Daniels intend to share this knowledge? Would he do anything to revise the situation? *No.* He didn't begrudge Dylan a single penny after all that he'd been put through. Could anyone else be aware of what had really occurred? *No, and nobody will ever find out, either*. At least Dylan could now afford to replace his mangled mountain bike with something special. He probably already had.

It was the many hours that Daniels had spent trying to analyse the final moments before his accident that had revealed the truth of Dylan's deception. Initially, after the concussion had subsided, his recollection had been patchy. He couldn't remember the crash itself and never would, but the events beforehand had slowly returned to him during his period of rest and recuperation. The first clues should have been apparent at outpost, had the assault team not been so preoccupied with their frenetic training regime and the succession of last-minute planning changes.

It had not previously occurred to Daniels that the bond formed between Dylan and Carver, while they were confined at Outpost, was the result of anything more than mutual boredom. In fact, the pair had far more in common.

Firstly, neither had volunteered to lodge at the mountain camp – both had been instructed to do so, despite agreeing to entirely different arrangements in their contracts. Secondly, both their lives had been put in danger. But it was the third factor that truly united the two civilians. Daniels could imagine how the conversation went as they sat out of earshot during McCowan's briefings: *I'm not getting paid enough for this crap. Yeah right, neither am I.* So when Dylan saw an opportunity, he knew that Carver would be willing to help realise its potential. All he needed to do was to make it to Carver.

Then there was Dylan's mysterious decision to loiter at Carver's beach house for a few days before making the return flight. He should have been desperate to get back home to his unstaffed shop, unless of course there was other business to attend to. Carver was doubtless a man with all manner of contacts, but it still would have taken some time to make the necessary arrangements. Maybe Dylan had opened a bank account; the transfers had been made somehow.

Daniels had given no second thought to Dylan's panicked flight from the clearing – it had seemed natural enough under the circumstances – nor had he reflected deeply on the value of the commodity they were about to destroy. He had been utterly focused on the mission's objectives and the need to remain undetected. Dylan had tipped out the explosive charge that he carried to the cocaine store, instead of leaving the whole rucksack. There had been no time for Daniels to theorise; his actions were spontaneous and pragmatic. He had simply rectified the issue before giving chase. But Dylan hadn't really panicked at all. In fact, *his* actions were driven by quick and clever calculation.

The full revelation had come to Daniels during his futile efforts to recall the fall from the cliff path. His memory stopped short every time, no matter how long or hard he tried. But the final seconds beforehand had played in his mind so frequently that he could see them almost as vividly as if he were still there. He could close his eyes now and relive them like watching a film. Chasing Dylan down the dark, narrow track, reliant solely on the night-vision goggles for navigation. He had caught up with the other Jackdaw and was just a few metres behind. But Daniels should have known he could never catch Dylan, not with all parameters being even. That final, synthetic-green image was clearest of all in his mind. Dylan's backpack was full.